BABYGIRL

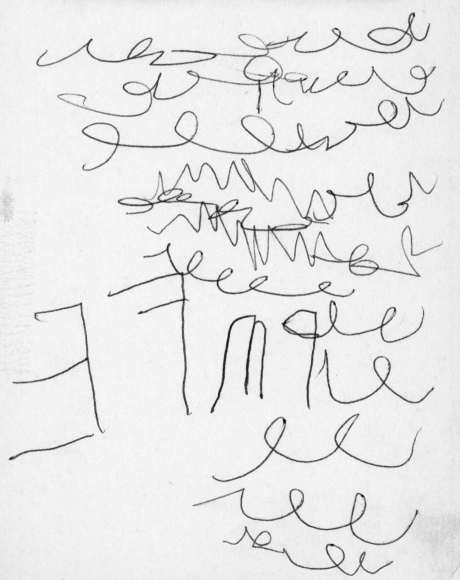

Also by Jihad

Street life

Anthology:

Gigolos Get Lonely Too

February 2006

BABY GIRL

JIHAD

www.urbanbooks.net

BABYGIRL

Urban Books
6 Vanderbilt Parkway
Dix Hills, NY 11746

ISBN 1-893196-23-2

First Printing October 2005
Printed in the United States of America

10 9 8 7 6 5 4 3 2 1

Acknowledgements

As always I have to give it to the creator. For without God, Allah, Jehovah, by what ever name you want to call him I wouldn't be able to do what I do and make the pen do what it do. I wanna thank him for my little King Zion Uhuru and I wanna thank Him for all of you who are reading my words.

Thanks Queen Arthine Frazier for giving me life and inspiration. Thanks Queen Pamela Hunter for always being there. Thanks Queen Lolita Files for believing in me enough to start a literary agency. Thanks Queen Victoria Christopher Murray for your editing, your friendship, and for just being you. Thanks and much love to Queen Reshonda Tate Billingsley for your eyes, ears, and being there. Thanks King Travis Hunter for making enough noise to get me my first book deal and thanks for being all the way down with me. Thanks King Carl Weber for not only signing me to Urban Books but your creative input and marketing efforts to make my books the success that they are. Thanks Queen Martha Weber for your incredible editing eye. And Thanks to my family of readers all over the world for your love and support.

Shout outs to my brothers Andre Frazier and Thomas Wiley. My sister La-Shl Frazier, nephew I-Keitz Garey, and D'Andre Frazier. Neices Ja-queitz, Sadaqa, Luscious, Jameese, and Shami.

My peeps, Eric Jerome Dickey, Thomas Long, Maurice Gant, Wayne, Corey Mitchell, Derrick Ward, Rodney Daniel, Shaheed, Roland Johnson, Nigeria Hunter, Katrina Frazier, Kendra Norman Bellamy, Toschia, Angelique, Angel Hunter, Stephanie Johnson, the rest of the Urban Books Fam, and to all that I've missed charge it to my memory not my heart.

Special special thanks to the HATERS keep on doing what you do, you are helping to get my name out there. It's okay that you won't buy my book because my name is Jihad but it's not okay that you won't even look the word up and find out that although it is a Holy War, it means Striving and struggling to bring others into the awareness of the oneness of God.

Thanks Deborah Burton, Tasha and the Queen Divas in the Turning Pages book club in Oakland, Ladies of class in the GAAL Book club in Atlanta, and Shunda Leigh of Booking Matters magazine

Shout outs to the Bruhs, and sistahs on lock down. Been there done that, that's why I'm gon' change that. We got to stop the madness and fight the system of ignorance and oppression instead of each other.

To leave comments or to learn more about Jihad, Babygirl, and Street Life go to www.jihadwrites.com and please tell the readers what you think of Babygirl and Street Life on www.amazon.com

Love and Life
Jihad

BABYGIRL

U promised me iced-out wishes and platinum dreams
If I opened my legs
U said I'd make the team
Now you mad cause I took you to the hoop
played you out all your green
I bet next time you'll step correct
to the Black Queen
Don't trip,
cause I ganked you for your grip.
I'm not to blame.
It was you who came to me
with that weak ass game
pulled up in a fat Range Rover
but at the end of the day
it was U
who got bent over
so next time
U see a fine pair of hips and thighs
don't play yourself
with them lame ass lies
cherish a sistah
as if she's a black pearl
if not
you'll probably get taken
by anotha

BABYGIRL

LOVE AND LIFE

JIHAD

PROLOGUE

"So I'm leaned back you know," he shrugged, "bout high as a mu' fucka, chillin' in the V-I-Peazy at Paradise Ceazy while this li'l White greasy weazy rides my Johnson like a pogo seazy.

"Mind you, I'm sippin' on Louis the whole time-teazy when out the corner of my eye I get a glimpse of this perfect melon indentation."

He paused to make a circle with his hands.

"Now a nigga bangin' the guts up out of this stripper, ya'll know how a real playa' do it. Pop, pop, I'm slappin' that ass, makin' it do what it do, while I'm doin' the do, and this melon movin' around the curtain we behind interruptin' my long stroke. Now ya'll mu'fuckas know Frank Lester's hodar is always on beep-beep."

"H-H-H-Hodar?"

"Yeah," he looked up and down, "radar for ho's, li'l nigga."

"O-O-O-Okay, okay, I feel you."

"Anyway, I got platinum horse tail all in my face, I'm dick deep in this be-otch's pussy, but this melon is fuckin' wit' my big head, interferin' with Big daddy nut-nut."

"B-B-B-big d-d-d-daddy nut-nut?"

He banged his fist on the table. "Lil' nigga, if yo' st-st-st-studderin' ass don't stop interruptin' me."

The others sitting around Frank Lester's entertainment room broke out laughing.

"As a mutha fucka was sayin', the curtain is bouncin' to the bass of Fat Joe's new jam Lean Back, and I'm leaned alllllll the way back, my eyes and my mind on the ass dancin' curtain while Big daddy nut-nut is slowly comin' in for a landin'."

"Ha-ha, d-d—d don't tell me you---"

"Got damn, studderin' Steve. Will you shut the fuck up and let me tell my got-damn story?"

"M-M-M-My bad, g-g-g-go head."

"Anyway, make a long story shawt, this bitch is in mid mu' fuckin' bounce when I grabs the Julia Robert's-lookin' ho's waist, pushes her off me, takes the jimmy off my Johnson, puts it in her hand with a couple hundred bones and rises the fuck up.

"A nigga ain't even bust a nut off in the be-otch, that's how this mystery ass in front of the VIP curtain had my curiosity up. Who owned the ass that was making the curtain move," I wondered.

"Yeah, F-F-F-rank who w-w-w-as the h-h-h-o that m-m-made you rise up off the p-p-p-pussy?"

"Interrupt me one mo' mutha' fuckin time, I'm o' put my foot so far up yo' ass you'll be shittin' shoe polish for a mutha fuckin' week." He paused to look the guy up and down, before saying, "Li'l nigga."

"Anyway the black knee-boot, platinum weave wearin' ho' gets attitude and shit cause I didn't give her the whole three-hun'. I damn near went Ike turner on the be-otch, but insteada' puttin' my pimp hand down, I just looked at the funky ho' like, is you fuckin' dumb, stupid, crazy, or all mu' fuckin' three?

"Next, I put my finger to her lips and shakes my head left to right. I pull my pants up, buckle and zip my shit, grab my bottle of Louis and heads west.

"Finally, I satisfied my curiosity. I pull the curtain back and damn near blinded the melon-ass bitch with my diamond Colgate smile. Mu' fucka was young and tender, just like a nigga like 'em. Yes sir, with that sweet lollipop drop-basketball-melon-ass.

"I give it to the ho', she tried her damnedest not to recognize a playa'. I guess she was trying to show respect for the lame ass L-7 square ass lookin' nigga that had her hemmed up in the curtain in the first damn place.

"I eased on up to her. I acts like I know the ho'. I strike up a conversation and pretty soon captain lame game faded back into black until he was a memory.

"I figure the pretty young be-otch is a star in the makin', so I pull summa' my Romeo and Juliet game up out the archives of my mind. Next thing you know, she humpin and bumpin' what and whoever I choose.

"Ain't that right baby?" Frank turned his head towards the high school-aged looking brown-haired girl sitting beside him.

She knew her response had to be quick and simple. Any little thing could send him into a violent rage.

Anyone in his circle who had lived long enough had, at one time or another, felt his wrath.

Trapping pretty girls and getting them strung out on the drugs he flooded the streets of St. Louis with was just a hobby.

"I said, ain't that motha' fuckin' right?"

"Yeah, daddy," she cooed.

"Say what be-otch?"

"Huh?" she responded in fear.

Pop!

She put her hands to her face and tried to move away from him, scared he was going to beat her in front of his friends again.

Instead he leaned into the white powder lined up on the glass table, pressed his thumb down on one end of his nose and snorted.

He threw his head back, shook it and pinched his nose before speaking.

"Be-otch, how many times have I told you to never 'yeah' me? You ain't back in redneck ville. This ain't Jefferson City.

"Speak the Queen's English like a proper White Ho' when you wit' me, cause I don't fuck with no alley talkin' ass be-otches."

"Yes, Daddy, I'm sorry."

"Don't be sorry, just don't do that shit again. Now go over there." He pointed to a man old enough to be her grandfather sitting on the other side of the mirrored table in a black chair. "And give that studderin' motha fucka some head."

She got up and walked over to the lounger. She got on her knees and undid his pants.

"Don't worry Julieliscious, Daddy got some get high for you when you finish with him and the others," Frank said.

The guy looked like balled up burnt paper with rat teeth, but anything was better than Frank's sadistic son tying her up and letting the dog mount her from behind, ripping her insides apart again.

She silently prayed, begging God for forgiveness and asking Him to end her life before she did it herself.

CHAPTER 1

MOMMA

I could remember it as if it were yesterday. Just thinking about my past brought chills to my spine and a fiery hatred to the core of my soul.

I massaged my temples as I maneuvered my platinum Range Rover around our horseshoe driveway. Oh my God, I'd just come from an exhausting and ridiculously crazy real estate closing. I couldn't believe how ignorant and infantile the spoiled rich behaved. I mean, I'd worked my butt off for Dr. Grant Herbert Daniels III. Just because he was the most prominent African-American plastic surgeon in the greater Los Angeles area didn't mean he had to be the most prominent butt hole, but he was.

The *LA County Industry Insider* reported that Dr. Grant Daniels was plastic surgery's Van Gogh, and he was here to stay. It was rumored that he'd worked on everyone from Latoya and Janet to Liz and Joan. If only the world knew what I knew. Despite all the praise being lavished on him, he was and would always be Dr. Death Daniels to me. I could have died from the breast job he botched.

He was in his mid-forties, medium height, sort of plain looking, with short, graying hair. His third wife was younger than his oldest daughter. For the last two years, he reported earnings in excess of three million. That meant he was doing at least double that, considering the kind of man he was. He'd recently made his last court-ordered twenty-thousand-dollar a month child support payment. His practice was booming. Money was the least of his problems, yet he, like most financially successful men, was a certified, card carrying clown.

He may have found the house, but it was me he called and begged to convince the owners to sell. Let him tell it, this was his house. The architects stole the design from his mind. I wasn't the least bit surprised when he sent me a copy of the original blueprints. What did surprise me was the fax he sent over to the RE/MAX office where I now worked as a clerk.

He knew how to push my buttons. Usually the seller pays a commission to the listing agent, who then splits it with the selling agent, after the broker gets their cut. No, no, no, not this time. This wasn't just any ole contract. If it was, I wouldn't have looked twice at it. But since I was no longer a licensed real estate agent in the state of California, I had to go over it with a fine tooth comb, making sure I covered myself in case the real estate commission or RE/MAX got wind of it.

I read over the numbers three times just to make sure I wasn't seeing multiples. Dr. Death offered me two hundred thousand dollars to close the deal. He even stipulated in a separate addendum that I'd be reimbursed for all expenses I incurred, whatever they may be. Dr. Death also stated that he would pay market value for the 7,487 square foot home. The deal he offered was merely a love offering for my silence for what he'd done to me on his operating table. He also knew that I was his best chance to convince the owners to sell. He'd witnessed my careful planning and relentless negotiation tactics.

After signing the agreement, I replaced my fuchsia Dolce and Gabbana heels with black Nike running shoes. I didn't change out of my black St. John's outfit because I wanted to be taken seriously. My platinum- framed Christian Dior shades completed my ensemble.

I rubbed my hands together as if I were trying to start a fire. My adrenaline was flowing. I boxed the air before I set out to do what I do. It was feelings like the ones I was having now that made it vividly clear how much I hated the mirage I lived. I mean, my whole life was just like L.A., smoke and mirrors, air kisses, and rubber handshakes. I owned the 'In' vehicles. I wore the 'In' clothes. I dined with the 'In' people. I was even married to the 'In' man.

My husband was thirty-five, tall, bald, not great looking, but handsome in a Fishburne sort of way. He was most proud of his Harvard pin, his Bostonian lineage, his golf game, and his successful insurance businesses, in that order. Missing from this list were his daughter and his wife.

Did I ever love him? No. Did I ever like him? Yes. He was what every young woman wanted, security spelled M-O-N-E-Y. I must have had a bad pack of pills, or he had super sperm, at least one. I married him more for the life that was growing inside of me than for the L or the M word.

We owned a home in Encino, less than two miles from Michael Jackson. You'd think I would be happy, especially since I'd been homeless, and had grown up in orphanages all across L.A. County. If I was happy, I wouldn't be popping Celexa and Lexapro like tic tacs. It didn't take much to convince Dr. Death Daniels to continue with the anti-depressant prescriptions even now, two years after the silicone bag burst inside my chest less than two weeks after the boob job he screwed up.

I hated my work, and I barely liked my husband these days. From the time our daughter was born, he was a ghost in our lives. The only time he spent with her was when he'd give her an occasional bath.

I guess—no, I know—I lived my life so my Babygirl could have every opportunity that I didn't have. She was, is, and will always be my purpose for breathing. That's why I dealt with headaches like Dr. Death Daniels and Corinne Hart, the owner of the estate home he coveted.

I'd been on the case three months before the private investigator got me the dirt I needed. Even I was shocked at the mountain he uncovered.

BABYGIRL

After my phone calls to the Hart residence went unanswered and my messages were not returned, I camped out across the street from the massive black iron-gated entrance. I peered through the gate's curved bars only to see a winding, uphill, runway-like driveway.

Three Magic Johnson Starbucks lattes and five hours later, a late model virgin-white Bentley raced down the driveway. I drove the Rover in right behind the convertible Bentley, just as the electronic gate was closing. Suddenly the Bentley came to a halt. I barely avoided a collision as I slammed on my brakes right inside the gate. Immediately, I jumped out of the Rover and ran up to the Bentley. The beige top was making its way up as I stuck my arm over the window.

"Mrs. Hart, forgive me. My name is L.J. Hawkins. I'm a real estate agent."

"And I'm calling the police," she said in a snobbish tone.

"Please! Just give me one minute," I pleaded. "Sixty seconds."

"I certainly will not. I have a maid, a gardener, and a pool person. I have enough of you people working for me as it is."

"You people," I said.

Ignoring me, she continued, "There is nothing you can do for me."

Oh no, she did not refer to me as 'you people.' I closed my eyes. Relax, breathe, stay in control, I told myself before I went 'you people' all over her.

To add oil onto ice, this b-i-t-c—you know what—had closed her convertible top on my arm. Oh, my job was about to get much easier and much more fun. Luckily, I had what I wanted in my free hand.

"Yes, police, I'm Corinne Hart, wife of Douglas Palmer Hart of Hart Pharmaceuticals." She looked at me and rolled her eyes through her peach-tinted Gaultier sunglasses. "I have a—" Her mouth flew open, and her eyes tried to push themselves out of her head.

"Hello. Hello. Mrs. Hart. Are you all right?" the invisible voice over the loud speakerphone asked.

"Yes, I'm-I'm sorry. False alarm. I thought, I thought I-I saw something."

"Yes or no, are you sure everything is fine?" the female voice shot back.

"Yes, I'm frigging sure."

Click.

"Where did you get that?" What do you want?" she asked.

"First, I want you to release my arm." The top went up just enough for me to free my throbbing limb. "I want your house."

"What do you mean, you want my house? Are you mental or something?"

Ignoring her insult, I went on. "I represent the person you and your husband are going to sell your home to. Now, my client will buy your home at market value, which is seven point five."

"You are mental." She took off her hat and cringed as if she had eaten a lemon doused with hot sauce.

"No, but it's obvious that you are."

"Surely you jest. It took well over a year and six and half million to build the Hart Estate. And since then, we've put almost another one point five into the indoor pool, the statues, and the landscape." She shook her head. "No, no way in Sam damn hell."

"Okay," I said, as I shrugged my shoulders and nodded. "If that's your final answer, I guess I'll have to show these to your hubby."

She cackled like a chicken. "My husband was there."

"I'm sorry." I put my hands together as if I were about to pray. "You don't understand. I am going to your husband simply because I need to appeal to someone who can understand what would happen once the Humane Society," I counted on my fingers,

"ABC, CBS, NBC, FOX, the *Times,* and the local authorities get a copy of these pictures."

I nodded while stretching my jaws into a smile so wide it hurt. "I'm sure there are laws against copulating with Doberman Pinschers. And I bet you don't find anything sick about forcing an animal to enter you. It's bad enough that you had to suck the poor creature off. What are you, thirty, thirty-five?" I put one hand on my hip and turned my head toward the sky before continuing, "You are, hmmm, at most a size three. Auburn hair, nice tan, great boob job, and all you can find to screw you is a dog. You are a sick biscuit."

I shook my head. "Here is my card. I'll have a contract Fed-Exed to you tomorrow. We'll close by the end of the month, and you will have until the middle of next month to be out of my client's house. Oh, and by the way, the sales price of seven point five is non-negotiable. Upon closing, I'll give you the negatives and all prints of these pictures."

"But," she tried to interject.

"No buts." I put a finger in the air. "Except for the hairy pale one that belongs to your husband. Yes, I have pictures of his butt with a clear tube protruding from it with what looks like a white rat moving around inside."

I felt her eyes burning my back as I walked off, smiling.

Ninety thousand dollars of Dr. Death's money and six months from the time I hired the two ex-Naval SEAL counter intelligence experts, I had a cemetery full of dirt on Douglas "rat in the booty" Hart and his mantelpiece, smart aleck, dog-molesting wife.

It turned out to be my own Black Friday. It all began at two o'clock in the afternoon on July 30, 1986. No one was more eager to get this closing over with than I was, or so I thought. We were all sitting at a long mahogany table at the expensively decorated offices of Jean, Tanner, and Cohen. The closing packet was neatly organized on the table in front of Sherman Tanner.

Prior to the closing, I'd explained in detail to Dr. Death how the deal worked. He'd get a seventy percent loan to value on the first mortgage, and he'd get another loan to cover another twenty percent, which meant he'd need to bring ten percent plus closing costs plus my fee to the table in certified funds. That totaled it one million, seventy-five thousand dollars. The morning of the closing, I called and told him he'd need an extra fifteen hundred dollars for miscellaneous closing fees that neither I nor the mortgage broker had anticipated.

As we sat at the closing table and Dr. Death reviewed the expenses, he turned into Mr. Hyde right then and there, going ballistic over a measly two hundred and twelve dollars. I pleaded with him to calm down. I explained that it was not uncommon for the HUD-1, which is the settlement statement of fees, to be slightly off.

He exploded out of his seat and started hollering about the personnel at banking and finance being crooks, and how he refused to pay out another dime. He would have blown the whole deal if I hadn't gone Medusa on him. My stare and the sharpness of my nails grinding into his arm instantly petrified his Mr. Hyde mask. I casually rose from my chair and led him by the arm out of the office, into the hallway of the glass high-rise office building.

"How soon you've forgotten about the Hollywood Heights Office Park Plaza scandal. Let me refresh your memory. You hired me to convince the seller to let you pull all the equity out of the plaza by doing an additional sales contract at the plaza's appraised value. That was five hundred thousand dollars more than the listing price of eight million, remember?"

I stabbed him in the chest with my finger before

continuing. "Because you wouldn't let the seller 1099 you to avoid paying capital gains taxes on the half-million dollar kickback he was giving you, the little old man blew the whistle on us. I lost my real estate license and you only lost the twenty-five hundred dollars you paid to have the bogus appraisal done."

With his arms crossed and wearing a smug look on his face, he asked, "Did I not have a fifty thousand-dollar check couriered over to you the day the board suspended your license?"

"Fifty thousand dollars was what I made on a slow month before you came along. And the only reason you gave me that was to buy my silence. Consider yourself lucky I remained silent this long." I snapped a finger in his face. He flinched. "Just like that, you'll go from being the scalpeled Van Gogh to Frankenstein Van Gone if I go to the press or the American Medical Association and tell them about the refurbished silicone implants that burst inside me that you," I stabbed his chest, "used on me."

Like Moses parting the Red Sea, it was a miracle how the evil Mr. Hyde of a minute ago was suddenly transformed back into a gracious, witty, calm Dr. Daniels. The closing went smoothly from then on, and I was out of there in no time with a check burning my hands all the way to the bank.

Not only did I have to wait in line thirty minutes to deposit the check into my account at the ATM, but I had to fight rush hour Friday traffic in L.A. It took me two hours to drive ten miles, I thought as I sat in front of our beachfront home in Santa Monica. I was too exhausted to get out of my Rover. I reached into my purse and came out with two Tylenols and some goody powder. After washing them down with a half bottle of Evian water, I took a deep breath, got out of the Rover, and stretched my back. As I walked up my cobblestone steps, I couldn't help but close my eyes and picture

8

myself sipping on a glass of Chardonnay while leaning against the jetted wall of my black Jacuzzi tub, listening to Will Downing as bath salts and oils rumbled around me, soothing my tired, aching muscles.

My imagined Calgon moment was abruptly interrupted. I could've sworn I heard Babygirl screaming over the loud classical music that was piped in all around the house.

CHAPTER 2

MOMMA

I fumbled with my keys before finding the right one. I opened the door, kicked off my heels, and ran in my stockinged feet toward my husband's voice. At the library door, I thought my heart was about to explode. I was barely able to stand as I looked in. My husband, my baby, my husband's best-friend's wife, and me. No, I shook my head. I was right here, so why did I see me in the library? My mind was playing tricks on me. I opened my mouth but nothing came out. They wouldn't look my way, so they had no way of knowing that I was falling. No, I was running. My legs were taking me the other way. My mind reached back for my baby.

I wanted to turn back, but I couldn't. I was in the kitchen. My eyes zoomed in on the speckled gray granite countertop in the middle of the ocean blue tiled floor. There it was, on the island, waiting for me in all its gleaming glory. In an arm wave of confused chaos, I swept the cutting board away to the floor, along with an array of sliced vegetables. Wearing the smile of a clown, I came away from the kitchen island countertop holding the butcher knife like Lady Liberty holding her torch.

I don't remember walking out of the kitchen and down the long open hall, but I must have, because again I found myself looking into the French glass double doors of our library, which was now open. And I was inside with the knife. No, I was outside looking in. It was like I was at a live horror movie. I looked at me as I growled in the middle of the library.

My husband was a statue. His face was frozen with emotion as he stood in front of Babygirl. I must have blinked, because I missed something. Now instead of holding his penis on the side of my baby's face, his hand was on his neck, trying to stop the blood that was gushing from it.

My baby ran into my arms. No, not my arms, because I was outside the library. I had never gone in. But, but who, how? I wondered while I was left holding the air instead of my baby in my outstretched arms. After blinking a third time, my eyes focused on the bloody, naked, screaming white woman in the room.

"No!" I called out as I straddled and cut the woman from neck to navel. I pinched myself. It hurt, and I wasn't in that library. I was losing my mind. No, I couldn't be, because if I was, I wouldn't know that I was losing it. I covered my eyes and prayed for God to wake me from this living nightmare.

Once I uncovered my eyes, my baby was crying at my feet. I found myself in the middle of bloody books, scattered papers, and new decisions. Councilman Ward's wife's legs spasmed while she lay sprawled on the floor underneath a twelve-foot cherrywood book case. My husband quietly stared at the recessed lighting on the two-story ceiling.

"Is Daddy in Heaven, Mommy?" my six-year-old daughter asked, pulling me out of wherever I had gone. I looked at myself.

"Mommy, Daddy and Auntie Gina hurted me." Oh my God. What had I done?

"Mommy, are we going to get in trouble?"

I shook my head. "No, baby." I kneeled onto the hardwood floor, trying to reassure my naked, sexually abused baby that everything was going to be just fine.

"I promise they will never hurt you again, baby," I said as I held her close to my heart.

"Thank you, Mommy." I nodded.

"Mommy?"

"Yes, baby."

"You promise, Mommy."

"Promise what, baby?" I asked, doing everything I could to stop from crying.

"Mommy, just say you promise."

"Mommy can't, can't say that if I don't know what it is I'm promising."

She broke out in tears. "You ain't going to never ever, ever, never, ever leave me."

I nodded my head, "Cross my heart; hope to die, stick a needle in my eye."

"I love you, Mommy."

"I love you too, Babygirl." Thank God I'd gotten there before my husband got a chance to penetrate my baby . . . or had he at another time? What had Gina done to my baby? I had so many questions, but too little time to look for answers. All I had time to do was run and run as fast and as far as I could. I knew what I had to do. I'd read it somewhere in a book. I took a deep breath.

"Babygirl, go upstairs to your room and watch your Little Bill video. I'll be up to get you in a few." She shook her head and started to cry.

"What's wrong, sweetie?"

"I don't wanna go up there." She pointed to the brass railed winding staircase. "You said you wasn't never gon' leave me."

"I'm not, Babygirl. I'm just going to grab some things. We are going on a vacation."

She just looked at me.

"Okay, Babygirl, you can stay with Mommy, okay?" She nodded.

I had no family. I was on my own. It was just Babygirl and me. I went to my husband's-my dead husband's bedroom closet. I walked into the middle, removed a couple of shoe boxes and opened his safe. After cleaning it out and grabbing my jewelry, I grabbed some clothes and some toiletries. Next, I pulled out a backpack and a duffel bag and threw everything in them. I rushed to Babygirl's room, grabbed a few of her things, put them into my bag, and with her following behind, we left in the Rover.

An hour later, I'd driven to the ATM and pulled everything I could from credit cards and debit cards. I estimated that I had close to thirty thousand in cash. Most of that came from the safe. After filling the tank and nearly cleaning out the snack food aisle at the Quicktrip, I threw all my cards and I.D. out the window. I kept only my driver's license, and that would be history in a few hours, I thought.

By 11:00 that night, we were out of the desert and into the bright city lights of Las Vegas. I would've loved to get a room at Caesars Palace or the Mirage, but since I didn't have any I.D., Babygirl and I settled for the Doo-Drop Inn truck stop motel.

Early the next morning over breakfast at the Doo-Drop donut shop and eatery, I overheard a trucker telling a waitress that he was on his way to Atlanta, Georgia to deliver a shipment of Sealy posturepedic mattresses. I left a twenty on the table, grabbed Babygirl, and rushed out into the mid-summer morning, blazing sun. I spotted it immediately. In blue and grey lettering on the side of the eighteen-wheeler, the sign simply read: UNITED MATTRESS, INC. A few minutes later, we were sitting on plastic covered mattresses, with a pen light on.

That was four long years ago.

CHAPTER 3

BABYGIRL

"I wanna thank You for this day, for every breath we take, and thank You for my Babygirl. Amen."

"Amen," I said. "Momma, can I hang out with you today?"

"Girl, you know Momma has to work."

"But, Momma."

"But, Momma nothing."

"I ain't gotta go to school, though."

"You *ain't* and *gotta* what?"

I sighed. "I do not have school today."

"That's more like it. But remember," she pointed in my direction, "Babygirl, you have school every day. There are no days off," Momma said.

"I know, I know." I shrugged. "Every day, every experience is a school lesson, so therefore it's up to me to discern and study it."

"Very good. Now, that's Momma's Babygirl. Tell you what, you can hang out with me until one, and then you go see Uncle Ben. Deal?" She stuck out her hand.

"Deal," I said right before shaking Momma's hand.

"Grab your bag, let's go."

It was a beautiful, cool Atlanta December day. The sun was waking up with the early morning rush hour holiday season traffic. Our neighbors were still dead to the world despite the noise of cars racing down the I-20 freeway that was over and under our cardboard box make-shift homes.

"Momma, look." I pointed to the other side of the street.

"Stay here," Momma said, as she ran into the street.

14

"Get up, fool. Are you nuts?" Momma shouted.

He sat up and turned his head. "You know I is, but that's beside the point, Babysis. I'd like to lay here and chat, but I gotta get back to work," he said, lying back down in the street. Car horns were blaring, people were cursing and driving around him.

"Don't try that crazy stuff with me. I am not the one. Not this morning. Now, you get your white behind out of this darn street right this minute, Shabazz," Momma said as she marched out into traffic, weaving her way around the busy street until she was standing next to Uncle Bazz.

"Look at your niece over there." She pointed to me.

"You are scaring her half to death. What kind of example are you trying to set for a ten-year-old?"

Shoot, I wasn't scared. Uncle Bazz was funnier than TV.

"What if something happens to me? Who's going to look after Babygirl?"

Beep! Beep!

Momma turned toward a bright red sporty Mercedes. "Calm down, we're moving!" Momma shouted as she helped Uncle Bazz up from the pavement.

"Get your fucking ass out of the street, you crazy whore," the driver yelled as he sat on his horn. Momma looked at me and covered her ears. I sighed before loosely putting my hands over my ears. Momma was crazy if she thought I was gonna miss hearing Uncle Bazz straighten this dude out.

Uncle Bazz got up from the street, reached in his pocket and came out with his taped-in-the-middle, single-lensed, brown plastic glasses. He turned his head toward the hornblower, hawked and spit in his direction before wiping the single lens on his dingy T- shirt. After putting on the glasses, he brushed himself off, still standing in the middle of the street.

15

BABYGIRL

Traffic was starting to back up as Uncle Bazz cracked his neck and his knuckles before walking toward the man in the Mercedes. The angry driver suddenly took his hands off the horn. He turned the wheel to the left as if he were about to drive onto the sidewalk.

"Motherfucking Elmer's glue, pasty-skinned, stringy haired, whip-cracking, son-of-a-rat-bitch, inconsiderate, late to work, racist, Jeffrey Dahmer- looking, pecker-wood, Fred Flinstone, bastard asshole. Who the mother, mother, fuck, fuck do you think you are addressing?" Uncle Bazz looked like a run-over Mr. Bobblehead on speed.

I turned my head so Momma wouldn't see me laughing. Uncle Bazz was so crazy. He knew he couldn't whoop nobody with his skinny self.

He pointed toward me. "Do you not see my niece over there, fuck-face faggot?" I had tears in my eyes and my face was all turned up, trying to stop another laugh attack.

By now, Popeye the Hornblower had turned into Wimpy the Scaredy Cat as he let his windows up and locked his doors. The man just about crashed into the car behind him, backing up and trying to race around Uncle Bazz. The man's fear only made Uncle Bazz curse louder and harder.

"You have the audacity to fucking curse in front of my niece, I will fucking rip off your Fred Flintstone neck and piss down your Cowardly Lion spine. That's if you have one, you, you—"

"Shabazz! Shabazz! Relax, he's gone. You made your point," Momma said.

Uncle Bazz walked over to my side of the street.

"Babygirl, I'm sorry. You know how your uncle be gettin' when any clown be, uhm, disrespectin' my peeps," he said.

I nodded. We were used to his antics, and Momma knew it would be a waste of time to try to stop him

16

from cursing somebody clean out when he was like this.

"Come here. Give your Uncle Bazz a hug, Babygirl." I was in his outstretched, dirty arms almost before he could complete the request.

Uncle Bazz was crazy as a bedbug, but I loved him anyway. I never knew his real name. I don't think anyone did, not even Momma.

As long as we knew him, Uncle Bazz was always falling down in department stores where mysterious pools of water appeared before the yellow wet signs showed up. He took his own roaches to restaurants, where they'd end up in his food after he'd finished eating, and then he'd go off on the waiters and the manager until they let him leave without paying.

"Shabazz, what on earth were you doing?" Momma asked.

"Well, you see, uh, I been uh, practicin', uh, ya know, to uh, get paid and shit, by you know, uh, getting hit by a you know, uh, a nice car. Dig, dig, uh, see, I got it mapped, racked and backed, dig, dig." He nodded and gestured. "Uh, you know it was, uh, you who gave me the game, Babysis."

"Stop!" Momma said while grabbing hold of the dirty brown jacket that concealed his pale, emaciated arms. "Are you high?"

He looked to the ground.

"Shabazz, you are high?"

He covered his bugged-out blue eyes with one hand and ran his other through his dirty blonde-brown stringy short hair.

"You are high. What are you doing? Are you trying to kill yourself? Go over there." Momma pointed to the edge of the highway's overpass. "Jump off. It's easier, quicker, and it would be less painful for me and Babygirl."

"No, no, no." He stomped his mismatched sneakers on the ground while shaking his head. "I gotta plan,

17

Babysis." He grabbed Momma's arms with his long, thin, hairy, dirty hands. "I-N-surance. You hipped me to the game. Dig, dig, dig you know how you be talkin' to us bout life I-N-surance, securities, real estate and whatnot, huh, huh, huh, ha, ha, yeah, yeah, represent, represent, star student, putting it down like James Brown, yeah, applyin' what you teachin', wearin' the crown, rep-resent, rep-rep-resent," he sang and danced.

"Rep-resent, rep-rep-resent," I sang along with him as we held hands and danced around Momma.

"Babygirl, what have I told you about dipping in grown folks' business?"

"Sorry, Momma."

"Stay in a little girl's place or else."

"Yes, ma'am."

"Shabazz, you are talking crazy. I don't want Babygirl around your madness today. Come on, Babygirl," Momma said as she grabbed my hand away from Uncle Bazz.

"A'ight, a'ight, a'ight, for real-for real-for real, ho-ho-ho-hold on, Babysis. On the real deal Holyfield now, I went to, uh, the book house and read on, uh, you know, uh, I-N-surance, you know. So, I uhm, I'm gonna get rich by, uh, getting hit by a car. Not just any car, but an expensive car, like that Mercedes. And it ain't gon' be no nigga Benz. It gon' be a Flintstone- driven fully, I-N-sured. You know a nigga prob'ly ain't got no I-N-surance.

"Dig, dig, dig, I'm gon' get my forty acres and a mule with interest. Them Flintstones got all the pie. I'm tryin'a get my piece. Just watch a nigga get that I- N-surance. You done empowered the right nigga, baby, Babysis."

"What did I tell you about that word?"

"Ah, yeah, my bad. Sorry, Babysis."

"And as for you, young lady," Momma stabbed the air in front of my face, "I don't see anything funny. Either zip it or go across the street and wait on me. I am not going to tell you again."

I bowed my head. "Yes, ma'am, I'm sorry," I said, dying to laugh some more. Shoot, I couldn't help it. He was funny.

I don't even know why Momma always used that finger to threaten me. She knew she wasn't gon' do nothin'. Talkin' 'bout she not gon' tell me something again. She knew she gon' keep tellin' me if I kept messing up.

Momma crossed her arms and shook her head.

"What? What? What, what, what?" he questioned.

"Shabazz, how many times do I have to tell you, honey? You are white."

"I can't help the skin I was born in. Come'ere." Momma leaned in to him. He whispered really loud,

"Somewhere down the road, them mu'fuckin' Flintstones raped my ancestors so much and so many times they, uh, impregnated them over and over until my mother ended up being a slave in oppressor's skin. You know good and got damn well this blonde hair and these blue eyes are just a mirage. Black ain't a muthafuckin' color. It's a state of mind, a state of being, huh, yeah, all eyes on me, right on for the right- ons, right, right, right," he said while bobbing his head.

"Babygirl, I see you over there. I'm not playing with you. Don't make me tell you again."

There she went again with that finger and them threats. "Okay, Momma, I'm sorry, for real this time." Traffic was steady. I'd gotten used to the confused stares of passerby.

"Shabazz, I love you. Babygirl loves you. We just want you to get clean. You are so intelligent."

He smiled, brandishing his yuk-mouth, deadwood-looking teeth.

"This car insurance fraud scam is too dangerous. What if—"

BABYGIRL

"Babysis, I uhm, peep game, peep game, peep game, dig. I got it mapped, racked and backed. I lose a foot, half a leg, so what? I get a nice hospital bed, and I get this monkey off my back. I get a mouthpiece to represent me in court. The I-N-surance company settles. I get a fat check and a disability check on the monthly. I get you and Babygirl off these here streets," he made a wide arc with his arm, "and we ball out for life, dig?"

"No, I don't dig. That foot, that leg could be your life. You always talk about getting back to black. How are you going to do that as a cripple? How can you place a price on what God gave you? Can't no man re- make or replace a leg or a foot." Momma tapped a finger on his forehead. "Your mind is the key, baby," she said.

"My mind, my mind is," he closed his eyes, "my mind is gone. Heroin is the slave master's overseer. He already got my mind. I'm in and out so much, I got standing reservations at the rehab. It's a wonder I got any blood left as many times as I've slit my wrist. Always some nosy, can't-find-they-business-nor-mind-they-business mu'fucka rescuing me. I can't, I can't," he shook his head, "break his chains. Every time I escape his plantation, he finds me and brings me back. That heroin overseer ain't nothin' but a damn Flintstone."

I never heard Uncle Bazz talk like this. A minute ago I was laughing my butt off, and now I was sad, about ready to cry. I wished so bad that I was grown. If I was, I'd help all my uncles and aunties on the streets.

"So, I figure if I'm in a wheelchair and can't get around too well, I can't be his slave no more. And then just maybe I can get my mind back."

"Shabazz," Momma put her arm around him, "I love you. Babygirl loves you. But that isn't going to do any good if you do not love yourself." She shook her head. "And I know you don't, because if you did, you wouldn't be killing yourself with that poison you shoot in

20

your arms.

"Go back to the library, the book house as you call it, and have Ben introduce you to the autobiographies of Malcolm X and Marion Barry. Learn how these strong African-American leaders escaped their drug plantations. By studying them, you're studying you. You may just figure out how to fall in love with yourself."

"Gotta go, gotta go, got business. I'll holla," he said as he unexpectedly ran off, trying not to let us see the scared and lonely tears that were escaping from the clouded window of his soul.

Momma and I walked off in silence. Twenty minutes later, we were at the BP gas station on Ninth and Peachtree. She went inside the store to get the key and the cleaning supplies from Ms. Lisa, like she had every day for almost three years now. Ms. Lisa owned the BP. She always worked the morning shift and if she didn't, instructions were left for whoever was there to give Momma the keys and the cleaning supplies. It was a good deal. We never had to buy soap or personal hygiene stuff. Ms. Lisa always made sure we was straight.

Momma always made sure that we washed up in clean bathrooms. Momma preached cleanliness to all the street people. She said just 'cause we on the streets don't mean we have to smell like the streets.

The Ninth Street BP had to have the cleanest bathroom out of all the gas stations in the city. We scrubbed the floors, the walls, the sink, and the toilet, until the tiny room sparkled like Mr. Clean had been there himself.

"Now, Babygirl, you go in wash up and brush your teeth. Momma has places to go, people to see, and money to make," she said as I took my backpack into the restroom.

Momma didn't think I knew what she was doin' to get money. But I did. I wasn't no baby. I was ten and a half, and I understood a lot more than she thought about a whole lotta things.

CHAPTER 4

MOMMA

"Babysis, why you always goin' in that place, baby? It ain't like you gots no mail. You just like all us."

Babygirl and I were downtown on Peachtree Street outside the Mailbox Etcetera next to the Can for Coins distribution center, listening to Two Can San.

"Outcasts. We's the only family you got, and ain't none us sent you no mail, baby," San spoke in a slow southern drawl.

Sometime during our first three months in Atlanta, I'd gotten the P.O. box. Of course, this was after we met Shabazz and he helped us secure the new socials, birth certificates, and state I.D.s. It cost me ten of the thirty thousand dollars I started out with, but it was well worth it. For one, I needed the P.O. box to establish an address for Babygirl's schooling. And two, I had to have a mailing address to take out the two million dollar life insurance policy. Just in case something happened to me, God forbid, I had to make sure my Babygirl would never have money woes.

"Girl, is you listenin' to what I's sayin'?"

"I'm sorry, San, my mind was somewhere else," I explained.

"I was sayin' . . . ah, forget it. It don't matter," San said with a wave.

Two Can San was a woman of indescribable size and undeterminable age. Even if it was 100 degrees in the shade, San wore several outfits all at once. You could say she wore her entire wardrobe daily. The fullness of her face made me think that she was a near-plus size woman. Her teeth were uncharacteristically white,

23

being that she lived on the streets.

"Yes, it does matter," I said pointedly. "I wanna hear what you have to say." Babygirl remained quiet, which was a surprise because that girl loved to run her mouth.

"I was just saying that, uh, ah, sugar honey ice tea, I forgot."

"You said we outcasts, Auntie Two Can, like y'all, and we don't have any family," Babygirl blurted out.

Two Can looked at Babygirl. "No, little missy, what your Auntie said was we is your onlyest family."

"I love all of you, as I do all God's children, but what have I told you about the power of words and positive thinking, San?"

"I hear what you be saying, baby."

"I don't think so, because if you did, you'd hold your head up and realize that we are not outcasts. We are real people who live in the real world. We don't need money, houses, fancy cars, and designer clothes to hide behind. We come as we are and live how we can. Like Sly says, we are everyday people.

"Now, that's real, and that's what we need along with family, San." I put out my hands. "Look at you. You are healthy, and you always have a shine on your face. You move with purpose. I don't know if I've ever seen you without a cart full or half full of cans. You own your own business, and you are successful."

"Successful?"

"Yes, successful."

"Pssh, go 'head on now, girl." She waved. "I ain't nothin' but a li'l old can lady."

"Only because that's," I pointed to the inside of her shopping cart, "how you see yourself. I see you," I looked up and pointed to the Russell Simmons Def Jam billboard in the sky above us, "as the CEO of Two Can San's cans."

"Okay, you seein' way, way too much," San said,

scratching her gray, shoulder-length wig.

"No, it's you who is not seeing enough. Ask yourself."

"Ask myself what?"

"Are you happy? And if you say no, then change your condition, girl. There are women all around the world who would trade places with you in a heartbeat."

"And they's damn fools too." She nodded.

"Go to the AIDS ward at Grady. Are they fools? Go to Shepherd Spinal Center on Peachtree around lunchtime and look at all the wheelchair-bound women sitting outside. Are they fools? Go to the women's prison—"

"Okay, okay," San interrupted. "I get it."

"Do you really?" I asked.

"Really what?"

"Get it."

"Yeah, I get it, I got it, and can't get rid of it. But what I don't get is why you homeless. I don't get why a girl so doggone smart, with so much mother wits, is on the streets. And to add butter to the cornbread, you gots this perty little angel out here too."

I touched her arm. "What makes you think that I'm homeless?"

Her eyebrows came together and she turned her head to the side. "You live in cardboard boxes and under blankets, don't ya?"

I smiled. "No, that's where I sleep."

She put her hands on her hips. "Same diggety dang thang, baby."

I shook my head in disagreement. "No, San. Home is not a structure. Home is where you live. Home is this entire city. Home is inside you. Home is where the heart is."

"Okay, what da address of your heart den? I'm o' send yous some mail." She winked as Babygirl snickered.

"Everywhere I am is home. Home is where you and all my family are. And as for my Babygirl, wow." I closed my eyes and took a deep breath. "She is being raised by the most beautiful people on earth. Who could show any more unconditional, non-judgmental love than her aunties and uncles on the streets? Who better to teach her about life than real people? San, you said it yourself, we don't have anyone but each other. I can't even fathom anyone loving Babygirl more than you, Shabazz, Big Ben, Baby Ruth, and the others."

"Well, you sho' nuff right about that," San said.

"Babygirl and I eat well every day at the mission, or the women's shelter, and when it's too cold or storming outside, we find a way to get a room."

"You make it sound like you livin' good."

"Oh, but I am. We are. I'm happy. My child is happy. We even get decent clothes from the women's care center on Sixth and Piedmont."

"I love you, baby, and God Almighty knows I loves me some Babygirl," she said, pinching Babygirl's cheeks. I cringed. I knew how Babygirl hated for anyone to touch her face.

"I'm going to let you get back to work. I got business, and I got to get Babygirl over to the library with Big Ben."

"Don't think I don't know what you doin', baby. The streets got eyes and ears that you don't always see. Like I said, you too doggone smart."

"I have to do whatever it takes within my power to keep Babygirl in St. Pius. You have no idea how expensive private school is these days."

"Why she gotta go to a—"

"Because she's my baby and no one or nothing is going to stop me from giving her the best education money can buy."

"That still ain't worth sellin' yo' soul for a jelly roll," San said.

JIHAD

"I'm not going there with you, San." I didn't want to go there; I couldn't go there. Now was not the time, nor would there ever be a time, with or without Babygirl being present. My business was my business, and the less others knew about the why and the for what, the better.

CHAPTER 5

BABYGIRL

The past two years were a rollercoaster. Momma was up one minute and down the next, but you'd never know by the act she put on. She thought I didn't know. I was twelve, not two. She kept it hidden real good, though. If it weren't for Uncle Ben being sick and not making it to the library where he worked, I wouldn't have got a chance to witness it for myself.

Although she had her flaws, Momma was still Oprah Winfrey, Susan Taylor, and Iyanla Vanzant all rolled into one.

She was a cool mom, but she acted like too much of a goody two-shoes in front of me. But I knew what she was doin'. She ain't fooled me one bit. Heck, I knew back when I was a little kid at nine or ten. Uncle Bazz had a big mouth, and I had even bigger ears.

Not no more, but it used to bother me that we didn't live in an apartment or sleep in a real bed. But as Momma always said, whenever you think you have it bad, look around you. There's always someone who has it worse. One thing I can say, though, is that there is never a boring moment living on the streets.

You'd think we was rich like most of the other kids at my school the way Momma strolled in like the Queen of England at my school functions. You'd think them multi-syllable look-me-up words tasted like fresh baked apple pie as they rolled off Momma's tongue while she spoke to my instructors. At my school we didn't have teachers, we had instructors.

While we walked or took the Marta over to the soup

kitchen after leaving the P.T.A. meetings or parent teacher conferences, I would use the three Fs like they were the only adjectives in the dictionary: Everything was fabulous, fantastic, and the parents were just flabbergasted.

Momma and I alternated roles, acting like the snooty, stuck-up parents and, as Uncle Bazz would call them, the I-N-structors. Whoever played the snooty, nose-up-in-the-air instructor was always touching whoever was the bourgeois parent, and starting most sentences with "To tell you the truth, Ms. or Mr. So and So," like they had been lying the whole time.

For real, though, school was all right, sort of boring. English was my favorite class because I loved reading. Math, hated it. History, too one-sided, so I hated it. Gym, hated it-well, used to hate it. I'd been a little black stick until this school year began. The boys really noticed me at gym now. Over the summer, my boobies went from seeds to oranges, and my little ooty was now a booty.

I didn't really have no friends in school because the girls were too Barbie and Ken, too Paris and Nicky. Even the two black girls who attended St. Pius were too white. The boys were too boyish, although they were a lot cooler than the girls.

The grownups living on the streets were my best friends and best teachers. They were always teaching me some new life lesson. Dolls, video games, and TV were over-rated. Living life was a lot more fun than watching someone else's life on a TV.

I was a little disappointed and excited at the same time when we went to the Fulton County Library and Momma found out Uncle Ben was out sick again. I loved Uncle Ben to death. He was like us, but he had a real live job. He was like a hundred-year-old Energizer bunny, and smart to death too. He'd be a gazillionaire if he went on *Jeopardy*. They'd have to call up God to beat

29

him. He knew everything, and I mean e-ver- ything.

I'd sit in the library on the third floor and read for hours until Uncle Ben got off of work. That's when he'd make me take whatever I was reading and apply it to myself and everyday life. He'd always say the message is the meaning and the meaning is the message. I'd have to tell him as many messages as I could that came out of the stories I read.

And guess what? Uncle Ben didn't even finish the eighth grade.

"Babygirl, I guess it's just me and you today," Momma said.

"I thought you had to work."

She waved her hands. "Nah, I'll just take the day off and spend time with you."

"But Momma, you ain't hardly worked since school been out."

She pulled out her cell phone.

I touched her shoulder. "Momma, I'll go with you, I don't mind. I'll wait wherever you want me to. I know we need money to get a room in case the storm comes like they say."

"Who's the mother here?"

"Me," I said.

"In that case, Moooommm, you can go to work with me."

"Okay."

We were heading for the library exit when Momma stopped.

"Babygirl?"

"Yes, ma'am?"

"I love you."

"I love you too, Mommy," I said before we hugged.

CHAPTER 6

MOMMA

Unbelievable. Talk about bad timing. I watched the morning sky wake up. It was as clear as glass and bright as a new baby's smile.

"I knew it was too good to be true."

"What are you talking about?" Babygirl asked. As if reading my mind, she said, "The weather, Momma. It don't—"

"It what?" I said as we were walking up the gravel driveway in front of the old, rundown-looking dull yellow house.

"It doesn't seem like December. We done had—" She caught herself, shaking her head. "I mean we have had nice warm weather and no rain or snow."

"That's about to change. Look at the sky." I pointed up. "It's about to pour down any minute," I said.

"There's a thunderstorm warning in effect until ten this evening," Graham said as he looked down while descending from the metal ladder on the side of the little house.

"Graham, this is Babygirl," I introduced.

He put the paintbrush down on a workbench in front of several bundles of roofing shingles and other supplies. He wiped his hands on his white paint- spotted coveralls.

"Well, well, well, aren't you just the cutest little girl? Uhm, uhm, uhm."

"Thank you, Mr. Graham."

"Mr. Graham was my daddy. You can call me G or Graham. Now, let's get out of this weather," he said while looking at me like I was dinner. He led us inside the

31

house.

"Where can she wait?"

"I didn't know you were bringing company, let alone your lovely daughter." He smiled.

"We can leave if you'd like."

"No, no, no." He shook his head.

I felt a little uncomfortable preparing to do business while Babygirl was with me. But Graham was always respectful. He seemed to have class. That's why I couldn't figure him out. I mean, he was in his early forties, intelligent, nice looking, respectable, and successful. He could have his pick.

"Hello, is anyone home?" He waved his large hands in front of my face.

"I'm sorry, I was just thinking."

"And may I ask what about, pretty lady?"

"Oh, her babysitter Ben was sick again. I was just a little worried about him. I almost didn't come."

"But you did, and I will."

"Aren't you Mr. Confident this evening?"

"I owe it all to the great presidents who have helped me build my self-esteem."

"Presidents?"

"Yep." He pulled out a rubberband-wrapped wad of bills. "Jackson, Grant, Washington, and Lincoln. I keep them close to me as often as I can."

"Where can Babygirl wait?" I asked again.

"Looks like she's already found somewhere."

"No, she's a very inquisitive young lady. She's looking around your house."

"Not much to see, pretty plain. Just a two bedroom, one bath ranch I bought a week ago to renovate and rent out. I guess she can wait in the front room."

"Babygirl?"

"Ma'am?"

"What are you doing?"

"Nothing."

Nothing and silence didn't work together with Babygirl. I walked into the front room where she was sitting on the floor cross-legged, looking over some old *National Geographic* magazines.

"Graham and I have to go in the back room and discuss some things. You wait out here for me, okay?"

"Okay."

Graham was in the shower. I waited in a back bedroom void of any furniture except a black Futon couch that folded out into a bed.

"Why aren't you ready?" Graham asked when he came out of the bathroom and into the bedroom with a towel wrapped around his tight, bronzed waist.

"I need to shower, if you don't mind."

"You could've got in with me."

"Uh, no I could not. Not with my daughter in the other room," I said as I walked toward the bathroom.

"A whore with morals."

I turned around slowly. "What did you say?"

"I just said a woman with morals." He shrugged.

"No, you did not. You called me a whore."

"Noooo, I know what I said."

I didn't stand for anyone disrespecting me. I knew what I did, but what I did wasn't what or who I was, and I didn't allow anyone to treat or talk to me like any less than a lady. That is why I chose my clients instead of letting them choose me.

I should have grabbed Babygirl, turned and ran. But I only needed another hundred dollars and I could get Babygirl into a real home. The house was just a little larger than this one. Babygirl would be so happy. We'd lived on the streets for six years.

If I didn't have to come up with eight hundred a month for Babygirl's school tuition, seventy a month for life insurance, ten dollars a month for my P.O. box, and oh yeah, fifty dollars a month for my cell phone, we would've been in a house long ago.

The older woman who owned the house that I was going to surprise Babygirl with, didn't ask many questions. She didn't have me fill out a lengthy application, nor did she ask for identification. "I know a sincere person when I see one. I can feel it in my bones. You are right for this house," she'd said. She went on to explain that her daughter had breast cancer, so she had to move to Chicago to care for her and her grandchildren.

Since I needed the money, I went into the bedroom and took a shower. When I walked back into the bedroom, Graham wasn't there.

I don't know why, call it instinct or a mother's intuition, something didn't feel right. "Babygirl," I called out. With only a small white towel halfway wrapped around me, I ran barefoot into the front room.

"Graham?"

"Shhhh," he mouthed with his finger to his lips before leading me to the back bedroom. Thank God, she was asleep.

"What were you doing?" I asked.

"Nothing." He shook his head. "Why?" He turned his head to the side. "What did it look like I was doing?"

"I don't know." I shrugged. But again, nothing was entirely too quiet, I thought as I crossed my arms and let the small towel drop to the bedroom floor.

"Okay, okay, you got me. You win," he said in surrender, throwing his hands in the air. "How much?" he asked as he let his towel drop onto the dirty beige hallway carpet while still standing in the doorway.

"How much for what? And can you please keep it down and close the door?"

"Let's cut the bullshit, okay?"

I put my hands on my hips. "What are you talking about, Graham?"

He picked up his pants from the floor and pulled out a stack of folded bills.

"What, another hundred, two hundred, what?" he asked, all wide-eyed as he peeled the bills off of his stack.

"Graham, you are scaring me. What are you talking about?"

"The girl. I gotta have me some of that young chocolate." He licked his lips as his eyes did somersaults in the back of his head.

Oh, my dear God in heaven. This man was truly insane. I closed my eyes. *Breathe, girl, breathe. Think, think.*

Very calm and relaxed, I said, "She's not for sale, but this one's on me. Call it an early Christmas present," I said as I put my hand out and started massaging his throbbing member.

He slapped my wrist. "Bitch, get your hands off of me. I want that little whore, and I'm gon' get me some of that there," he said before he turned around and marched out of the room.

"Graham, she's only twelve," I pleaded as I followed behind him.

"That's what I'm talkin' 'bout. Prime cut, low mileage. Hell, if she can bleed, she can breed," he said, rubbing his crotch like he had crabs.

"I'll die first!"

He backed into the bedroom with me on his back and my teeth in his neck. "Funky bitch, I'll kill you!"

That was all I heard before he flung me off of him, slinging me into the window on the other side of the room. Glass shattered on and around me, letting the outside rain come in. I woke up just in time to see a large foot on a collision course with my face.

CHAPTER 7

BABYGIRL

Momma, please hurry up, I willed. She was takin' forever in the bathroom while this nutball stood over me. Although I played sleep with my eyes closed, I knew he was there 'cause of his breathing. He sounded like he was about to have an asthma attack.

Deep down inside, I wished he would. I was scared, and I just wanted to leave. I didn't care 'bout no storm or nothin'. I just had to keep playin' the sleep game. My momma ain't raised no fool.

I must've really drifted off, because next thing I know, I heard Momma and that man arguin' and fightin' in the back. I jumped up and looked around until I spotted this big ole hammer on the kitchen counter. With it in my hands, I ran to the back room.

"Momma!" I screamed.

He was naked as the day he was born. He stood over Momma with one foot in the air, 'bout to stomp on Momma's face. He turned in my direction just in time to see the hammer coming his way.

"Babygirl?"

I heard a nasty, crunchy sound as the hammer busted him in the middle of his forehead. His blood jumped all over my shirt and my chin. He took a step and reached out to grab me. I screamed right before he crashed to the floor.

"Babygirl?"

I was trembling so hard, I almost dropped the hammer. "Momma," I said, as I crouched at her side. "You bleeding like crazy. What are we going to do? Momma. Momma."

"Babygirl, calm down. Everything will be all right.

36

Help me up," Momma said in a strained, barely audible voice.

"But Momma, you're bleeding really bad."

"Just . . . Just help me up, girl."

I was still shaking, but not enough for me to drop my hammer. Momma was just gon' have to get up the best way she could, using my hammerless arm for support.

"Wait for me by the door. I'll be there in a minute." I closed my eyes and vigorously shook my head from side to side. "Noooo, I'm staying in here with
you."

"Damn it, Babygirl." She pointed her finger at me and gritted her teeth. "I said leave this room now and wait at the dang-on door."

I was so scared I didn't know what to do. I ain't never heard Momma curse. I left the room crying. What was she gon' do? Why did I have to go? Was he dead? Why we couldn't just leave? Was I going to jail?

"Bitch, you try to kill me, and now you tryin'a rob me."

As soon as I heard him, I ran back in the room, just in time to see this man bent over Momma, banging her head into the hardwood floor with one of his large, King Kong hands.

"You funky whore, I'm gon' kill you and that li'l bitch of yours."

I held the hammer with both hands as I ran toward them, screaming. "Momma! Momma!" Before he could react, I was swingin'.

"Leave her alone," I said as I swung. Blood and all kind of stuff flew out of his head. I don't even know how long or how many times I hit him. The stink made me stop. I heard him poot. Then I looked at him and I saw it. He done went on himself. I dropped the hammer and dragged him off Momma, holding one hand over my mouth and nose.

37

"Momma, Momma." I shook her.

She stirred, and after a minute she spoke.

"Babygirl, I need, I need," she breathed, "you to . . ." She paused.

I waited.

"To be a big girl. Can you, can you do that for Momma?"

"Yes, ma'am."

She reached up and grabbed my arms in a death grip. "I'm going to need you to listen to me and do exactly as I say," she said while looking me in the eyes.

"Do you understand?"

I wiped the tears from my face and nodded.

"Take this." She put a wad of cash into my hands.

"Go to the bathroom, look in my pants pockets, and bring me my money and my phone."

Reluctantly, I did as I was told. It was killing me to see Momma like this. I walked on rubbery legs, but I had to keep going. I had to be strong for me and Momma. If we were going to make it out of this, I had to do what she told me. I had to be the momma now. She needed me to take care of her now.

"Here, Momma," I said, returning with everything she asked for.

"No, you put all that in your pocket," she said while squeezing my hand with another wad of bills.

"Now give me the phone, and go outside to the mailbox. Get me the address for this house."

Although we didn't go to church, Momma taught me that church was not a building, it was in you. She said God was everywhere, and I needed Him like I've never needed anything or anyone, so I took a minute to pray and cry in the rain.

By the time I got back to Momma, I was drenched. She was on the phone with what had to be 911. She motioned for me.

"Sixteen thirty-two," was all I said before she put

38

her index finger to her lips, motioning for me to be quiet. She repeated what I'd said, followed by the name of the street, before dropping the phone to the floor. Momma looked like a red, grown-up ragdoll lying propped up against the stained wall, surrounded by broken glass scattered all over the floor.

"Momma, can we go now?" I asked, fighting a losing battle to keep my tears inside my head. I was hoping the rain and the wind that were coming in from the broken window next to Momma would hide my tears and my fears.

"Babygirl, you have to listen to me, okay?"

My heart was in my feet. My body started a gentle tremble. I nodded.

"No, come here beside me."

I felt the tears, but I sucked them right back into my eyes. I shuffled my feet with concrete legs, slowly moving to Momma's side.

"We don't have long. Now, you know Momma loves you more than anything on God's green earth, don't you?"

"Yes, Momma. I love you too."

"I know. But Babygirl, just listen to me, okay?"

I nodded.

She grabbed my arm weakly. She grimaced in pain as she seemed to strain to look me in my face. "The police and the ambulance will be here shortly. You know these streets like the back of your hand."

"Momma . . ."

She shook her head. "I need you to go find your Uncle Ben or your Uncle Shabazz and tell them what happened. Stay with them until I come and get you."

"But . . ."

"But nothing. You have to go now. Momma will be fine. You can't be here when the police come. Please tell me that you understand what I am saying to you."

"Yes, ma'am," I said while losing the battle to keep

my emotions in check.

"There are the sirens now. They are getting close. Go, Babygirl. Go now."

I knew what Momma was talking about. I had killed a man. I was going to jail if I stayed. I moved in slow motion as I backed up toward the door.

"No, Babygirl."

"Momma," I cried out, "his fingernails are in my leg. Let go. Let go," I shouted.

My heart was beating furiously. Momma was trying to crawl to where I had dropped the hammer. I couldn't break free. The sirens were right outside. I kicked and screamed. He wouldn't let go. He wore the smile of Satan on his face. I kicked at his hand. I had to break free, to remain free.

CHAPTER 8

SHABAZZ

"Nigga, shut yo' ole ass up. You blowin' my muthafuckin' high-high-high-high with that bullshit," I explained to him while noddin' in and out of I don't know.

"That's the shit," Big Ben paused to take a sip out the brown paper bag, "I am talking about. Respect. Now, now." He pointed a long, crusty, dead-lookin'-ass finger at me.

"You see, you are a victim, a prisoner of your own doing. I hope you are listening to me, Wonderbread," he said, stumbling, trying not to sit on a couch spring.

"Only thing I'm a victim of is siety, and-and yo' ole, black Sigmond Fraud philosophyin' ass."

"You mean society," Big Ben corrected.

"What the fuck ever. Nigga, I'm high. You know what the hell I mean." I twisted my head to the side.

"And gon' be high 'til I die or reach the mu'fuckin' sky." I pointed a finger at him. "Now, put that in your bottle and drink it."

"I know you are high. I am not debating that." He pointed a finger in the air. "But, as you see, I am quite inebriated, but that doesn't mean I have to speak like my condition precipitates, Wonderbread."

I pointed my finger at him. "You doin' that shit on purpose. Why you always fuckin' with me?"

"How am I," he took another sip, "fucking with you?"

"Wonderbread. Nigga, you know I hate that shit. My name is Shabazz. S-H-muthafuckin'-bazz." I coughed after beating my chest for emphasis.

I wanted to break his finger off as he waved it at me again. I was getting dizzy following it. "You mean S- H-A, not S-H," he said while signing the air with that crusty damn finger.

I grabbed at my crotch. I didn't find it, so I settled for my thigh. "S-H-A on these N-U-T-Zees. Did I spell that shit right, muthafucka?"

"You detest me calling you out of your name, and yet you call me nigga, ole man, and motherfucker. I accept your colloquialism," he said as he folded one leg over the other and took another swig from the bag.

"Dere you go with them big-ass one-page words. Spell it, muthafucka."

"I-T."

"Spell collo-collo-collonalism."

"Colloquialism, Wonderbread," he said before taking another swig.

"That too, nigga. Hell, you know a nigga don't know what the hell you mean, but you still let them big shit words diarrhea out your nasty old mouth."

"Ah-ha!"

"Ah-ha what, muthafucka?"

"Ah-ha is that you obviously are suffering from a paranoid schizophrenia type of an identity crisis."

I was smiling through nods. The clouds were starting to fade. I was finally seeing what Big Ben was doing to me. "You trying to get me all in my feelings." I pointed a finger in his direction. "Nigga, you know I ain't crazy. You just like fuckin' with me. I bet that shit get your ole shriveled-up dick hard, don't it? Don't it, nigga?"

He sighed after turning up the bottle, in which a loud, obnoxious belch followed. "Penis envy now, hmmm." He paused to ponder. "You are white, a cracker, honkey, Caucasian, cave man, a Billy, a pink toe, all of these and more, yet you want to be me so bad that you call yourself what your people have been calling us for

42

hundreds of years. You shoot that heroin because you hate yourself. You hate being white. You hate being associated in any way with your oppressive and evil-doing ancestors. You hate you."

He had one more time to point that damn finger at me.

"So much, you've taken on the identity of not only a black man, but a revolutionary black man. And you truly think that you are a proud descendant of black African heritage, like me." He stuck his chest out. "You are merely a drug addict, wanna-be Nat Turner in white skin." He laughed.

"Fuck you, nigga. I'm a nigga and you a nigga, whether your Uncle Tom, Clarence wanna-be Thomas ass wanna be or not, and you know I'm a nigga. I'm blacker than your white-talkin' ass ever was and ever will be. Ole tight-ass, one-page word using Oreo, left- in-the-oven-too-long Saltine, pseudo-synthetic, house- ass nigga."

"Wonderbread, you know I'm just fuckin' with you. You know you are my number one white bread. Every time I go to the grocery store, I buy Wonderbread. Hell, I'm gon' buy you for real as soon as slavery is reversed," Ben said as he got up off the old, stained beige couch.

"You needs to quit fuckin' with me and fuck with that old-ass couch you done damn near got stuck in. Put a brick under the muthafucka or somethin'. I'm gettin' sea sick watchin' the bitch rock back and forth like a crippled rocking chair."

"At least I have a couch."

"A couch. Where? Nigga, you got an ouch. When a muthafucka sit down on one o' them springs and it be done stuck 'em in the ass, they scream 'Ouch!' "

"Ah-ha!" Ben pointed at me.

"There you go with that shit again. Nigga, you make my head hurt. Ah-muthafuckin'-ha what?"

"You seemed to get overly exuberant upon

expounding upon the springs in my couch sticking in a man's behind."

"Don't go there. D-don't even do that. You know I don't play them faggot games."

"Ahh, homophobic, are we?"

"Fuck you."

"Is that what you really want to do?"

I don't know why I let his ole dried-up decrepit ass get to me. As I marched past his ass, I smiled at the thought of busting him in his big mouth just one good got damn time. I mean, just one, just one muthafuckin' time. Always calm and shit. Lookin' like a dried, burnt-up Farakkhan, chastisin' a muthafucka.

"I hope you realize that you are talking out loud."

"I gives a fuck. You make a muthafucka wanna O.D.," I said, as I walked to the other side of the room.

"And where, may I ask, do you think you are going?"

"To lay the fuck down. You done made my head hurt. I'm high, and I'm tired," I said as I sat on the mattress.

"Don't you even think about bothering Johnny number seven," Big Ben said.

I looked at him like he just flew over the cuckoo's nest. He looked like he was 'bout to say something else smart until some muthafucka banged on the door like the police. Lock me up, I didn't care. I just wanted to lay the hell down. Fuck the police. A nigga wasn't 'bout to get up. They just had to bust down the door and carry my black ass off to jail. Fuck 'em. They was too late. I shot up everything that looked like dope. Muthafuckas wasn't gon' find shit on me.

It was a comedy act watchin' Big Ben run around like a one-legged midget in a butt-kickin' contest. Funny how all of a sudden that nigga was sober as a surgeon as he went lookin' for drugs and shit. That's what the nigga get for fuckin' wit' me. Hell, I'm a professional dope addict. I done smoked and shot up everything that resembled dope in that room. Shit, heroin too hard to come by.

"I'm going to jail because of someone else's malfeasance again. Shabazz, if I go back, I will kill you, and when you are dead, I will kill your ghost," Big Ben said right before he opened the door then backed into and fell over a blue milk crate overflowing with old records.

CHAPTER 9

UNCLE BEN

It was, let's see, 1956. I was the hippest cat in coolville back then. I sported a jelly roll, slick-back hairstyle just like the hippest cat-daddy on the planet. Nope, ain't never gon' forget it. I'd finally gotten the opportunity to lay my eyes on the cat mostly responsible for my success with the dollies and paper shakers.

It didn't happen in the sixties or seventies; oh, it started way before then. The movement began with one cat, Nathaniel Adams Cole. Yeah, that's right; Nat King Cole made it hip to be black. I mean not just black, but crayon, coal-crude oil black.

Me, hell, until the fifties rolled around, I was called light post, burnt tree, Black Ben, and other names. That was before Birmingham discovered Nat, and when they did, they discovered me.

Now, Nat the King Cole was jamming way back in the late thirties and forties, but Birmingham was always behind the times when it came to black folks' music. Folks say I was his illegitimate son, being that I was said to be his twin and only twenty-three at the time.

Well anyway, I was decked out in my best threads as I entered Municipal Auditorium in Birmingham. Cat Daddy Cole was playing for a packed segregated audience. It was fat city in the joint that night until some Billies pulled Nat off the stage and attacked him.

I had to put Stinky in a chokehold to stop him from leaving the Colored section in the balcony and jumping down on them Billies who had Nat. Nat was cooler than a polar bear's toenail as he got back on stage and jammed on jelly for the rest of the night.

JIHAD

After the show, me and Stinky was on our way to my chariot when we overheard some Billies talkin' 'bout how they'd taught that singin' nigger a thing or two. Next thing I know, Stinky done run off. I looked up the dirt parking lot cross the street just in time to see them Billies pounding on my baby cousin. Before I knew what I was doing, my new midnight blue, size twelve Stacy Adams was giving one of them Billies an enema. His buddy was trying to breathe as I held him in a five-finger chokehold.

By now, Stinky had left me and run off. Didn't take long for all the Billies in Alabama to be on me. When I woke up the next day, I was a purple pumpkinhead in the Birmingham County Jail infirmary. I considered myself lucky to wake up at all.

Three months later, my case went to trial. I was charged with two counts of attempted murder with a deadly weapon. If I knew a wing-tip Stacy Adams shoe could get me in so much trouble, I'da worn a pair of Buster Browns.

The fact that I was the only one hospitalized didn't matter. Nor did it matter that I fought half the dang city at one time. I guess Old Jim Crow decided that since I hadn't been hung, he'd string me up in his court system. It took all of three days to find me guilty. Imagine the amazement on my face when the judge sentenced me to twenty-five years to life.

I was too numb to cry, too shocked to move as I was roughly manhandled by two burly closet Klansmen in bailiff uniforms. The pink-faced, filled courtroom laughed, cat-called, and applauded as I was taken away with my legs dragging across the white speckled floor.

I spent my first five years in a small, dark cell in a basement-like dungeon. For twenty-three hours a day, I was alone with a steel slab and a blanket-thin mattress that I went to callin' Johnny. Johnny wore an old, mildewed, off-grey wool blanket and a jaundice-yellow,

47

piss-and-I-don't-know-whatever-else-stained sheet.

See, Johnny was my bed and my best friend. We spent hours, days, months, years discussing everything and anything. Other than Johnny, there was only a single overhead light in my dungeon that I turned off and on by screwing and unscrewing the forty-watt bulb.

It wasn't until my third year that the prison took my slop bucket and put in a metal seatless toilet. I will say this for the hole: There were no roaches. The rats made sure of that. I enjoyed their company. I just wished they weren't so scared of me.

The one hour a day I was let out of my cell, I had the choice to shower or go outside into a cage for some fresh air. I chose the shower six times out of the seven days in a week. I was content not talking to anyone in the hole but Johnny.

We started reading the dictionary my first year in, and we often had heated debates on words and their meanings.

If it weren't for my sixth grade education, I wouldn't have made it through prison. I may not have been able to read very well at first, but I could read. And I did. I got much better as I perused the few books I had access to.

When the book cart finally got to me on Tuesdays, the only thing to pick out were dictionaries and Encyclopedia Britannica. By the time I got out of the hole, I'd read and discussed the dictionary cover to cover, fourteen and a half times, and the A's through the N's of the Encyclopedia Britannica twenty-six times.

Because of the way I began to talk and the words I used, I became known as Professor for the next twenty-one years. I didn't exercise or play games. I just ate, slept, read, debated with Johnny number two, my mattress in the cell I was moved to once I got out of the hole. Occasionally I went to the toilet after coming in from digging ditches on the chain gang I was assigned to.

I grew to enjoy being left alone. I didn't care for people all that much anymore. People were noisy and worrisome. I guess that's why me and Johnny number two were so close. We gave each other plenty of space. We knew when to talk and when to remain quiet. He was much more comfortable than Johnny number one, and more intelligent. We had the most interesting conversations.

In the twenty-six years I spent in prison, I never once got into a fight or had an altercation with the hacks. Hell, everybody thought I was plum crazy, and I was content with what they thought. I never proclaimed my sanity or tried to correct their incorrectness.

I was forty-nine and had spent most of my life in Holman State Penitentiary, down in South Alabama. I hadn't given much thought as to what I'd do once I was released. Hell, I never thought I'd be released. After the third time the parole board turned me down, I refused to go back.

But when they did finally release me, I caught a cab to the Greyhound in downtown Mobile and bought a ticket for the next bus leaving out of Alabama. I was too afraid to stay in a state that could sentence a man to twenty-something years in prison for the crime of being born black.

Twenty-six years they took from me. Twenty-six years of digging ditches, picking cotton, and cleaning toilets, and all I had to show for it was a hundred-fifty dollars, someone else's discarded, penniless penny loafers, a pair of slacks that had been pressed too long, and a white-and-yellow stained button-down long sleeved shirt.

In all, I'd spent eighty-five of the $150 I'd received from the prison for my two decades of service. I couldn't believe a bus ticket to Atlanta cost forty-five dollars. Even worse was the cab ride to the bus station. It was forty dollars. If I wasn't so anxious to get out of Alabama, I would've walked and hitched my way out.

I'd never been to Atlanta, but I figured anywhere, U.S.A. was better than the nowhere that I'd come from. The next few years were a roller coaster ride, from one Waffle House and fast food restaurant job to another—until I met Mrs. Parker. I was at my usual table in the back of the library simultaneously finishing up the *Post, The Times,* and the *Journal* when Mrs. Maggie Parker made my life a whole lot simpler.

Mrs. Parker was the head librarian. She was a sweet, older white woman who had an obsession with cleaning and organizing. While she worked, we conversed for a little over an hour before she offered me a custodial assistant position. I was caught off guard because I'd been coming to the Fulton County Library downtown on Peachtree for close to a dozen years now, and Mrs. Parker and I had never exchanged more than a few gentle pleasantries.

Of course I took the job. It didn't pay much, thirty cents over minimum wage, but I was content. My schedule never wavered. I went to work every day, whether I was scheduled or not.

After my shift, I'd go to the third floor, grab the *Journal,* the *Post, The Times,* and the *USA Today,* take a seat at the back, and read what happened that day around the nation. Afterwards, I'd get whatever book I was reading out of my employee locker and read until I left the library two hours after it closed at ten.

My next stop was Green's liquor store on Marietta Street. I went there to buy lunch and dinner daily. I made a third trip on payday to cash my check. After leaving, I often ended up sleeping on the street somewhere nearby. I wasn't homeless. No, never been that. I was just usually too tired or too inebriated to get back to the boarding house I was living at.

Now, don't get it wrong. I wasn't an alcoholic. Not

50

even close. An alcoholic had problems functioning like a normal, lucid, sane, citizen. An alcoholic had a drinking problem. Neither of those scenarios applied to me. As long as I had a drink, I had no problem. And no matter how much I drank, I never expressed myself in a manner befitting a drunk. Well, not until I let another person into my quiet and comfortable existence.

It took ten years and I was up to Johnny number fourteen by the time I took in another friend. We didn't have anything but misery in common, but somehow I took to this pathetic-looking blonde Mick Jagger. The crazy thing was that the boy actually believed he was black, and if I were blind, you couldn't tell me he wasn't.

Funny how we met. No, I take that back. It was frightening.

I was walking down the street drinking my dinner, minding my own business, bothering nothing but the concrete I walked on when I saw two brothas kicking this white kid to sleep. I would've kept going if I hadn't seen the same pleading, hopeless look I'd seen almost forty years ago after a Nat King Cole concert. How we'd locked eyes, I don't know.

I guess I don't have to tell you what I did, but I will 'cause I get angry every time I think about it. I'd only had a sip. Now, I don't even buy the good stuff, 'cept on special occasions, you know, my birthday or Christmas. And it was my birthday. Well, almost. My birthday was only two days away.

It cost me twenty-seven dollars, and I'd only drunk maybe one dollar's worth before I baptized one youngblood with a bottle of Grand Marnier, and cut the other with shards from the broken glass.

From that day forward, I couldn't get rid of him. He was the dog that wouldn't run away. Shabazz, as he called himself, was a damn good con man. His downfall was the cancerous tumor-like monkey he shot in his veins every day.

My days of listening to the wind sing and the trees blow were over. His mouth killed quiet, and it never stopped running. One thing I can say about him was that he was the cure for boredom. High or sober, the boy was a one man play.

He was usually higher than the star on the Macy's Christmas tree in December when he met me outside the library after I got off of work. No matter how high he got, he always entertained me with stories of the latest schemes he'd been planning or the ones he'd already executed. Shabazz was never broke, and yet he never had money. He was a survivor living on the edge of sanity.

Shabazz's and my life drastically changed when this needy but extremely aggressive and intelligent woman walked—no, ran and jumped into our lives with the sweetest little girl this side of heaven.

CHAPTER 10

BABYGIRL

"Babygirl, whachu, uh, where yo' momma at, sweetie?"

I didn't care that his nose was running. I didn't care that he looked half out of it. I just needed him now. "Uncle Bazz, I killed him. Momma's still there. I mean she, she, she stayed."

"I'm here. You just calm down. You're safe now, sweetie. Uncle Bazz got you. Everything's gonna be all right," he said while holding me in his arms.

"No!" I shook my head. "You don't understand. It ain't gon' be all right. It ain't!" I tried to pull away from him. "I'm tired of grownups always telling me that. Didn't you hear me?" I shouted. "I killed him."

"Killed who?"

I let out a shrill scream.

"Muthafuck," Uncle Bazz shouted before grabbing me to keep from tripping over Uncle Ben, who was trying to get to his feet.

"Babygirl, you okay?" Uncle Bazz asked. I shook my head. "No."

Uncle Bazz must not have been paying attention to Uncle Ben, 'cause he almost jumped to the ceiling when Uncle Ben put a hand on his shoulder.

"Nigga," Uncle Bazz turned his head, "you 'bout scared me to damn death. Now, see what you done gone and damn did. Sneakin' up on us and shit," Uncle Bazz said.

"Watch your mouth, and relax," Uncle Ben said as he took his hand off Uncle Bazz's shoulder and stepped

53

around him.

"I'm sorry, Babygirl. I must've fainted or something."

"Negro, your drunk butt fell," Uncle Bazz corrected. Uncle Ben ignored him. He bent down and took my

hand as I sat in a ball crying.

"Shabazz, go get a towel, and look in the milk crate by Johnny number seventeen, and get one of those white packets, and put on some coffee.

He turned his head back to me. "Babygirl, your hands are freezing. Girl, you gon' catch your death out in that rain." He smiled. "Now, slow down and tell your Uncle Ben what happened."

My hair was dry and I had two cups of nasty, sugared-down coffee in me by the time I finished my story.

"Babygirl, you stay here while me and Ben go down to Grady and see if they brought your momma in," Uncle Bazz said.

"How you know they ain't took Momma to

Crawford Long or Georgia Baptist?" I asked.

"I don't, but we closest to Grady, and they got one of those Lo-Jack computer systems that can locate anyone that checked into any hospital in the city."

"How do you know that?" Uncle Ben asked.

"The police used it to find me that time I broke into the clinic pharmacy and exchanged all the methadone in the rehab for aspirin. Hell." He shrugged. "Wasn't my fault they got me off one drug and hooked on another."

"What did that have to do with the hospital computer system?" I asked.

"Uh, I sort of O.D.'d on the stuff. I tried to shoot it like it was H."

He called hisself whispering in Uncle Ben's ear. He knew he didn't know how to whisper. "Anyway, somehow I ended up on the sidewalk outside the emergency room at Crawford Long."

"You are the biggest dumb white boy in the world. I see why they don't want you in their race," Uncle Ben said.

"Ya momma! But let's not get started on her now. Ben, how much money you got?" Uncle Bazz asked.

"Let's see." He pulled nothing but air out of one pocket and some change and a crumpled-up bill out of the other. "I got two dollars and twelve cents."

"I got three. Hell, that ain't enough to get us a cab."

"Here." I pulled out the money Momma gave me and gave it to Uncle Ben. "Momma gave it to me before I ran."

"Come on. Yoda will charge a dollar, but we can call a cab on his phone down the hall," Uncle Ben said.

"Who's Yoda?" I asked.

"The black walrus that lives down the hall," Uncle Bazz said.

"And where do you think you are going?"

"With you two."

"Babygirl, you should wait here. I promise we'll find your momma," Uncle Ben said.

"I'm not staying here. She's my mother. She needs me. I don't care what you say, I'm going." An hour later, we were walking through the sliding emergency room doors.

"St. Elsewhere don't got Jack or Jill on Grady Hospital. Niggas just dying to get in," Uncle Bazz said.

"You are truly an uncouth and disrespectful imbecile," Uncle Ben muttered.

"Sticks and stones and bricks and bats may break my back, but them one page words just make my head hurt."

"Ignoramus, that does not rhyme nor does it make any sense. You have almost as much sense as God gave a goose."

"Quack, quack muthafucka," he replied as he puckered his lips, stuck out his chest and flapped his arms.

"Please stop it. You two act like you're the child and I'm the grownup," I said as we walked to the administration desk. Uncle Bazz was right, though. The emergency room looked like the aftermath following a stampede at a Jay-Z concert.

"Excuse me? Ma'am?"

"Fill out this application legibly," a nurse said while attempting to hand Uncle Bazz a clipboard with some papers on it. "And take those over there." The bubble gum-chewing, ancient-looking nurse pointed to a workstation to my left.

Uncle Bazz smiled his best stained-tooth smile.

"No, I am not seeking treatment. I am desperately looking for a patient brought in here. Uhm," he massaged his goatee as he paused, "earlier this evening," he said in his best white man voice.

"Take this and wait over there." She gave him a slip of paper with the number 174 on it and pointed a crooked brown finger in the direction of the standing room only emergency waiting room.

Uncle Bazz placed both hands on the desk, leaned over as far as he could, and slowly spoke. "Look, I was taken out of homicide," he put his palms in her face, "ten days ago because her majesty, Mayor Pamela Hunter so ordered. Since then, I've been forced to live like a drug addicted bum. I haven't had a shower in three days. I've been busting my white ass working undercover on some big city government homeless prostitution and extortion case.

"Now, my informant, Lavette Hawkins, has been taken down. Either you get on that computer and find her now or I take that phone," he pointed to the phone next to her, "and place a call to Sleeping Beauty. Imagine what will happen when I tell Mayor Hunter that you

56

are hindering me from doing the job that she so ordered."

Uncle Ben's eyes watered as he stood back by the Coke machine looking like he'd swallowed a mouse. I had to hold my head down so no one could see me fighting to keep from exploding with laughter.

"No, no, that won't be necessary, uh, uh—"

"Detective Shaft, John Shaft."

"That is L-A-V-E-T-T-E. Is that correct, Detective Shaft?" she asked all pleasant-like.

"Precisely," he said as he nodded.

"Are you sure she was brought here? The system doesn't show anyone by that name."

"I'm not a hundred percent sure. Can you just check the system and see where she was taken?"

"Yes, sir. It'll take a minute," she kindly explained. People were getting antsy as the line backed up, waiting for service. I said a silent prayer, hoping no one said anything. You know how Uncle Bazz could get, especially if a white person huffed and puffed up at him. Thank God he just stood there like a cucumber.

"Nope." She shook her head. "No Lavette Hawkins admitted anywhere in the city today. You sure it was today?"

"Sure as shit stinks."

"Excuse me?"

"I said very sure."

"I don't know what to tell you, but if you give me your card, I'll continue to check the system and give you a call as soon as I find something."

"As I told you, I am deep undercover, I mean deep with a capital D. I don't carry cards or I.D. Give me your direct number and I'll call you, Mrs. Partridge."

"That's Miss." She smiled a crooked denture smile as she scribbled a number down on a yellow sticky paper.

Four days later, we still had not heard anything. I cried until there were no tears left in my head. I half-

57

slept in Johnny, Uncle Ben's single mattress bed at night, and ran around with Uncle Bazz checking the hospitals and beating the streets for information during the day. Uncle Ben would've been with us, too, if he didn't have to work.

Now, ten days had passed. I was in Uncle Ben's room taking care of Uncle Bazz. He'd been throwing up and shaking like crazy the past few days. No way was I going to let anything happen to him. I didn't have anyone left in the whole world but him and Uncle Ben.

"What are you doing home so early, Uncle Ben?"

He sat down on the old Goodwill reject couch he'd been sleeping on and covered his face with his hands.

CHAPTER 11

SHABAZZ

One of us gots ta die. At first I thought I could be as scarfaced as any nigga. Now, I just didn't know. The muthafucka was getting the best of me, throwin' blows at my ass like Mike Tyson.

It had been, I think, a week now. I'd been broke down, beat down, insides all fucked the fuck up. I couldn't shit, I felt like I was pissing glass. My mouth tasted like sandpaper. My head felt like a bunch of midgets were wrestling inside it. I just knew I was going to explode any minute.

Just going to sleep and waking up was murder. It even hurt to breathe. My pain had pains and my hurt even hurt. I wanted to scream so bad, but wanting hurt so much, I never made it to the scream. And even if I did scream, I'd scare Babygirl, and that wasn't happening.

The monkey on my back turned into King Kong on steroids. All I had to do was feed the son of a bitch. But hell, by the time I was strong enough to leave Big Ben's room, some of the fight went out his ass.

It still hurt to hurt, but I was kind of glad to get out and help Ben, if only for a couple of hours.

In the beginning, the nigga attacked my head like brain cancer. I gotta take that shit back; the monkey couldn't be a nigga. A nigga ain't got that type of mind control power. Nah, the monkey on my back had to be a straight up Flintstone from Bedrock.

And Lavette, that woman just don't know the hell she'd taken me through. Made me think she did this shit to make me get straight. Wherever she was, I bet a

59

million dollars when she thought of me and Babygirl, she knew I'd kick or die trying. She knew I loved that little girl harder than I loved life. Hell, only known the two of them six years. I still remember the day they crashed my party.

*****

Earlier that day, six years ago, I had staked out my spot for my going away party. Doing the survey in the parking lot was part of the preparation for that evening. I was clean. Showered up and dressed like a real square John. Dressed to kill, or better yet to die, was what I was. I had me a clipboard, paper, pen, fake glasses and all.

It took me three hours of faking. Three hours of asking every Jack and Jill in the parking lot to participate in a survey to monitor the most frequently prescribed drug administered by physicians on a daily basis. First, I'd show them the colorful Caribbean Island brochure that I'd taken from the travel agency down the street the day before. Then I'd explain that J & S travel was raffling off tickets for a seven-day all expenses paid Caribbean Island vacation for two. I explained that the drawing was going to be held on the following day at ten A.M. at the travel agency. To enter, they just needed to show me their prescription and donate a dollar to receive the little blue ticket.

No matter how many times I pulled a scam like this, it never ceased to amaze me how gullible people really were. No one had called J & S travel or reported me to anyone in the drugstore.

When I found the mark—well, the Maria I was looking for—I watched and waited. When she finally came out of Walgreens, I went into action. As she was about to get into her car, I came up from behind and snatched her Walgreens bag. While running, I checked the bag just to make sure she had the benzodiazepine sleeping pills. All of this scamming in the hot sun for some damn sleeping pills, I thought as I ran.

Later that evening, I was dressed and ready, going as I was, no bags, just a razorblade and an empty pill bottle. It was just supposed to be me and my two slit wrists and my razorblade-first-class-ticket to hell. Hell wasn't my first choice, obviously, but anything was better than living. Once I got there, I figured I'd scam ole Satan into putting me on the up elevator.

That night, I was in my own world, minding my own, on my way to the next life, bleeding and sleeping behind a dumpster. Two days later, I was damn near blinded by this big ole sparkling-ass smile owned by this pretty-ass sistah-girl. And there was this miniature version of her holding my hand.

Although she'd saved me from myself when I didn't ask to be saved, I owed it to Lavette to clean myself up at least until we found out what the hell happened to her. I had a bad feeling we wasn't ever going to see her again. I had a worse feeling that I was going to have to stay clean and get a real job to take care of Babygirl. That scared me worse than what I thought may have happened to Babysis.

CHAPTER 12

UNCLE BEN

As far as I was concerned, a black life in this country was worth no more than it was a hundred years ago.

I was seventy-three and in my lifetime, I'd seen black folks go from one form of slavery to another, and most don't even know they still slaves. Hell, I figure the only reason the Emancipation Proclamation was signed was because it was only paper, and paper ain't worth the ink used to write on it.

Words on paper don't make a slave. Black folk still ain't got a clue. Being a slave is a conditioning, and black folk had been conditioned three hundred some odd years before Lincoln signed that paper.

Just look back in the early forties when I was 'bout Babygirl's age. The system treated Blacks worse than a mule. Hell, I ain't ever seen a mule lynched. But black folks were strung up on a tree and lynched for so much as smiling at a white woman, as we still are today. The difference now is that the tree is the media, and the rope is the court system.

As long as you are a house Negro, you straight. You just have to be that boy that Master sent you to them big, fine schools and universities to be. He'll even loan you the money to go to his schools and learn how to be more like him. And after you earn your degrees and become a master slave, you have to spend the next lifetime paying him back for loaning you the money to go and learn how to be a more profitable slave.

He will put you in glass offices to oversee the field Negro. He'll make you mayor of the poor and warden of the less fortunate. And every time you lash your whip on the back of another Black, he'll smile and pat you on yours. He'll even mistakenly call you Lassie instead of Leon. You'll graciously thank him, and name your unborn child after him like your ancestors have done since the slave master beat all the Kunta Kinte out of Toby.

You'll do whatever it takes to stay with him until you're too old to be of any use to him. Then he'll put you out to pasture like all old horses. He'll give back a pittance of your sweat that you gave him for thirty, forty years, and call it retirement and social security. Now, back in the good old days, Master called you nigga to your face. There was no doubt where you stood: behind him and in the 'For Colored Only' section.

It was for these very reasons that I had to do what I had to do. I was that field Negro they'd wrote off, that field Negro they deemed as useless and a threat to no one but himself. I was old, but my light was still shining. Oh, you better believe I was going to find that girl's momma.

I quit drinking, and wasn't going to take a sip until I got to the bottom of what happened to Lavette. I started my days off drinking black coffee and skimming through the obituaries.

I knew one thing, I had to hurry up and find that woman. This sober stuff was killing me, and I couldn't die until I made good on my word. Hating being dry was an understatement. Being sober was horrible. I mean it was a pure nightmare. I was seeing the world again for what it was, and I could hardly handle it. I was weak. I couldn't bear the pain of every day. Every day, waking up black and helpless to change the condition and mindset of America. It was like I was standing behind a glass wall watching my mother, sister, and brother die daily.

I held conversations with my mattress because it had more sense than today's black folk.

I'll say this, though. That dang-on Babygirl sure knew how to make me smile in a world of sadness.

And her momma, huh. Well, she could bring out the good in Satan. Yes, sir. That woman was the sugar in lemonade.

Having no luck on the seventh day, a thought came to me while mopping one of the library restrooms. In all these years, I never half did my job, but today was different. I 'bout had a heart attack twice, running to catch the next 126. On the bus, breathing like a locomotive, a tear somehow snuck up in my eye as I thought back.

I will never forget the sadness and desperation in Babygirl's voice the night she showed up at my door all wet and crying. I remembered every word. That's why I was on this bus now.

Thirty minutes later, I pulled a pen out the pocket of my blue work coveralls and wrote down the information I needed. It was 5:45 by the time I made it to City Hall. This was one of those rare times I needed Shabazz. No, I take that back. I needed Shabazz's mouth.

Some chubby, weaved-up, tight rent-a-cop uniform wearing little girl not even old enough to drink told me that since they closed at six, I had to come back in the morning. While she was talking, I looked at her sideways, trying to figure out what was wrong with her bobbing neck and flip-flopping eyes. When she finished, I looked at my watch then at the clock on the wall.

"The clock reads five forty-five." I pointed.

"No, it is five for-ty-six. The line cut-off is at five for-ty-five. Can't you read the sign?" She talked to me like I was one of Jerry's kids. Ain't that a blip. Hell, she was the one that looked like she got off the short bus. And then she pointed to some tiny little something on a wall five miles from where we stood.

"I'm old, not deaf," I said.

"You'll have to just come back to-mor-row, pops."

"But there is no line." She shrugged. "Rules."

I stuck my index finger in the bubble she was blowing.

"Now pop that," I said, turning to leave.

"Old-ass billygoat."

I turned back around. "Oh, so you finally found him," I said.

She sucked her teeth. "Found who?" She placed her flea market jeweled arms and hands on her extra-wide horse hips.

"Your father, the billygoat. It's about time your Isaac Hayes-looking mother finally came clean," I said before I left the building with her curses bouncing off my back.

The next morning I returned, this time with back-up. Babygirl was sound asleep when we left. Shabazz was still sick, but well enough to help Babygirl out. I gotta hand it to him. He'd do just about anything for that little girl and her momma. Hell, I would too.

"Graham Jefferson," I said as I read the tax record report.

"I know that name. Where the hell from, I don't know. But I'm tellin' you I know that name," Shabazz shot back.

"Are you two finished?" Baby Kong interrupted.

"Call the President. I done found one of Sadaam's weapons of mass ugly. Oh no! Run! It's Boozilla, Godzilla's illegitimate son."

She crossed her arms. "You got one minute to get out of here, scarecrow."

"Ohhhhh, I'm scared. Whachu gon' do, bite me, Cujo?

"Okay, trash bag, you, your boyfriend, lover, this building. Out."

"Bitch, buy a verb." Shabazz jerked his arm out of her grasp. "When you speak to me, talk in complete sentences. I don't understand Rot-weiller. And you put your fake gold-wearing paws on me one more muthafuckin' time, I'll bite the bat shit out ya ass and we'll see how you like living with HIV."

She took two wide steps back so fast she almost

lost her balance. As soon as she half gained her composure, she went to screaming in her two-way.

"Let's go, Shabazz, before we get arrested," I said.

"That's it." Shabazz snapped his fingers.

"What is it?"

"That nigga. The big-time preacher man over at First Corinthians."

"What are you talking about?"

"You know the man the police found all banged up on the south side." He put his hands over his mouth.

"Oh shit."

I nodded. "But I don't recall reading anything about a woman being at the house."

"Of course not." Shabazz held his hands out.

"Graham Jefferson, Sharon Jefferson. And you always calling me dumb.

"Congresswoman Sharon Jefferson. Let's go," I said.

"Where to?"

"To hell if we don't pray. But for now, you better get back to the house."

"I'll be all right."

"You are not all right. Boy, the way you look, you'd scare off night and make daylight cringe. And besides, you need to get back before Babygirl wakes up, if she hasn't already."

He nodded.

I hate to say it, but I was sort of worried about him. He had grown on me like a bunion you couldn't get rid of.

A little later at the library, I found out that Sharon Jefferson's husband was none other than old Graham. Even more amazing was the Jane Doe that was found in the house. I made a couple calls and found out that a Jane Doe was found in that small yellow house, and she was being held at the county morgue. I read the papers daily, and there was never any mention of a woman found in the house with Graham.

What I saw on that slab in the county morgue was hardly the jubilant and glowing beauty who always had a kind word and a positive outlook on any and every situation. No, this was a woman who'd lived hard and died even harder. The mask she wore daily was now removed. The pain of living as she did was written all over her face. It'd been almost fifty years since I cried.

CHAPTER 13

BABYGIRL

It had been six months to the day since my old life ended and this one began. I knew Momma was dead before Uncle Ben opened his mouth. I knew the moment I let go of her cold, clammy hands that dreadful rainy night that I'd never see her smile again. I couldn't admit it. I wouldn't face the truth until the hardest man I knew walked through his bedroom door a broken man.

Surprisingly, it was Uncle Bazz who stayed clean. He hadn't used, smoked or drunk anything harder than a Coca-Cola since Momma died. Uncle Ben was a different story. He'd embraced the bottle like it was his long lost son.

I was young, but I was wise for my age. I could see that life had beaten Uncle Ben down so bad that he couldn't handle living without drinking. His drinking had nothing to do with the love I had for him. It never had and it never would. He was still a great uncle and the worldliest, most intelligent man I'd ever known.

Uncle Bazz had gained a lot of weight in such a short time. He wasn't fat or nothing like that, but he was healthy. His skin was peach-pink instead of the old yellowy-grayish white I'd always seen through his dirty and tattered clothing. Now he was clean as the Board of Health, and he put on a suit every day before leaving our new two-bedroom apartment.

He left home every morning carrying his portable workstation, a brown or black leather briefcase. And almost every day, he came back with an awesomely funny story of how he'd tricked somebody out of some money.

68

"Babygirl, please come into the kitchen. I have to talk to you."

"Hold on. Let me put my Sims game on pause."

"Girl, I hate that your friend Nigeria got you hooked on that thing," he hollered back.

I got up and walked into the kitchen. "Yeah, Unc, what's up?"

"Niggas, baby. I love me some black folks, but I hate niggas. Babygirl, you know I've been going down to Family Mutual two, sometimes three times a week trying to see how to claim the two million dollar life insurance policy your momma had."

"Yeah."

"Every time, and I mean every damn time I go down to that big-ass building, I have to take a number and wait on Weavy Jefferson or Shenika Hood Rat to get off the phone. Between the *child, please*s and the *girl, shut yo' mouth*s it was obvious that they were on personal calls. I can't believe such a professional atmosphere employs receptionists that are so unprofessional.

"And when I finally get service, they can't ever get shit right. They should be called can't-get-right Rita and wrong-way Wanda. It just frustrates me to have to tell them how to do their job, and half the time I don't know what I'm talkin' about."

He had me cracking up. I didn't know where he was going, but I hoped he took his time and kept on with the story before he got to the point.

"Well, to make a long story not so long, I'll just spit it out. We hit like shit."

"Huh?"

He sighed. "Five and a half months of damn near living at that dang insurance building and they give me this. The MF, SOB A-holes played you and your mother. Read this." He handed me a balled-up letter.

Although we at Family Mutual share your pain and are

grieving with you, we regretfully inform you that under further review, your claim has been denied. Clearly stated in Volume 12, article 27, section 14-7, line 68. In cases where there is no autopsy to determine the cause of death, then no monies will be awarded to any parties. This is due to our suicide clause, explained in Volume 7, article 13-2, line 33.

If an autopsy is ordered within six months of issuance of a death certificate, then the case will remain open for an additional calendar year.

From our family to yours
Sincerely, Larry Trimble, CEO Family Mutual

"Funky-ass corporate pigs. Insensitive muthafucka ain't even sign his name. I just can't get over this bullshit. I done had to play super white man all this time. Hell, Babygirl, I even cut my hair."

I nodded.

"I went each time, suited and booted, wearing my lips sucked in and walking like a constipated robot on speed trying to fit in with the white world, and they still treat me like a nigga."

"Don't worry, Unc. No amount of money can ever bring Momma back. It ain't no big deal."

"Hell if it ain't. Your mother wanted the best for you. She sacrificed everything so you would not have to end up like her, and now everything she lived and died for is down the drain with the stroke of a pen and some fancy paperwork. Family Mutual been dragging me along for six months, just long enough so that bullshit autopsy clause could kick in. They knew what the hell they were doing."

He dropped his head. "Babygirl." He shook his head. "They got me good. Somehow, we gon' get they ass. They gon' pay. You understand me, Babygirl?"

"Yes." What else was I going to say? I didn't know what the heck he was talking about, but he needed my reassurance. He may've been the adult, but it was me who took care of him.

"By the time school starts back, they'll be done figured out your momma passed. And we are going to have problems."

"Why is that? Momma owes them, not you."

"Yeah, but I can't afford to keep you in private school."

I reached out and grabbed his hand. "I don't care about any private school. I've learned more hanging out with you and Uncle Ben the last few months than I could ever learn in some private school."

"See," he pointed an accusing finger at me, "that's what I'm afraid of. The last thing you need is to be picking up my game."

"Game? What is life but a game? Uncle Ben taught me that life is a big ole poker game. He who has the best face, not the hand, always wins."

"Can't argue with that."

"If I pick up all of yours and Uncle Ben's game faces, then I'll win too, right?"

"I guess you got a point there," Uncle Bazz said.

"So then, it's a done deal."

"What's a done deal?" he asked.

"I'll go to Washington High in the fall and you will put me down with the game."

"I don't know."

"Why don't you know? Is it because I'm thirteen?"

"No, it's not that."

"Then what is it?"

"Look at you." He extended his arms out toward me. "You are a young lady."

"No you didn't. I can't believe you. You always talking about," I bobbed my head and circled the kitchen, making all kinds of exaggerated gestures, "the white man this and the white man that, and yet you are just as prejudiced."

"Prejudiced?"

"Yes, prejudiced," I said with my hand on my slowly filling out hips. "A male chauvinist is what you are, Uncle Bazz."

"No, Babygirl, you don't understand."

"Okay then, make me understand."

"It's dangerous out there. Your hustle goes bad, the mark peeps your game, calls your hand, and who knows what'll happen. You could get killed."

"And if I was a boy I couldn't?"

"Well yes, but."

"But what?"

CHAPTER 14

SHABAZZ

My birthday, damn. High 'til I die and smoke 'til I choke used to be my theme. Since I was thirteen, I'd been getting high on my birthday. I started out sniffing gas and glue before smoking weed, dropping acid, doing speed, snorting coke, and finally graduating to shooting junk.

Who would've thought I'd ever become a sober, half-ass square? I say half-ass 'cause I still played the long and short con to survive.

I tried it straight for a while, got a job at Kroger. Hell, I even worked for four hours before I walked out the back door with a hand truck stacked up with five cases of Newports. Working a straight gig just wasn't my thing. I couldn't deal with no one telling me what to do and where to go. I couldn't cope with making money weekly or bi-weekly. I had to get paid every day. That's why I did what I did and do what I do. I know I had responsibilities and all, but shit. I'd given up dope. A hustler wasn't who I was. It was more than that. I breathe, eat, piss, and shit game better than Parker Brothers and Milton Bradley.

It had been two years since Babysis had passed. I know it's fucked up to say, but her passing saved my life. I enjoyed waking up every day. I looked forward to hearing how Babygirl was putting it down at school, pitching quarters for dollars and selling bootleg DVDs and CDs that we'd downloaded and copied.

I should've been on the school payroll, as much as I was down there getting her out of one jam after another last year. At times, she had me madder than a black Muslim at a Klan rally. I didn't get mad at the game. I got mad that she had gotten caught.

73

CHAPTER 15

BABYGIRL

"You must think I'm Betty Ball, believe it all." I put my hand on my hips, catching the attention of the bellman and anyone else in ear's range. "Gino, save that drama for ya bald-headed wooden-toothed momma," I said, shaking my finger in an exaggerated fashion. I was a seven, but the size five white nurse's skirt I had on covered me like melted Velveeta.

"I seened you with that bald-headed, wig-wearing, Auburn Avenue two-dollar hooker."

I changed the cell phone to my other ear, took the nurse's hat off and shook my head so my long hair would fall over my shoulders. A button popped off the top of my shirt, almost freeing my crowded C cups before I continued. "Could've fooled me. You had your tongue so far down her throat I thought she was gon' choke. Oh shit."

I put my cell phone back in my Dooney and Bourke purse as I ran in my ugly white nurse shoes over to the overturned potted palm tree.

"I-I apologize, sir. Please accept my—"

"Fuck, are you blind or what? You've probably ruined a tie that cost more than you make in a friggin' year, asshole." The little man trembled and frantically moved his mouth back and forth while the other continued cursing as he wiped the dirt from his tailored pinstripe suit.

"Are you friggin' blind?"

"Yes, and he's mute too," I said.

"Excuse me? And?" He turned his nose up at me like I was fried shit. "Who the hell are you?"

74

JIHAD

"My name is Wanda Berry, and this is," I pointed to the little red dingy baseball cap wearing, fragile looking, hunched over, shivering man who held onto my arm as if his life depended on it, "Stu, Stuart Martin, and he is," I paused for emphasis, "blind and mute, as I was trying to explain."

"Well fuck, how am I supposed to know the guy's friggin' blind?" the man asked in a voice three octaves higher than his normal tone. He walked toward the elevator, still shaking palm tree dirt off his leg.

After exiting the golden electronic glass swivel doors of the Ritz-Carlton, Uncle Bazz folded his walking stick, took off his Ray Charles glasses, and threw the red cap in the garbage outside the hotel. We raced to our Crown Victoria police special that was double parked in front of the next building. Uncle Bazz removed the blue light he'd stolen from a detective's car a while back, before we jumped inside and sped off.

"Damn, damn, green eggs and ham. Ass face was loaded," Uncle Bazz said while going through the mark's brown wallet.

"Must be at least a gee there," I said while circling the block.

"Eight hun."

"I know we keepin' some of it, Uncle Bazz."

He looked at me cross-eyed. "You know better than that. Just take down his info and look for the lotto number."

The lotto number was the mark's social security number, and his info was credit card numbers, bank name, expiration dates, the three-digit security code on the back of the cards, and driver's license info. We'd been hitting big money suckas like that dude for a couple years now, and we never took a dime out of their wallets.

After circling the block, we pulled over. Uncle Bazz put on some dirty construction jean overalls, a black

75

wig, and a construction hat. Then he got out of the car, marched right back into the Ritz-Carlton, and dropped the wallet off with the manager, claiming he'd found it in the area of the commotion a few minutes earlier.

I remember one time the mark was in the lobby of one of the hotels we hit when Uncle Bazz went back inside. The mark saw the exchange between the hotel front desk manager and my uncle. Not recognizing him, the mark immediately thanked Uncle Bazz then pulled out a twenty and offered it as a reward. Of course, Uncle Bazz took it.

I still recall when Uncle Bazz first put me up on the game. It was only after I begged and begged and kept getting into trouble for nickel-and-dime hustling at school.

"Babygirl, rule number one: If you want more, do more," he said as we walked through Lenox Mall. "But never scam the poor. Rule number two: Pay your tithes by giving some of each take to the needy. That's God's way of protectin' the greedy. Rule number three: Listen, watch, and wait. If it's meant to be, the mark will always take the bait. Rule number four, and the most important one of all: Stay true to this one and it will protect you from takin' a fall. One day, somebody will peep your game, but they can't trap you if they don't know your name."

"I understand one, two and four, but it seems you can lose out if opportunity knocks and someone beats you to the door," I said.

He extended his arm out toward some bleachers in the middle of the mall. "Have a seat, Babygirl."

People were rushing from one store to another. It was crazy. The day after Thanksgiving always was. I loved it. The holidays were when people were the most gullible for game.

"Why take the chance and rush to charge up a card that will be clipped at any time? Why take the small change out of a mark's wallet, making him suspicious of what other information you may be in possession of, when you can be patient and screw all his credit cards at your leisure, arousing no suspicion whatsoever?

"See, Babygirl, all I need is their driver's license number, date of birth, home address, and social security number. I can make another license, put my picture on it, and duplicate the credit cards with my credit card embosser."

"Embosser?"

"It's a simple number pressing machine anyone can buy on E-Bay for two grand. It's the same machine credit card companies use to press their cards. You see, before you know it, we got five and ten-thousand dollar limits.

"I buy laptop computers, jewelry, and special order items I can fence over at Spanky's pawnshop and used car lot, and I can sell my laptops to Rodney over at Discount Electronics.

"And if I ever get a hold of some blank American Express platinum cards, we'll be featured on MTV's *Cribs* with Russell Simmons and Puff Daddy. Shit, we'll be richer than Godiva chocolate dipped in syrup. Babygirl, I'm talkin' 'bout cards with hundred thousand-dollar limits on them."

"Why can't you get Amex? You get all the others." He shrugged. "The Koreans I buy my blanks from can't get 'em, but," he pointed, "if they ever do, I gotta have them no matter what the price tag is."

"How do you know what card has what limit?"

"I just call the credit card company. Remember, I have all the mark's information; I become the mark." Listening to Uncle Bazz laying down game was inspirational. With his knowledge and street savvy, he should've been the Donald Trump of street game. I could hardly wait to take what he was teaching me to the next level. He didn't realize that I had assets he didn't. One was my ass, and it was set to mesmerize and hypnotize the marks out in the world on a whole other level.

CHAPTER 16

SHABAZZ

Babygirl was turning into a real pro. Many folks would think I'm fucked up in the head for corruptin' such a sweet little girl. Them the same broke muthafuckas bustin' their ass on somebody's job, living one paycheck away from the welfare office.

The finance companies fuck people like me in the ass every damn day. They'll finance a car, and by the time you end up paying for it, you'll have paid four and five times what you bought it for. They'll put you in a pretty house, and when it ain't so pretty or it gets too small, you sell it and you owe the same amount you owed on it when you first bought it ten years ago. Not me. Never would be. I bought the custom three hundred-thousand dollar home Babygirl and I had been living in for the past year and a half using a dead man's identity. And the mortgage was being paid by the trick of the month, whoever that turned out to be at any given time.

Hell, I ain't nothin' but an opportunist. No, better yet, I'm a capitalist in a capitalist country. I'm just a product of my environment and my upbringing.

And anyway, since Babygirl had been striking with me, she'd stayed clean at school. This year she'd made me proud. She didn't get caught one time. She was a pro now. If there was a hustler's pro bowl, she'd be a rookie all-star. My Babygirl was handling her business. No suspension or detention. I ain't never seen a C on any of her report cards. Either she figured out a way to change her grades, or she was really bustin' her ass with all A's and occasionally a B or two. At any rate,

Babygirl was putting it down like James Brown, doing the damn thang.

I did get pissed off when I caught her using my shit to make somebody a driver's license. My thing was it ain't wrong unless you get caught. But my encoder, my printing machine and embosser were off fucking limits. Those few pieces of equipment were what kept the mortgage paid in the four-bedroom home we lived in, in Kinsley Estates.

Babygirl was at school and I was in my basement office encoding a fresh credit card with the new information I'd bought from the Koreans up the street that owned the Verizon Wireless store. Somebody with a fat-daddy limit was about to get credit jacked. Suddenly, the high-pitched chirping of my yard alarm interrupted my thoughts. I hit the remote on my TV to see who was coming up my driveway.

"Shit!" I grabbed a shirt out of the dirty clothes hamper. I didn't have time to go upstairs. Fuck, I had to get my wallet, but which one? Shit.

"Open up! Police!"

Shit! Shit! Shit! I grabbed my cell phone, pressed speed dial, and walked out of the back door with the phone pressed to my ear while they were coming in the front door.

Running was how criminals always got caught. That is exactly why I unchained my neighbor's dumb-ass Collie, and was walking it out of my subdivision when one of my happy-ass help-the-police neighbors pointed me out.

Tires screeched and sirens blared as the squad car sped my way. God and I weren't all that cool, but I said a silent prayer, hoping Babygirl checked her cell phone messages before she got home.

The car ran all up on the curb and into someone's yard, cutting me off. It wasn't that serious. I wasn't even attempting to run. I just stood there waiting for the cop to get out of his vehicle.

"Freeze, asshole," the cop said with his gun drawn and pointed at my head.

The dog ran off as I dropped the chain and held my hands in the air.

"Tavarus Jackson, the legend himself," the little circus sideshow-looking cop said as he slapped the cuffs on my wrists.

"Legend? I'm just an average Joe. Why you harassing me? Is this the best way you guys can waste my tax dollars?" I asked in my best John Q white man voice.

"Tax dollars? Ha! You must be joking. I doubt if you've ever filed."

He was right. Hell, I didn't even know what a 1060 tax form looked like.

"We got him," and "Have they found the girl?" was all I heard before I was roughly shoved into the squad car. "Punk muthafucka, you's a bad man when a nigga all hemmed up in cuffs. Old Uncle Tom, Aunt Condolezza, Clarence Thomas-ass nigga," I said to the little man in blue.

Mini Mouse opened the door, "What did you say, white boy?"

"You heard me, midget muthafucka, kindergarten-tender, dick-in-the-booty-ass cop."

"A white boy named Jackson. That's a new one on me."

"White boy these nuts."

He laughed and looked around before pulling out a flashlight damn near the size of his short ass. I bent over for cover just in time. The nigga beat my back like a drummer performing a solo at a rock concert.

As I was getting the shit beat out of me, I hollered at the man upstairs one more time. I prayed that Babygirl somehow got away and that somebody was getting this Happy-Meal, Prince-sized, Mickey Mouse muthafucka on video.

"I bet you like that young black pussy, don't you, white boy? You make her a fake I.D., too, huh?" he said between blows.

"Suck a dick, bitch," I barely uttered between the pain of each blow. Shit, I wished I would pass out. Fuck, this shit hurt. My back had to be broke.

"We got your credit card-making machine, your cameras, and a slue of forged payroll checks. You gon' make some brotha a good wife in the penitentiary."

"Let me out and take these cuffs off, and I'll make your bitch-made ass my wife." After I said that, everything went black.

CHAPTER 17

BABYGIRL

Almost over, I thought as I headed toward my last class, the most depressingly boring one.

Washington High's student population was ninety-nine percent black, but all the mystery teachers were white. I called my sixth period class mystery class because it sure wasn't history. Then again, it was somebody's story. It just wasn't mine. Uncle Ben made sure that I knew my history, not the fragmented, watered-down, non-violent, non-radical non-story they call Black history that is taught in schools all over the country.

From the first time I went into the library, before I could read the *Cheetah Girls*, or novels by Stephanie Perry Moore, Uncle Ben made sure I read stuff by black historians like J.A. Rogers, John Henrik Clarke, or Carter G. Woodson.

In Ms. Chandler's class we read about America's forefathers, the history of the constitution and the presidents. It was funny how she would always say our forefathers. Hell, my ancestors weren't the forefathers, they were the foreslaves. My forefathers didn't have any say-so when that fake-ass bullshit document called the Constitution was drawn up, and my forefathers didn't wear no punk-ass white wigs.

"Damn, Babygirl, you 'bout fine as the shine on my ride." Marcus Jones twisted his big head to the side and leaned against the locker beside mine before he continued. "When you gon' treat a bruh to some of your sweet, sweet sugar between them candy-cane legs?" he whispered in my ear.

"When the Winter Olympics are held on the south side of Hell, and George Bush becomes the national

83

spokesperson for the Nation of Islam."

"Damn, girl, you got a foul-ass mouth."

"And you still all in it." I put one hand on my hip as I held my pink bookbag in the other. "Obviously you like this mouth." I teased him with my puckered lips.

"Nah, shawty, as long as that mouth ain't on me, it ain't nothin' but a noisemaker."

"Yeah, right."

"You must think that pussy got diamonds inside it or something."

"You'll never find out."

"Shit, I can have any of these chicken heads I want. I look good; I'm the star of the basketball team, and I'm declaring myself for the NBA draft next year." He looked at me with a devilish smile on his face. "Who wouldn't want to kick it with the next M.J.?"

"Me! Now be gone, Marion Jones." I waved him away as my cell phone fell out of my locker.

"Ha ha, you got jokes now. Marion Jones, the female track superstar. You know I got moves like Jordan," he said, trying to touch my butt.

"Stop, boy," I said as I moved out of his reach.

"Damn, girl, I see why you ain't servin' me. Somebody got you on lock. Damn, he blowin' you up," he said, picking up my cell phone off the hallway floor.

"Give me that, fool." I snatched my phone out of his hand. Three missed calls. Something must've happened. Uncle Bazz knew I was at school.

I'd have to wait to check my messages. Because of Marcus, I was running late for class. I was doing good this year. I hadn't gotten into any trouble. I didn't need to start now. Fuck it, I'd call him back after school, I thought as I headed toward the classroom.

"Babygirl, wait up," my girlfriend, Nigeria, called out as she ran to catch up with me.

"What's up, girl?"

JIHAD

"This stupid history class," she said as we were about to enter the hall where Ms. Chandler's class was located. "Did you see the police running into the Admin office?"

"Police?"

"Yeah, just now."

I cut her off. "Girl, I gotta run. You ain't seen me. I'll call you later," I said as I dashed down the hall toward the fire exit.

I ran to the student parking lot, hoping dumb-ass Marcus hadn't left. He was one of those baby player seniors. You know, the ones who had all their hours to graduate. They just came to school and took some electives to hang out and try to screw all the hee-hee and stop-you-so-silly-boy girls that would open their legs for any "I love you" line they threw at them.

"Marcus, wait up." I ran toward him and waved as he was pulling off in his new '97 drop-top.

"Changed your mind, huh?" he said, flashing the two golds he had in the front of his mouth.

"I need a ride," I said as I got in, flashing a whole lot of leg.

"What a young nigga get out of it?" he asked, running his hand down my leg.

I wanted to say a broken hand, but instead I said,

"Just drive, boy. If you act right, we might just be able to work something out." As if I didn't have enough problems. I was in the car with Horny Harry and some shit was going down at my crib.

"So, Babygirl . . ."

"Shhhh, I'm checking my messages," I said while turning down the music.

"Babygirl, I ain't got long. Do not come home. The crib is being raided. Either I'm about to get away or I'm going down. Don't worry 'bout me. You know I'm gon' be all right, regardless. Go to Wachovia and use your key to get in the safe deposit box. Get the papers, the money

85

and the pre-paid phone. Get rid of the phone you have, and all your I.D.'s. I'll call you when I can. Shit, gotta go, love you," Uncle Bazz said before his voice cut off.

"Babygirl, you all right?" Marcus asked.

"I'll be fine. I just need a minute," I said, covering my face with my hands. I had to get my feelings under control. Crying wasn't going to change mine or Uncle Bazz's situation. I knew my role. Now I had to play it.

I took a second to figure out my next step and what to say to Marcus. I put a hand on his leg.

"Marcus, you were right. I just didn't want you to think I was like all the silly underclass little girls that would do anything to ride in your fancy Corvette and get a crack at the money you are about to be making when you go pro next year."

He smiled. "Babygirl, I know you ain't no groupie. Girl, I've been in love with you since I first laid eyes on you. Baby, I have a lot of decisions to make, and a lot of growing up to do. See, I need a woman by my side. I ain't trying to just fuck for the sake of fucking. Been there, done that. I want you to be my girl, my Babygirl, and ride with me all the way to the hall of fame," he said as his fingers slowly walked up my skirt.

That bullshit he spit gave me just enough time to clear my head and figure out my next move. "Oh, Marcus, I hope you are serious," I said in my best fairytale voice, "because that's what I want." I grabbed his hand and squeezed. "And I want to be sure my first will be special."

"Babygirl, you ain't still a virgin, are you?"

"Yeah, sort of." I fidgeted in my seat. "Well, I ain't no goody-two-shoes." I dropped my head and lowered my voice. "I mean, I've went down on a couple of guys. I ain't no freak or nothing, but it's just something about," I closed my eyes right as he looked over at me, "having a man in my mouth and making his body dance as I play his penis like a trombone."

"Fuck, girl, you tryin' to make me wreck. You got me harder than Chinese arithmetic."

"You so crazy, boy." I hee-hee'd. "You think you can take me by the Wachovia on Wesley Chapel? My father wants me to get some money out of our account for his trip."

"Why is he sending you?"

I dropped my head. "I'm all he has. My mom died," I sniffled, "in a car wreck two years ago."

"I'm sorry to hear that."

"Yeah, it's just me and Daddy." I sniffled again.

"That's why I left school early. An emergency came up and he has to fly out to Boston for the weekend. He didn't have time to stop at the bank. And somebody broke into his Benz outside the gym yesterday and stole his I.D. and credit cards."

"Okay, no problem."

I went into the bank and did just as Uncle Bazz instructed. I put the new cell phone in my purse. I was about to drop my old driver's license and social security card in the trash with my old cell phone until I remembered that I was in a bank with surveillance cameras. I had to conceal the ten thousand dollars that was already in ten neat stacks of bundled hundred-dollar bills. The only way I could do it was to roll up two stacks and put one in each bra cup. I even had to take off my shoes and put one stack under each foot. The others went into the small black Louis Vuitton purse I swapped out at Macy's with a knock- off Louis Vuitton I bought from the flea market.

I took a deep breath and walked out of the bank. I got back into Marcus' Vette, crying and nearly hysterical.

"What's wrong, Babygirl?"

"This is just like what happened to Momma."

"Huh?"

"Daddy didn't get a chance to say goodbye to Momma either, and now his mother, my grandmother, had a stroke and is in a coma. The bank account is frozen because Daddy reported all his cards, I.D.'s, and checks stolen. Now I can't get any money, and he might not ever see his mother alive again, just like Momma." I shook my head in despair and cried even louder.

"How much? How much do you need? I mean, how much does he need?"

I pushed my breasts into his chest. I felt the money pressing into me while I hugged and cried on his shoulder. "Oh, Marcus, what am I going to do?"

Again, he repeated, "How much does he need?"

"The flight is nine hundred thirty dollars."

"I know I have eight hundred, but I can get some money out of my dad's account," he said.

"He has to rent a car, and it's at least one hundred dollars," I said, thinking I should have pushed for more.

"My bank is right across the street. I'll loan it to you," he said, speeding out of the parking lot with me damn near in his lap.

"No," I shook my head, "I can't ask you to do that. That's over a thousand dollars. I'd give it back to you when Daddy got back. No, you don't know me like that. I couldn't—"

"Babygirl, it ain't no problem." He wiped my face with his hand. I was surprised that I was actually crying real tears. "And at a time like this, you'll need someone to be there for you while your pops is gone."

I nodded. "Yeah, you right. Will you spend the weekend with me at my house, Marcus?" I asked as he pulled into the Bank of America parking lot.

"That's the least I could do. I don't, uh, suppose you on the pill, are you?"

"Yes, I am. I take them because it helps with that, you know, time of the month."

88

JIHAD

As he was getting out of the car, I said, "Sweetie, after you come out of the bank, I need you to take me home so I can help Daddy get it together and catch the earliest flight out. As soon as he leaves, I'll call you."

"No problem. I'll run you home soon as I get back with the money," he said before closing the door and walking off.

In ten minutes, I had eleven hundred dollars added to the ten thousand I got out of the safety deposit box back at Wachovia bank.

"I thought you lived in Kinsley Estates."

Shit, I don't remember telling this fool where I lived. "No, my dad's ex lives over there. She's really cool, and I hang out with her a lot," I said while scoping out the house in some subdivision I had him to turn into.

"So where do you live?" he asked as he slowly drove around some winding street that I'd never been on.

"Just right around the corner. Pull over right here." I pointed to a deserted looking house that was in desperate need of a lawn man.

"But you just said around the corner."

"I know what I said, baby. I'm just not paying attention, you know, with my grandmother and all," I cooed as I played in his close-cropped hair.

"Give me a couple hours. I hope you like steak, because that's what I'm cooking for dinner for my man tonight," I said as I rubbed his chin. "We don't have any ice cream, so I'll have to do for dessert, if that's okay with you, sweetie."

He nodded like the obedient puppy dog he was.

I slowly sashayed toward the house as he pulled off. I waited until he was out of sight then I walked back down the driveway and to the street before I called a cab.

CHAPTER 18

UNCLE BEN

I was sitting comfortably in my recliner. I had the vibrate mode on while my wide screen television was watching me sleep.

"So, what happened?" Babygirl asked as she barged through the front door of my apartment.

I was too old to jump, but not too old to be scared half to damn death. "Damn, girl, you trying to give me a stroke? Have you heard of knocking?"

"I'm sorry, Uncle Ben, but you didn't answer your phone, and you didn't call after Uncle Bazz got sentenced. So, what happened?" she asked, kneeling in front of me.

"He was sentenced to five years," I said as my beige leather massage chair electronically eased me into an upright sitting position.

"Five years!"

"Babygirl, you know he was going to do time. Come on, now. He took a plea."

"For thirty-six months."

"I know. I know. But after the court took into account his priors and the murder, the judge gave him the maximum sentence," I explained.

"Murder? What murder?"

"Babygirl, you should have seen your Uncle Shabazz. That boy put on a one man show that would've earned him an Emmy if his case were on Court TV.

"The judge sat perched on his high bench, with a smug look on his face, glaring at Shabazz. Shabazz remained calm and unfazed. His sorry excuse for an attorney sat at the defendant's table looking like a drunk with his wrinkled blue off-the-rack suit.

90

"After the judge gave him permission to address the court, he stood and took two steps to the left, then turned sideways so the judge and the crowded courtroom could see his face. Shabazz seemed to survey the nervous men in orange jumpsuits waiting for their fates to be determined as their loved ones sat behind the first two benches, praying God would show mercy on their fathers, brothers, and sons.

"Next thing you know, he went to preaching and politicking about justice and how he was merely a victim. Victim of what, I don't know, but it sure sounded good. Hell, you'd a thought he was the white Johnnie Cochran."

"Uncle Ben, you said murder. What did you mean? Uncle Bazz didn't kill anyone," I said shaking my head.

"Don't worry about him. Knowing Shabazz, he'll be running the Atlanta Penitentiary in no time. Heck, he's in his element. Let's just hope he gets his head straight in there and picks up a trade. He sure can't keep scamming and credit carding."

"Uncle Ben! Stop trippin'! Tell me about this murder, pleeeeeeaaaaasse."

I looked at Babygirl for the first time in a while. Wow, she had grown up on me. She was standing in the living room of my apartment getting very frustrated.

It had been ten months since Shabazz had been arrested. Babygirl had turned out to be a very strong, intelligent and resilient young lady. She was absolutely, breathtakingly lovely. She looked like one of those Dark and Lovely models you see in *Ebony* magazine. You know, the ones with the sprinter's bodies and the *Jet* centerfold faces. Yes indeed, she'd grown into a lovely, Hershey bar-brown, kinky dread- haired, dark- skinned beauty.

I just couldn't get over how much and how fast she had grown. She had a little bit too much Shabazz in her for me, though. That mouth of hers could bring the strongest man to his knees. I just hoped she'd learn how to tame it.

"Uncle Ben?"

"Okay, Babygirl. Calm your nerves. I'm going to tell you. But," I pointed, "you have to promise me you'll never tell Shabazz. He doesn't even remember telling me."

"I won't say anything. I promise."

"Well, back in the day, before we even knew you and your momma, Shabazz would shoot up, and I'd be drinking, and we'd shoot the breeze about some of anything and everything." I paused to get more comfortable in the beige leather massage chair Shabazz had bought me from a Brookstone catalog with a fake credit card.

"You better sit down and make yourself comfortable, Babygirl." She sat cross-legged on the floor next to me. I looked around the apartment as I prepared to tell her the story.

Speaking of apartments . . . Hell, I had to start saving now, 'cause come two months, my lease would be up, and I couldn't afford this loft. I'll say this, though: Shabazz knew how to spoil a man, leasing this loft full of furniture and paying my rent up for the last three years. All I had to do was pay my utilities. Hell, he could've just let me move in with him and Babygirl and saved the money.

"He was a good man, I'll say. He never forgot where he came from."

"Uncle Ben, stop stalling!"

"Calm down, okay, Babygirl. I'm going to tell you."

"You keep saying that, but you keep going off on another subject."

"Okay, okay. Well, one night, we met up at my room in the boarding house. Anyway, we sat around playing the dozens and telling lies as usual. It was just a regular ole Friday night, nothing special. I was sipping on Rose, and he was nodding off into another world. I reached under the couch and got my recorder out. I thought I'd have some fun, like I used to do when you were 'sleep. I knew he was about to start talkin' crazy. And in the mornin', we'd listen to the tape and have a good laugh.

"Anyway, soon as I got the tape ready, I looked over at Shabazz and I see this stream of tears running down his face. A second later, his skin brightened. His neck became a tree of viney veins as he looked up and stared me down with blind man's eyes. If I hadn't been so inebriated and anxious to see how this scene would play out, I would have thought twice before I pushed the record button as he started to speak."

Babygirl nodded.

"Babygirl, I'll be right back," I said as I got up.

"Where you going?" she asked.

"I have an idea. You just wait right there."

A minute later, I was back in the den looking at the naked wall right above the stereo system Shabazz and Babygirl bought me last Christmas.

"I think it would be best if you hear it from him, in his own voice."

"You recorded him?"

"Yes, I did. And to this day, I've never told him."

I put the tape on, pushed play and turned the stereo up. It was time Babygirl knew of Shabazz's past, I thought before sitting down and closing my eyes. It hurt something terrible when he first told it to me, and I figured it wouldn't feel too much different now, ten years later.

The tape started.

CHAPTER 19

SHABAZZ

Little did they know my army was right around the corner, ready for war. The Apaches were going about their daily tasks of dancing and trying to conjure up ways to kill all the women and children in town. I was about to send a scout to the back of Daddy's sunken- in TV chair when he stepped on my army.

"Janice!"

I scurried past Mommy and crawled under the old rusty metal dinner table in the kitchen. When Daddy shouted in his deep devil voice, there was sure to be trouble.

"Yes, Larry, and why so loud? You're scaring your son," she said, drying her hands on a dishtowel as she met Dad in the archway.

"Tell me that this is not what I think it is. Tell me." He grabbed Mommy's arm and jerked, flashing some papers in her face.

"You're hurting me. Please."

"Please my ass. Look at these."

I couldn't see very well from where I was sitting, but I did see Mommy put her hand over her mouth.

"Where did you get these?" she asked.

"Is it true?"

"Let me go."

"Is it true?"

"Yes. Yes. I'm black. My mother was Creole, and my father was a white Navy officer.

"No, Daddy, no!" I shouted as I came from under the table.

"Run, Junior, run!" Mommy barely was able to say as Daddy clamped his huge hands around her small neck.

94

"Let go of her. Let go, Daddy."

"Ow! You bit me. You stupid little shit," Daddy said before he shook me off of his leg and kicked me in the back.

"Leave, leave him—"

"You say something, wench?"

Momma had a coughing fit after Daddy released his choke-hold and slammed her to the floor.

"Noooooo," I cried out, barely able to move.

While she was trying to catch her breath, Daddy grabbed her hair and dragged her over to the pantry. After kicking her inside, he slammed the door.

"Boy, bring me a chair unless you want me to kick the dog again." He pointed to the pantry door, where Momma was kicking and screaming.

"She ain't no dog," I muttered.

He took off his belt. "Boy, you sass me?"

"No, sir," I said as I got up and slowly walked over to the kitchen table, trying my best to stop sniffling. My back was hurting really, really bad. I could hardly carry the chair.

After putting the yellow chair under the pantry door handle at an angle, he made me give him my belt. I started crying because of the beating I was sure to get. Instead, he grabbed me and used the belt to tie my wrists to the black wood-burning stove.

I was too scared to ask why he was doing this. The only thing I did was pee on myself as I cried my nine-year-old heart out. I jerked and yanked, but that old stove didn't budge. Momma was screaming and banging on the door. It wasn't like anyone would hear us, since we lived so far off the road.

Daddy was mean when he'd been drinking, but he never did anything like this.

So what? Momma was a black person. I didn't understand why Daddy was so mad. I was white, and until now, I thought Momma was too. She looked white, so why the big deal?

Were black people mean? Did they have diseases, what? It had to be something wrong with them to make Daddy go crazy. Most of them lived on the other side of town, so I ain't had a whole lot of contact with them.

I heard a car coming, thank God. Daddy had to let us go now. My wrists were ripe from struggling with the belt strapped around them.

"Charlie, Matt," I heard Daddy say. They were a couple of Daddy's friends. "Follow me into the kitchen, fellas," Daddy said.

"What's up, Lar?" It sounded like Matt. He was the one with the red beard and the long belly that hung down to his stubby little legs.

"Got damn, what the hell goin' on, Lar?" Longbelly asked.

They were all standing in front of the kitchen table like I wasn't even there.

"I'll get to that in a minute. Right now, I need you guys to help with somethin'. It's very confidential. I'll give you a thousand bucks a piece."

"For that kind of money, you must want us to kill somebody or something." Charlie, Daddy's Herman Munster-looking friend said.

"No." Daddy shook his head. "Not something," he said.

"Come again?" the tall one asked.

"Where you gon' get that kinda money?" Longbelly asked.

"Don't you worry 'bout all that. Now, we all brothers, and brothers help other brothers, right?"

"Right," they chorused.

"Take a look at these," Daddy said.

Longbelly let out a loud whistle. "That's your wife."

"No shit. You hear all that noise she's making in the pantry," Daddy said.

"I was sort of wondering why you had your wife

locked up in your pantry," Longbelly said.

"But it says here that she's a nigger and your son, he's a nigger too," the tall one said.

"I didn't know." Daddy shrugged. "I just found out. I should've known something wasn't right when she told me she was an orphan and she agreed to uproot and move here from Louisiana without so much as a why or a when."

"How'd ya find out?" Longbelly asked.

"I had a guy I know do some checkin' up on her. For the last ten years, she'd taken trips back home twice a year. She never took him." He pointed to me.

"And she never let me go with her. Said she was going to see friends. I thought she was stepping out on me until the guy I hired brought me this original birth certificate, unlike the one we used to get the blood test before we were married. And these pictures of her with her family."

"Hell, Lar, I thought she was one of those Orphan Annies," Longbelly said.

"I did too. I can't believe I was married to a nigger bitch for ten years and didn't know it."

"And how about you been our chapter leader for three of the last eleven years you been in the brotherhood? Hell, boy, everybody knows you gon' be the next Grand Marshal," Longbelly said.

"Not if word gets out that I'm married to a nigger. I called you two because we'd done this before down in Greenville. I trust you two. Like I said, we are brothers in the order and—"

The tall one cut Daddy off. "You wants us to kill her and help get rid of the body?"

"No, I want you to help me get rid of the body. I'll do the killing. But I'll let you two have some fun with the whore before I do her."

"What about the boy?" Longbelly asked.

"He got nigger blood in him too. He gotta be dealt

with just the same," Daddy said.

They were going to kill me and Mommy. My eyes were wide with fear as I listened. Instead of crying, the thought of being shot and buried in an unmarked grave made me twist and turn like crazy. They were going to cut me up in little pieces and throw me in the river. Tears of fear ran down my face as I imagined all types of horrible ways to die.

They ignored me as they opened the door to the pantry and dragged Momma out onto the kitchen floor.

"No! Leave her alone!" I screamed. The tall one grabbed a lock of Momma's hair, and Daddy got hold of her kicking legs while Longbelly took a hunting knife and cut her red-and-yellow flower dress down the middle.

"Baby, cover your eyes. Don't look," Momma said as Longbelly got on top of her. I tried not to look, but I couldn't turn away. Daddy laughed and cursed while the two men did some of the worst things you can imagine to my Mommy. She screamed until her face went from red to blue. The torture went on forever.

And after forever was over, Daddy lifted her lifeless head off of the bloody white-and-gray linoleum kitchen floor and slid the black-handled shiny hunting knife across her throat.

That's the last thing I remembered before the smell of gas woke me up. It was dark and I was in a moving vehicle. My head was throbbing. Something in a plastic garbage bag was next to me. I was tied up, so I rubbed up against it. Then I remembered. Mommy. She was gone. I wasn't tied up tight. My feet weren't tied at all. I easily worked my hands out from under the rope.

The car slowed down. I had trouble, but I managed to tie the rope back around my arms. I no longer heard the car's engine. The smell of gas was fading. Hearing the slamming of car doors made me realize that we had come to a stop. I closed my eyes as the trunk was opened.

"You think he's dead?"

"Put your hand on his chest and see."

"Hell no. You do it."

"You the one who wants to know if he's dead."

"As hard as Larry hit him with that iron skillet, busting his head wide open, if he ain't dead, he should be on his way. Hell, he looks dead. Besides, I just can't kill no kid. I got morals."

"Morals? You just raped a nigger woman earlier, and you did it to her again after she was dead."

"She deserved every minute and every stroke. She won't be stealin' no more seeds, taintin' and poisoning the white race."

"Whatever. Come on. Help me get her out and then we'll get the boy."

They took Mommy out. One of them said, "Might as well take her on down and throw her into the river. We'll come back for him. Ain't like he goin' nowhere."

I waited until I was barely able to hear the sounds of twigs and leaves under their feet. Then, I freed myself from the rope, turned over and rose up out of the trunk just in time to hear a faint splash of water.

"Hey, kid!" one of them yelled from the river bank.

I climbed out of the car and ran like crazy. I didn't look back. I ran through those woods like I knew were I was going. I ran and I ran. My heart was about to explode. My mouth tasted like cotton. And when I could no longer feel my legs, I still kept running. I couldn't see where I was going. It was darker than black in whatever woods I was in. I heard footsteps. They were catching up. I saw a light up ahead. I ran to it on burning legs, and I almost made it before I fell.

I woke up dead. First thing I saw was the white light. They say that's what you see when you die. I turned my head to the side. Everything was fuzzy, but through my haze I saw God. She was holding my head in her big ole brown arms. I opened my mouth, but nothing came out. I was in black people heaven. God must have made a mistake.

I wanted to tell her, but I couldn't speak, and didn't for months. God turned out to be black herself. Her name was Hattie Mae Jackson.

I don't remember hearing a dog, but Momma Jackson said her German shepherd, Roy, barked so much that she came outside with her shotgun to see what all the racket was about. Instead of finding coons or some other wild animal in the trash again, she saw me laid out on the ground near the woods in her dirt backyard.

I wrote down what had happened to me and with my eyes, I pleaded with her not to send me back. She must've heard me, 'cause I was still there the third day, when she found out that everything I had written down was true. Mommy's body was found on a bank down the Mississippi, not too far from where I told Momma Jackson she'd been thrown.

It was three months before I talked. By then, I was family. Momma Jackson turned out not to be God, but I sure hoped God was like her. She was a widow woman with one son. Her son Harold was a part-time pimp/hustler/con man/drug dealer. You name it, if it was profit in it, he was game for it. He became my big brother and mentor.

I wasn't worried about Daddy finding me. The only time a white man came on our streets was when he was coming to take somebody off to jail.

It was in the early eighties and we lived in a neighborhood that still had dirt streets and alleys. The poor were even too rich to move into our hood. I'll say this for us: We didn't have rats. Shoot, we wished a rat would dare come on our street. That's all we needed to have a barbecue.

Since I would never tell her my name, although I'm sure she found out, she started calling me T.J. after her late husband, Tavarus Jackson. Harold eventually got me a fake birth certificate, solidifying my new n^me, Tavarus T.J. Jackson.

Five years later, I was on my bike coming home from school when I saw this man getting out of a new pickup. Memories of Momma's screams, her cries for mercy, my tears, riding in the trunk of a car with my dead mother, all flooded back. But it was one horrific memory that made me come to the decision that I had. It was the man that I'd called Daddy for nine years, wearing that grotesque, sadistic smile as he stood standing over Mommy's dead and defiled body. If I lived to be a hundred and ten, I'd never forget that look on his face.

I reached into my Levi's blue jeans pocket just to make sure I still had the twenty I picked up the night before from the weed drop I made for Harold. I didn't waste any time as I followed my mother's killer into the hardware store.

I knew exactly where the tools were. I picked up the biggest crescent wrench I saw and walked toward the counter just in time to see him leaving. I didn't think. I just ran up behind him and swung that wrench as hard and as fast as I could. The first blow to the head dropped him. A woman inside the store screamed. Ignoring her, I continued smashing his face with every ounce of strength I could muster, while others in the store just watched. Everything happened so quick, I couldn't think. In a matter of minutes, I was back on my bike, speeding down Main.

I went home as if nothing happened. Just as I finished telling Momma Jackson what I'd done, the police came busting in our screen door.

I was only fourteen, but the D.A. still tried to have me charged as an adult for capital murder. I was assigned a public defender. He was a young Jewish kid, fresh out of college. Momma Jackson seemed to trust him, so

I did too. He proved to the court that I was the dead man's son, and that he killed my mother. I even helped to convict Longbelly and the tall one with my testimony. Still, I'd killed a man, and I was convicted and sentenced to Milledgeville Correctional Institution for boys until I turned eighteen.

Longbelly and the tall one accepted a plea, and were given a one-year suspended sentence plus fifty hours of community service. Momma Jackson told me that they were dumb for taking a plea, 'cause everybody knew even in 1980s Mississippi, a white man killing a black person was the equivalent of a black person killing a dog.

And if I could go back to that day, I'd kill him again. I'm just mad I didn't have no weed to celebrate after I smashed his face with the plumber's wrench.

CHAPTER 20

BABYGIRL

Sometimes I have to ask myself was it yesterday or was it three months ago when I came through the door of Uncle Ben's small one-bedroom apartment that dreadful morning.

After a long night of selling fantasies, dancing naked at the Parrot, I usually came over to Uncle Ben's to get some sleep. This had been my routine since I started dancing six months ago. By the time the club closed at three and I left at close to four in the A.M., I was too tired to drive the thirty minutes it took to get to my apartment in Buckhead.

Before I walked in the door that morning, I heard the scratchy, static sound of Uncle Ben's surround sound big screen television system. I remember thinking that this was weird. Uncle Ben never left the television on overnight. He was too bill conscious, although I'm the one who had paid his bills since Uncle Bazz went down. An eerie feeling crept up on me as I walked through the dark and into the television light of the den. Electric snow and squiggly lines were racing down the fifty-seven inch television. I looked at the screen for like a minute before I dropped my purse and my overnight bag onto the dark carpet.

I walked into Uncle Ben's sunroom without turning around. I broke off the greenish-brown dying leaf on the five-foot elephant-ear plant that sat in there. I momentarily lost myself in the night that I observed from the horizontal plate glass windows.

I was in no rush to move away from that spot, that place in time where everything meant everything and everything meant nothing. Finally, I dropped my

103

shoulders and turned to face Uncle Ben's chair. A line of tears started to form, dropping from my eyes to my face to the carpet as I took timid baby steps toward the reclined figure of what I thought was the definition of a man. Uncle Ben, my Uncle Ben was gone. I kneeled onto the carpet by his side, holding his cold hands and looking at his peaceful face through the television light for the longest time.

This was three months ago, and I was still mourning like it was yesterday. Lord knows I had to pull myself together and get my eyes back on the prize. I'd spent a grip times two on the funeral arrangements, but I wouldn't have had it any other way. After all, Uncle Ben was like a father to me, and ain't no way I was going to let the state put him away in a wooden box in an unmarked grave. It took most of my nest egg, fifteen grand, but no amount of money could replace the love I had for Uncle Ben. I was happy to be able to send him away righteously.

I just hated that Uncle Bazz couldn't be at the funeral. I wrote, telling him how I'd found Uncle Ben and how he'd died peacefully, but as usual, my letters went unanswered. Now, I had to focus and get back on track. I'd invested too much time and money in myself and my apartment.

I liked my little spot. I'd done too much redecorating and added too much high tech video equipment to lose it. I knew what the peach piece of paper was before I snatched it off my front door.

I was two months behind on my rent. The high-rise I lived in boasted indoor tennis courts, a state of the art business center, and a gym. There was an extensive waiting list to get in. If the leasing manager wasn't a man, I wouldn't have gotten the apartment at all. After the way I played him to get my apartment, I knew I couldn't go to him for help now. As Uncle Bazz would say, "Fuck it in a bucket." I had to get my butt in gear, stop grieving and get back on the grind. I had ten days to come up with $3,763. That was last month's and this month's rent plus late fees.

I could go down to the Department of Vital Records and pull all the birth and death certificates for the year I was born until I found someone that had died the same year I was born. Afterwards, I could get a certified copy of the deceased birth certificate. From there, I could go to the social security office and apply for a number. It would take about two weeks, but after receiving a social security number I could get a Georgia I.D. and driver's license. From there, I'd open up a couple bank accounts and start writing checks between the two, using each bank to cover each check, building an imaginary balance.

Nah, that shit would be too much trouble and would take too damn long. I only had ten days. Been there, done that. Way too much stress, and not enough rest for a diva.

Hell, I was twenty, but I told men I was eighteen. I had a pretty face, a cooty-cat, and a mouthpiece. And the way the three worked together, it was no wonder that I tricked the money right up out of men's wallets. I was seriously thinking about trying to get a merchant account and a credit card machine for the guys who didn't carry cash. I decided against this when I decided to quit dancing and strike out on my own, just five minutes earlier. I needed too much money, too quick, and I had all the tools to get it without putting my body on display for every pervert that had ten dollars to get in the Parrot. I got my butt up out of my California king sleigh bed and put my three best assets to work.

It was a beautiful spring Monday morning. It was the beginning of the week, the best night to go to the number one pick-up joint in town, Crunch Fitness. The sun was peeking through my blinds as I finished pouring a bowl of Captain Crunch. While eating breakfast, I got on NASA (that's what I called my state of the art Dell computer system) to check the weather. Fifty degrees, it read.

A minute later, I replaced the cherry-colored Victoria's Secret bra I had on for a cream-colored sports bra. After putting on some matching shorts and old green-and-white Nike Air Max's, I was out the door and jogging down eleven flights of stairs. It was too nice a morning to waste working out at the apartment gym on the third floor.

An hour later, I was back from my five-mile jog. I stripped off my wet clothes and put them on the shoe rack by the door. Naked as a newborn baby, I went out onto my balcony, stretched, and took a deep breath as I looked over downtown and Buckhead.

I rolled my electronic telescope to one wall. Next, I lifted one long, sweat-glistening leg over the stainless steel balcony railing while the other leg helped brace my body. I stretched my arms forward, touching my strawberry-painted toes. The sweat from my back tingled as it ran down my spine to the crack of my behind. After stretching the other leg, I wrapped both of my hands on the top rail, placed my feet between the top two rails, and slowly leaned back at a forty- five-degree angle until my shoulder blades rested on the green-and-black slate tiled patio surface.

The muscles in my quads, hamstrings and calves were slowly loosening as I stretched. Beads of sweat were racing down between my legs as I arched my back. "Oooh," I shuddered as a cool, swift breeze snuck up on me and kissed the sweat-lingering lips between my legs. I closed my eyes and imagined that the gentle wind between my thighs was LL Cool J. He eased his way up the smoothness of my tight stomach. He worked in harmony with the beads of sweat that were now racing and dancing on and around my suddenly swollen pink-and-burnt-brown nipples. That LL Cool J wind had me moaning to his groove.

My fingers awoke. They too wanted to get in on the LL Cool J wind groove. And who was I to deny them? His wind, my index and long finger. Oh my God. LL and Usher. A threesome. At first the LL Cool J wind and my Usher Raymond fingers worked in unison. Then Usher got greedy and began using that long, curved, violin-stick finger and played a slow, melodic beat, to and fro, back and forth, "Ohhhh," gently messaging that, that pulsating ball in the middle of my shaved forest.

The LL wind was still there, however faint. My heartbeat started to increase as if I were running again. Sweat was racing down my legs, trying to get to the concert that was playing between my lips of love. My legs started to spasm. My eyes lost themselves somewhere in the back of my head. Usher was speeding up the tempo. LL was everywhere now, competing. He played the same tune as Usher.

From somewhere deep down in the core of my soul, glass-breaking octave sounds of ecstasy were released from my mouth. My eyelids shuddered as my gushing juices of joy spewed over and around LL and Usher. They'd already soaked my waxed heart-shaped mound of pubic hair, and now the flooding river was on its way to drown the ground.

And then I went limp. My morning ritual was complete. I loved me a beautiful, strong black man, but I didn't need one to make me feel good about being me, and I sure didn't need one to make me feel like a woman, I thought as I got up on weak legs and made my way through the bamboo hardwood den to my bathroom.

After letting the steaming water run over my body, I massaged myself with shea butter soap and a sponge. I felt a whole lot more than the heat from the steaming water, and I would've let that feeling take me where it wanted, but I had work to do.

After drying off and slipping on some black stretch

jeans, a fuchsia Baby Phat breast-hugging baby tee, matching Nine West open-toe sandals and some Michelle Thompson shades, I picked up my cell phone and called my hairstylist and sometimey friend, Tracy. She did most of the girls' heads at the Parrot. And not just because she was the sister of one of the girls that danced at the Parrot. She was the absolute bomb when it came to laying a head out.

She picked up on the first ring. "No, no, and hell double no."

"Well, hello, and how the hell are you doing this bea-u-tiful morning, sweetie?" I asked.

"No, bitch, no. Today is my only day of rest, and I am not doing no damn hair."

"Girl, I'm sorry, I know how hard it must be running the shop, working six days a week."

"More like eight. Even God rested on the seventh," she said.

"Well, girl, you get you some rest. You can catch him another time."

"Catch who?"

"That's why I called. But girl, you right. You got to get you some rest. I'll call you tomorrow." I hung up and began to count. "Nine, eight, seven, six, five, four, three."

"Hello," I said after pressing the answer button on my cell phone.

"Catch who?"

"Huh?"

"You said something about catching someone."

"I know you heard that Morris Chestnut's in town shooting a couple scenes for his next movie out near Sugarloaf Parkway."

"Girl, everything I hear is second-and third-hand information from the girls who come into the shop. I don't know when I've listened to a radio or seen anything on TV."

"Anyway, Morris is going to be at Crunch Fitness tonight getting his sweat on."

"You lyin'."

"No, for real. Pshhh, it ain't no big secret. Ask anyone who works out at Crunch. Matter of fact, if you don't believe me, I'll call a guy I know on three-way that works there." I paused. Okay, she didn't say anything, so she was calling me out. "Hold on, girl."

I hung up on her and called the gym. "Yes, can I speak with Dominic Morgan, please?"

"I'll see if he's available. Please hold."

"Crunch Fitness, may I help you?"

"D'nic, what's up, cutie pie?"

"Who dis?"

"Your future baby's momma."

"Must be you, Babygirl. I'd know the world's biggest tease anywhere."

My phone beeped.

"Hold on, cutie. Don't hang up, D'nic." I clicked over and said, "Girl, what happened? I clicked back over and you were gone," I lied.

"I don't know. Try calling the gym again," Tracy said.

"Hang up. I have to clear my other line. I'll call you right back, Tracy."

I clicked back over. "D'nic, you still there?" I asked.

"I don't know why, but yeah."

"I need two favors. One, I need a guest pass for a friend, and two, I'm going to call you back. When I do, I'll ask you what famous person will be working out tonight. You have to say Morris Chestnut."

"Girl, are you crazy? Don't get me caught up in no more of your bullshit. You almost got me fired for putting you in the system for a year. And you still owe me for that."

"Look, I ain't got much time. Tell you what. I'll come pick you up. I live right around the corner, and I'll give you what I owe and more on your lunch break. Just do this for me."

"You gon' give me some of that pussy for real this time?"

So crass, no taste, and no tact, I thought. "Ain't that what I said? And if I don't, you don't have to leave the pass for my girl." My phone beeped. The caller ID read TRACY. "I'll be there at one. Call you right back," I said before hanging up and clicking over.

"Tracy, sorry 'bout that. I just got my period, and you know how that is."

"You going to call or what?" she said, sounding impatient and unbelieving.

"I can't believe you don't trust me. I'm hurt."

"Make the call, girl."

"Okay, hold on." I clicked over and dialed the number. I clicked back over. "Tracy, you there?"

"Yeah."

"Crunch Fitness, may I help you?"

"Hello, may I speak to Dominic Morgan, please?"

"He's with a guest. Can I take a message?"

"I think the ba-baby's coming," I said as I moaned.

"Please."

"Dominic, emergency, line one. Dominic Morgan, emergency, line one," I heard before she put us on hold.

"Girl, you's a real fool."

"Or very smart," I shot back.

"Crunch Fitness, may I help you?"

"Dominic."

"Don't say anything. Let me talk," Tracy said before I could say anything. "Dominic, you don't know me, but I heard a special someone will be at your facility this evening."

"Yes, Morris Chestnut."

"Oh, okay, thank you. Sorry for disturbing you."

"Twelve-thirty," was the last thing he said before I

110

clicked him off the line.

"What does twelve-thirty mean?" Tracy asked.

"I don't know. The receptionist said he was with a guest. He must've been talking to them."

"I thought you were bullshittin'. Girl, I apologize, but you know how you are. You'd say anything to get me to do your hair."

"Speaking of doing hair, girl, I look a hot mess. I can't meet Morris Walnut, Peanut, Chestnut or any other kind of nut looking like this."

"Meet me at the shop in fifteen minutes," she said reluctantly.

I'd cut my dreads out a year ago. I was letting my hair grow. I was almost twenty-one now, and I wanted to have more of an Ashanti look by my birthday in six months. Right now, I looked like a dark-skinned China doll with the short hairstyle I currently wore.

The day went by uneventfully. Later that evening, I pulled into the Tower's Place underground parking lot in my red Volkswagen bug. Tracy had laid my hair out. I got out of the car sporting the platinum Halle Berry look that she wore in X-Men. The sixty thousand square foot gym was located on top of the parking garage. I got out of the car and stretched. The platinum and diamond belly button ring was a nice accent to the flat, muscled stomach I had on display for the men in the gym, and it matched my hair.

"Damn, girl. You might as well be naked with some Nikes on," Tracy said as she approached.

"Look at you, looking like a dance hall diva with all that red on," I lied. Tracy was all right with me, but tonight she was doing way too much, looking like a fire engine, wearing a mountain of red. She was one of those super-sized sistahs who tried to squeeze into Happy Meal clothes. Her stomach looked like a winding road map with all those curved and crooked stretch marks exposed under her Mount Everest breasts. They looked to be suffocating in the world's biggest sports bra. The fire engine red biking shorts she squeezed over her big ass were just downright nasty looking.

"I am full-size fine, ain't I?"

"Girl, you doing the damn thang," I said as we walked to the door.

Monday night was the busiest night at the gym. I guess everybody was trying to make up for not working out on the weekend. After scanning my card, I told the girl at the front desk that there should be a guest pass for Tracy.

"Who'd you speak with, ma'am?"

"Dominic Morgan."

"He's with a guest. If you'd like to wait, I'll let him know you're here when he's finished."

"That's okay. I'll find him."

I turned toward Tracy. "Girl, sit down over there." I pointed to a group of chairs near the door. "I'll go on a Chestnut hunt and I'll straighten this out with Dominic. Don't worry, girl. I'll be right back."

She looked crushed, but what else could she do?

I was on my way up the stairs to the free weight area where all the wolves gathered to lift and look down at the half-naked women in the aerobics studio below.

"You ain't shit," D'nic mouthed as I crossed his path. He was with a guest, obviously trying to sucker her into buying a membership like he tried with me six months ago.

I met him around the corner and whispered in his ear, "Don't hate the player, hate the game."

"Damn, baby, can a nigga pay your rent, buy your clothes, make the car payment, what?" some cornball brother spewed. "Fuck the three Js. They ain't got shit on you, chocolate sunrise."

I smiled at him before asking, "What are the three

112

Js?"

"Not a what, but a who. Janet, J-Lo, and Jada," he said, counting on his fingers.

"Cute, but still corny."

"But it served its purpose."

"And that was?"

"To get some conversation. My name is Dwayne, Dwayne Tate." He pulled out a card from the front pocket of his shorts.

Okay, he was doing way too much. He worked out with business cards in his too short, tight white tennis shorts? I took the card. "Oh, you are an attorney."

"Yes, I own the law offices of Norris, Williams, and Tate," he said, smiling.

I wanted to tell him not to ever smile. He was okay looking until he smiled. His teeth looked like he'd been chewing on the sidewalk. I just could not understand why men with so much money didn't take the time to get their teeth fixed.

I shook his extended hand. "Nice to meet you, Dwayne," I said before walking away.

"You think I can see you again?" he asked.

"Sure, I'm here all the time."

He shook his head. "No, I mean maybe I can take you out to Sambuca's or to Dante's."

"How did you know I liked jazz?"

"You look like a jazz woman."

"Really, and how does a jazz woman look?"

"Like you. Tell you what. I just traded in my SL for the new Porsche Cabriolet. How about going for a ride with me after you work out?"

He was begging for me to get his ass. He did everything but tell me he had money.

"I'll find you after I finish my workout, Derrick," I said, walking away. I felt his eyes all on my ass as I swayed and sashayed.

"That's Dwayne, Dwayne Tate," he reminded me.

I waved my acknowledgement of his name. A jacked-up grill and little-ass feet were my biggest turn off, and Dwayne "rent-money-payday" Tate had both.

I went back down to check on Tracy. She was gone. Oh well, I shrugged. I'd take care of her later. I hated to play her, but shit, I was desperate. And I didn't want to go back to dancin'. I loved me too much to degrade myself like that again.

I left the gym, went home, and got on the net. I put D-W-A-Y-N-E, T-A-T-E, A-T-L-A-N-T-A, A-T-T-O-R-N-E-Y in the Goggle search engine.

Jackpot! The fucker was loaded. Forty-nine? Shit, he was old enough to be my daddy. He had three kids and a wife who was a family practitioner. Shit, she had all the money. Her teeth were straight, and her feet were probably bigger than his. Shit, I wished she was him.

I made a gesture, pulling down an imaginary slot machine lever. "Ching, ching." He'd been married for twenty years and was up for a judgeship.

I was back at the gym in five minutes.

"Dwayne." I put my arm around his sweaty broad shoulders.

"I saw you leave."

Okay, he had the stalker gene, I thought. "No, I just went out to meet a friend. I was hoping you'd give me a ride home."

"You don't drive?"

"Yes, but I jogged here."

"You live pretty close, huh?"

"Right around the corner."

"Sure, okay, let me take a shower and change. I'll be right out."

"Come on, you can use the shower at my place. I don't like waiting." I smiled seductively.

Five minutes later, we were at my building and on the elevator.

"Can I get you something to drink before I get in

the shower?" I asked, as I took off my top, ignoring his wide-eyed stare. The look on his face said it all. Men were so easy.

He shook his head, though his eyes stayed on my breasts.

"Okay, if you change your mind, there's the kitchen." I pointed. "Help yourself." Numb nuts still just stared in awe. You'd think he'd never seen a woman's breasts.

I closed and locked my bedroom door. It took me about three minutes to set up the cameras I had hidden in six different places around the room.

After I showered, I took a bottle of cocoa butter lotion into the den. He was sitting on the edge of my ivory leather love seat. After handing him the lotion, I dropped my towel and turned my back to him. I heard him make a disgusting swallowing sound. "Think you can rub some lotion on my back, Daddy?"

"Su-su-sure." After about three minutes of his timid ass trying to drown my back, I told him to take a shower and come back and let me massage lotion into the pores of his beautiful, taut muscled skin.

For an older short man, he was light on his feet. He was through the French doors of my bedroom in no time. Once I heard the water running, I ran around the bedroom, clicking the cameras on. I then wide-stepped into the kitchen. I was under the sink, checking the video monitor when his voice interrupted me.

"You know, I never got your name," he said.

Did he see me? Couldn't have. He was too nonchalant. "Call me what you like. Names are not important," I said, walking out of the kitchen. Shit, I hoped the cameras picked this shit up. What a waste of a man. Oh well, another dickless wonder.

I grabbed his hand and led him toward the bedroom. I put my hand over his lips. "I like to role play, Daddy. Let me do the talking." I lightly circled my pointed finger around his left nipple before I continued. "You do as I say, and I will take you on a ride to Boogie Wonderland."

"Earth, Wind, and Fire," he interrupted.

"No. My earth." I cupped my breasts. "My wind." I opened my mouth and blew. I closed my eyes and touched the tip of my nose with my tongue. "My fire." I let my head fall back and gently rubbed three fingers from the bottom of my vagina to the top.

By now he was Jell-o pudding, soft putty, Play Doh. I gave him the pink panties and bra I had laid out on the bed. I whispered in his ear, "Daddy, go put these on, so Mommy can get real wet." I placed a finger over his lips. "Shhhh." I shook my head before he could protest.

Without a word, he went to the restroom. A minute later, he walked out of my bathroom looking like a baby Barry White in drag. I had to bite my tongue to keep from laughing.

"Baby, you look so, so damn tasty," I growled. "Get on your knees and bark for Momma."

"Woof, woof."

"Show Momma that tongue."

He obediently licked out his tongue.

I squatted right above his face. "Lick Momma's wet pussy." He put one hand on my thigh. I slapped his hands. "Unh-uh, not with your hands. Your tongue."

He went to licking and slobbing all over my cooty-cat. It felt kind of good, but thinking about that upside-down-crooked-tooth monster mouth of his turned me all the way off.

"Lay on your stomach."

He turned over as I stood up.

"No, on the bed," I said.

After he got up and flopped on my bed like a little kid, I got on top of him and in one quick motion I ripped off the panties he wore.

116

"Hey!"

"Hey yourself," I said, as I repositioned myself on top of him in such a way that his needle dick couldn't penetrate me. I rode him like that for a good three minutes.

"Oh, oh shit, fuck. Yeah, Daddy," I said while I tried to figure out my next move. "Whose dick is this?"

"Yours, yours baby. Oh, Lisa, oh shit, I'm cu-cu-cumming."

Oh shit. The fuckhead shot hot cum all over my shit, and my leg. Fuckin' little-dick moron. Disgusting, I thought as I jumped off the bed and wiped his cum off of me with the sheet that would soon be in the trash chute. "Dwayne, what is your whole name? I mean middle name too," I cooed while using the sheet to wipe myself.

"Dwayne Douglas Tate," he said, proud as a politician. "Why?"

"Just curious." I shrugged.

"I have condoms in my wallet. We can do the real thing now," he said.

"No, I can't do it. I'm not that type of girl."

He was standing behind me, massaging my shoulders. I could feel his little thing rubbing up against me. I turned around and put my hand on it then started massaging it while I nibbled on his nipples.

"Oh shit. Damn, baby. Oh my goodness-gracious. Oh, son of a muthafuckin' son of a bitch."

"Push me on the bed hard and take me however you want me. You be the rapist and I'll play the victim. Be a warrior and ignore my pleas for mercy. Show me how much of a man you are. Take me, Dwayne. If you ain't a punk, you'll take this pussy," I whispered in his ear.

He grabbed me by the waist, lifted me up and threw me on the bed. Then, he dove on me like I was a fucking swimming pool.

"No!" I screamed.

BABYGIRL

He held my arms as he tried to straddle me. I squirmed and made a feeble attempt to fight him off.

"You're raping me! No, stop. I won't tell, I promise, Dwayne. Please stop," I shouted.

"Black-ass whore, this is my pussy, and you better act like it or I'll knock you silly."

Knock you silly, what the fuck was that? "No, quit, stop, you're hurting me," I said, getting back into character. "Don't hit me again, please?" I said before shoving him off of me and kneeing him in the groin.

"Ohhhhhhhh," he groaned while balling up and rolling off the bed.

I ran into the kitchen and got my gun from under the cabinet.

"You crazy bitch, what's wrong with you?" he said all Mickey Mouse-like.

"R-A-P-E, muthafucka. Can you spell, Mr. Lawyer Man? You raped me. I told you to stop. Get the fuck out of my apartment before I call the police."

He went for his pants.

"No, leave your clothes and your wallet."

"Are you nuts?"

I jerked the chamber, putting a bullet in my nine. I started counting, "Five, four, three." I threw his keys in the hall as he ran past me.

After taking a shower, I was up half the night, laughing and editing the mini-movie I starred in earlier. I napped a few hours before waking up and putting the package together. I wanted to have the letter, the tape, and his wallet all packaged up neatly before I had it couriered over to the Law Offices of Norris, Williams, and Tate. His wallet was intact, just like Uncle Bazz had taught me.

Oh shit, Uncle Bazz, I forgot. I hadn't thought of him in a few days, and I couldn't wait. Uncle Bazz would be home in eighty-three days.

CHAPTER 21

SHABAZZ

You know the country is truly fucked up when you gotta go to prison before niggas accept you for who you is. I mean, I looked whiter than the whitest white man, but once I opened my mouth, a nigga know I'm one of them.

I spent all my life trying to be accepted and niggas, white and black, played me to the left at every right turn. But not in the joint. In here, it didn't matter if you were white, yellow, brown, or midnight. If you lived in a cage, you was a nigga. If you wore a badge and went home every day, you was a Flintstone. Didn't matter what color you was.

I was either the blindest or one of the dumbest cats in the world. I had wasted my whole life hatin' a whole damn race for what one evil, sadistic, sperm-donatin', pink-faced Flintstone had done. I got high for half my life trying to escape the pink skin I was in. In essence, I was getting high to die. All the dirty needles I'd used, I was lucky that killa virus ain't snuck up on my ass.

It's a damn shame it took me thirty years and a prison stint to half-ass wake up. I say half-ass 'cause I was still doin' shit I know was foul, but doing wrong for so long, I didn't know how to do right.

I wasn't nothin' but thirty-three, but a nigga look fifty-three and shit. But like my nigga Jay Z say, I done lived a hard knock life. Bein' me, livin' my life, made this prison shit seem like one of those Hawaiian vacations I used to trick squares with.

On the real, this wasn't shit compared to trying to figure out where my next blast was gon' come from when I was shootin' that shit in my arms, legs, and anywhere else I could find a vein. The food was fucked up

119

in here, but it was better than standing in the back of Burger King, waitin' 'til after closing time to eat some cold, greasy fries and burgers they had to throw out for the night.

Yeah, the Pen was full of a bunch of muthafuckas just like me. White niggas and black niggas so tired of tryin' to figure out where they fit in that they started jackin' otha muthafuckas for they spot in the puzzle of life. Hell, you know you can see when a piece of the puzzle is forced in a spot it don't belong. One-time, the po-po, five-o, take your choice; somebody gon' point your misplaced-piece ass out. And it was gon' be somebody you once called friend or family. That's how eighty-five to ninety percent of the cats in the new age prison slave plantation got here. The other ten to fifteen percent told on themselves by the dumb shit they did, like my dumb ass.

I was duplicating driver's licenses and printing credit cards like I had a pass from Bush. And from the very place I laid my head every night. Yeah, I was doing time for being stupid.

I tell you one person who ain't the least bit stupid: Babygirl. That's my heart. I think about my shorty every day. What she's doin', how she livin', a little bit of everything. But what I don't do is worry about her. Hells no. Babygirl is a no-limit soldier. The nigga who cross her is the one you gotta worry 'bout. That's gon' be one fucked-up-fo'-sho'-ass nigga.

The reason I ain't wrote her was just like I said in that first letter I wrote when I touched down in this piece. I wasn't putting her on my visiting list, nor would I write or call. I got busted, not her. I made my bed, and I was going to lay in it by myself. Babygirl wasn't gon' ever see me in no cage. I know she didn't like that I was shutting her out. She was probably all fucked up inside. So was I. But whatever. It was what it was, and she'd get

120

over it. Besides, she knew I was gonna make this time work for me.

Like I always told Babygirl, you come in this world by your damn self, and you gon' leave this mu'fucka by your damn self.

I was lying on my top bunk, staring at the gray concrete ceiling when my big country bodyguard and friend came bouncing through my blue metal cell door.

"Whachu doing, li'l buddy?" Big-hungry asked.

"Trying to figure out why I didn't get a yellow slip in the mail from J'doves people." I sat up and put my legs over the side of my bunk. "And trying to figure out why I pay you."

Big-hungry took a seat on the stainless steal seatless toilet in my eight by ten foot cell. "Uh, buddy told me that his woman was gon' bring some hair-on in through the visiting room tomorra." He looked up at me and smiled as I jumped down from my bunk.

"Damn, what the fuck I pay your Bigfoot ass for? You just can't get my shit straight, can you?"

They called him Big-hungry because the big Sasquatch mu'fucka didn't know the meaning of the words "diet" and "enough." I mean, the nigga never missed a meal, never turned down food, and was always chewin' on somethin'. He took care of my business, though, at least most of the time.

"I'm sorry, li'l buddy. I just thought you wanted your money any way you could get it."

"I do. Junk ain't dead presidents, though. I don't fuck with dope. You know that. We been down three years, runnin' dog house and A ward, the hardest cell blocks in the Pen."

Big-hungry nodded.

"You know how long it took for me to organize and lock down the gamblin' in here. Now we got this nice little set-up with Lieutenant Wilkinson on day shift, C.O. Jones, and Case Manager Dawkins. If all of a sudden I start pushin' H or coke, the stakes go up, we'd have to get down wit' some gang shit for real and who knows? All types of shit might blow up in our faces."

He shrugged. "You want me to put a whippin' on ole boy, J'dove? You just say the word, li'l buddy, and I'll whip him like a runaway slave caught readin' a book. It might start a war, but you just say the word, li'l buddy." He nodded. "And I'ma sho' nuff be on it."

"All I want, Big-hungry, is to get my money. I need to be able to go to mail call and wait on the C.O. to hand me an envelope with a yellow slip that say five hundred is in my commissary account. That's what the hell I need to happen."

"You ain't said nothin' but a word. I'm gon' be on ole boy like stink on shit."

"The nigga shouldn't play if he can't pay. I want my money in three days, Big-hungry."

He just nodded and stood there like a tree.

"You ain't gone yet," I said.

"My fault. Didn't know we was finished," Big-hungry said, leaving my cell.

Four years ago, I was takin' bets for a couple of ex-mob players on the inside named Big Mike and Leo. To put me down with their game, I had to make them think that I was the white boy that could get the action from the brothas without any threat of being welched on.

They told me that since I talked like black folks, I could get them to place their bets with me. Leo and Big Mike must've figured that I knew how to speak nigganese or some shit. You know, the language of the natives. Whatever they thought, they didn't do enough of it. They was right about one thing: I did get the brothas to come to me when they wanted to place a bet. See, Big Mike, Leo, or none of their horses could get the respect of the brothas, and if you can't get respect, you can't get paid.

Once I had two gees saved up and a subscription to *USA Today,* and the *Atlanta Journal,* I hired the strongest, biggest, blackest muthafucka in the joint, Big-hungry. I subscribed to the papers' to get the betting lines from the last page of the sports section. I compared the two papers' betting lines and set my own spreads. From there, I'd go to the law library, take a sheet of paper, and type up the games and the odds for that day. After making a hundred copies, I handed them to Big-hungry to pass out to our regulars.

I made Big-hungry think that we were partners. As long as I made sure he kept a locker full of goodies and a little money on his books, Big-hungry was satisfied. I even bought his big ass a bag of bud every Friday after evening chow. Me, I was still straight. I ain't did nothing harder than Tylenol since I kicked. Sports booking was my new drug of choice.

So, when I divorced Big Mike and Leo and told them to respectfully kiss my ass, they knew they had been fucked. But what could they do? The joint was the one place where Blacks were the majority, and most importantly, we ruled what happened behind the wall, which is what everybody on the inside called the penitentiary. And Big Mike and Leo knew if they tried to have me touched, they'd be starting a war they could not win.

Take two tablespoons of Ray Lewis, a dab of Shaquille O'Neal, two dumptrucks of ugly, and a boatload of big, and you got Big-hungry. Fortunately for me, I was the only one who knew that Big-hungry was just a big ole teddy bear.

Big-hungry was the proud father of a six-year-old boy. He was happily married, and had been for over ten years to his high school sweetheart back home in the small country town of Dublin, Georgia. He'd been a high school football star and heavily recruited by college scouts from all over the country. But he never went. He had no intentions of ever leaving Dublin for more than a week's time. He loved the country, the people, and his little family.

His world went from green to gray on April 8, 1995. That's the night he was pulled over at a truck stop about thirty miles outside of Sweetwater, Texas after picking up a load on his rig. It was a blue-black, clear, humid summer night when Big-hungry was stopped by two Texas State patrol cars and was ordered to step out of his eighteen-wheeler. He had just touched the pavement when he was dropped to his knees with a large black nightstick. From there, he was strip- searched, handcuffed to a railing on his rig, and forced back onto his knees, wearing only his Fruit of the Looms as state troopers searched the rig's trailer. An hour later, the state troopers emerged from the long, gray trailer with several shrink-wrapped packages of marijuana.

Even after his attorney proved that Big-hungry had no idea that the pallets were full of much more than the Dell computer equipment that was on the invoice, the jury still found him guilty of drug trafficking. After the judge sentenced him to eighteen months in Federal prison, Big-hungry went ballistic. He kicked over the large attorney-client oak wood table, swatted two court deputies off of him like flies, and attacked and beat the judge until the seventh bullet put him down.

This lone act earned him twenty more years.

The Pen was full of Big-hungries just waiting for a man like me to take care of them. Thanks to him, I was the top dog, booking everything from prison softball to pro football. I had five thousand on my books and thirty thousand more in an account my attorney, Dalton Parker, had set up for me. He was a shady muthafucka, but a damn good mouthpiece.

Dog house is where I did the do. D house, or dog

house, was the most notorious dorm for drugs, gambling, and prostitution behind the wall. Yeah, that's right, I said prostitution. There was enough gumps around selling head or ass that no one had to take no booty. Sick shit, I know, but the gumps' best clients were married men. That's an altogether different story, though.

Later on that day, I was on the yard. I'd just finished liftin' and I was waiting my turn to play handball when J'dove and his punk-ass flunkies stepped to me. He had his arms and hands in a gangsta prayer mode. His head was swaying like Stevie Wonder. I looked at the fool like *what, nigga?*

"You got somethin' ta say to me, nigga? Say that shit to me. I ain't one a them scared, booty-suck-ass niggas you used to fuckin' with," J'dove shouted to be heard and seen.

This buster was violatin' my space. I closed my eyes to tune him out while I calmed myself and chose my words carefully. "You know how the game goes, playa." I shrugged and nodded. "J'dove, you bet, you lost. You owe, you pay."

"Fuck that." He bobbed his head and took a step toward me. "Nigga, you shawt. You got eighty-somethin' days before you max out and step back into the free world." He looked me up and down before continuing. "Old bedtime-havin'-ass nigga. You might as well charge that five spot to the game, 'cause my account is closed. All I got for you is hard dick and bubble gum, nigga." He spit out a wad of gum onto the pavement where we stood, next to the handball courts. "Oops," he said. His boys laughed as other inmates stopped what they were doing out on the yard to see what was going on.

Big-hungry came outta nowhere. "You ain't gon' be callin' li'l buddy too many more niggas."

"What? You want me to call him light-skin, or better yet, white boy?"

Big-hungry took a step forward. I held my arm out.

"Sit this one out, big man. I got this half-man, half-bitch-ass nigga," I said, staring J'dove up and down.

He took off his shirt. I should have stole his ass in the mouth then. "What? You want summa dis, or do you want this dick?" he said, turning his face up and grabbing his crotch.

I pointed my finger in his face. "Half-bitch, trick-ass, gump-fuckin' puppy, piss-weak, faggot muthafucka. All's I want is my money plus anotha hun' for disrespectin' the game, ni-ggaaaaa. Three days, bitch-made-ass nigga, that's all you got," I said before signaling Big-hungry, turning and walking away.

"Get yo' money like the Red Cross. In blood, nigga," J'dove shouted to our backs.

"What the—"

Without any warning, Big-hungry shoved me to the ground. "What the—?" I had to break my fall with my knees and hands. I turned and sprang to my feet just in time to see something shiny go into Big-hungry's stomach. He dropped to his knees as I lunged for J'Dove. I grabbed his arm as he was takin' some sort of metal coil out of my friend.

I pit-bull-bit his ass in the neck like Dracula. As he went for my head, I released my teeth from his neck and grabbed at the metal thing he dropped to the sidewalk. J'dove dove at me to try to get to it. His boys were stomping Big-hungry when I caught him somewhere in the vicinity of the teeth marks I'd left a second ago. Blood was gushing from his neck like a red water fountain.

I could barely hear the jingling sound of metal and booted feet approaching as the deafening sound of a fog horn exploded through the air. Suddenly, sticks and booted feet were raining down on me. I looked to my left as I sat on my knees being handcuffed. Big- hungry was to my right, laid out on his stomach as two guards struggled to put cuffs on his gargantuan wrists.

For some odd reason, all I could focus on was the thin silver chain around his neck, the one that supported an oval silver locket. Inside the locket was a mini-picture of him and his then-three-month-old son taken almost six years ago, right before Big-hungry got busted.

CHAPTER 22

BABYGIRL

Last time I looked over at the red lights of my clock, it read 2:07 A.M. I was in the bedroom, lying down on the red satin sheets on my bed. My arms were resting behind my head on top of goose down pillows. The hip-hop jazz version of Anthony Hamilton's jam, "Charlene," was piped into my speakers from my computer. I had the books *Cash Rules* and *A Preacher's Son* beside me. I couldn't decide which one to start reading. I heard they were both off the chain.

So, instead of reading, I closed my eyes and thought back to a year ago when I was lying in this same spot, acting out a rape scene worthy of an Academy Award. It had been a year since I hit the blackmail lottery with the little lawyer man. I smiled as I thought of how excited I was when I checked my savings account balance and it was fifty-thousand dollars fatter thanks to attorney what's-his-name. He was so easy. All he asked for was my computer hard drive and any other evidence of the evening we spent at my place. No problem. I had everything couriered over to his office as he requested.

See, I wasn't so bad. I'd only blackmailed a real estate investor and an investment banker just as rich, pussy-hungry, and as dumb as attorney what's-his-name was. Being greedy is what got you on the news as being dead or missing. I wasn't trying to be the movie of the week. I was a one hit wonder. I hit you once, and you never had to wonder about seeing or hearing from me again.

I had fifty thousand in the bank. My Z 4 Beamer convertible was paid for, and the lease on my high-rise was paid up through the year. So, why was I so miserable?

Stop kidding yourself girl, you know why, I told myself. Every time I loved, I lost. My mother, the one person who gave it all up so I could be here, gone. The man who reminded me of Ossie Davis, Martin Luther King, and Malcolm X, the man who loved and taught me what it meant to be black and a woman, my Uncle Ben, gone. My brother, my protector, my sounding board, my street educator, the man who never talked to me as if I were a child, the man who always treated me with respect and love, the man who made me laugh when I was in the worst of moods, the man who gave up his whole way of life to raise me when Momma passed, Uncle Bazz, gone. Well, might as well be. He wasn't getting out; at least no time soon. He'd killed a man a couple months before he was due to come home. No telling when he'd get out or if he ever would. I had so much planned for us.

Other than random calls I received from Uncle Bazz's attorney, Jonathon Parker, I hadn't heard from him since he got locked up. That's why I knew before I even read the letter that something foul had happened. After reading it and taking it all in, I collapsed onto the living room floor and pulled my legs tight into a ball.

How could he do this to me? How could he let someone get him off of his square when he was so close to freedom? How could he? I cried.

A few days later, his next letter came. By then, I'd calmed down and rationalized the situation. Of course Uncle Bazz would not have provoked what happened. While reading the letter, I laughed and cried as Uncle Bazz recanted his prison ventures and adventures with some guy named Big-hungry. What a nickname.

I knew I shouldn't, but I worried so much about Uncle Bazz. He used to always tell me that worrying wasn't gon' make nothin' change or happen any faster than it's gon' happen. But still, I couldn't help it. He'd taken a man's life. And he was being held on Death Row because of overcrowding in the twenty-three- hour-a-day, two-shower-a-week segregation unit.

His letters started coming less frequently after a few months. His writing and his language seemed a little peculiar, not melancholy or anything like that. It was like he'd found religion or something. I don't know. At the conclusion of all his letters, he'd ask me if I was following the rules of the street.

It was weird. It was like he knew I was taking it all and not giving any back. I was living foul, and his letters caused me to reflect on the lessons of everyone who'd ever loved me. And they all said the same thing about giving.

I had to make some changes and make them soon. I hadn't given anything back to the streets I'd grown up on since Uncle Bazz left.

Momma raised me to help people, not hurt them. And look at me now.

*****

The room was bright and colorless except for the red stains leading up to her. Her back was to me as she rested in a praying position on her knees. Her naked back was taut with tense muscles. Her arms were extended toward the largest diamond ring I'd ever seen. It sat on a big, hairy white hand. The ring's blinding shine blocked out his face.

Curiosity had me now. I was timid as I walked forward. Who did this white hand belong to? And why was she begging him? As I got closer, I noticed the woman's head moving up and down.

Once I made my way to the side of them, I gasped. My hands jumped up to my open mouth.

JIHAD

The hammer was on the ground in front of her. My eyes slowly began their climb. Blood was dripping onto her stomach. Her soul was exposed. Her face held an empty look as a stream of bloody tears ran down her cracked face.

She ignored me and looked up to him. Out of her mouth poured the words, "Babygirl. My Babygirl, but, Mr. Sir, you said, but, Mr. Sir, you said," she repeated. The faceless man replied in a deep, laughing tone,

"You should have read the fine print." Then she begged and pleaded over and over as the bloody tears cascaded down her face.

"Who are you, and why are you doing this to me and my mother?" I asked the faceless man.

"I am but a version of you, my darling."

"Nooooo!" I shouted.

"Yes. My first name is False and my last name is Hope. See, that's what I give. In the form of, hmm, let's see . . ." He put his free hand to his temple. "Maybe a life insurance policy that most likely will never pay out or—"

"Noooo!" I bounced up off of the pillow and swept my books to the floor. "Momma," I shouted while reaching out to the air. I blinked and wiped tears from my eyes. I stumbled out of the bed and into the kitchen where I fixed a small bowl of butter pecan ice cream. Afterwards, I went back to bed.

Huh? I was confused. What was I doing at work? The stage was moving. Oh shit. I must be drunk. The Parrot was bumping with Ugly People's new jam, "Street Life."

Whatever, however, whenever, I had to get that paper, so I started climbing the pole while the other girls were clapping their butt cheeks around the stage. I was making love to that pole like it had my greatest dreams inside, waiting for me to make them explode out of it. I seductively and slowly slid down the sixteen-foot golden rod with the white four-inch heels of my catwoman boots

131

pointing in opposite directions.

Let's see them butt cheeks clappin', bitches. Top this, I thought as I looked into the crowd from the top of the gold pole, with my legs going from a "V" position to a perfect "L." As I tried to flip around on the pole, I lost my balance. My ass didn't do much to break my fall as my back collided with red-carpeted stage floor.

I looked up from the round, spinning, red-carpeted, elevated stage to see Two Can San, Uncle Ben, Uncle Bazz, Momma, and all the folks I'd known who lived on the streets. They all started chanting, 'Babygirl, but you said.'

Next thing I knew, I was being helped to my feet. I was about to respond until I turned to thank the person helping me up. I was temporarily blinded by the same sparkling diamond ring from earlier. I jerked my hand away from his. His laughter was deafening.

"Momma." I bounced up into a sitting position on my bed. The Parrot disappeared. Everybody disappeared. "Momma, Uncle Bazz," I called out. Nothing.

I frantically scanned my surroundings. The books I was trying to decide on before I drifted off to sleep were still right beside me. For some strange reason, I thought I knocked the books to the floor and went to get some ice cream. I knew that was impossible because my freezer was out. I touched my sweating face before running my hand over my damp bra and chest. My heart was slam-dancing against my skin.

I don't know if it was a sign, but I knew I had to change my life right then.

Just like my dream, the man with the big ring was fucking the poor, and I was fucking the rich. That's what he meant when he said that we were the same. He was right, but that was all about to change. No, I wouldn't stop scamming the wealthy, but now I was going to rob the rich and give to the poor. As Uncle Bazz said, I had to give back. Oh, I was going to always pay my tithes, I thought as I smiled.

Hell, I had the money. All I had to do was go to the library and find out how to do the do. I spent four months researching, talking to attorneys, and speaking with others who had non-profit organizations. In less than a year, SAID was a reality. Sisters Against Ignorance and Deprivation was the reason for my newfound happiness. I was going to give back. I was going to make a difference.

I rented a tight little spot I'd use as my work headquarters. It was not too far from my place in the Midtown area of downtown Atlanta. I took some fellas off the streets at St. Luke's kitchen to help me paint and tile the place. We were finished and had the sign up in lights in two weeks' time.

I spent the next year working towards my dream. I still had to go to the gym and to clubs like Twist to land a trick or two to continue financing my venture until the grants started rolling in. Tax advisors, attorneys, and non-profit business owners I talked to had me all hyped up. They said all I had to do was incorporate the name and get my federal tax-exempt 501c3 status, and money would be pouring in. They said all I had to do was apply for the free grant money the system was trying to give away.

In a year's time, I applied for twelve grants, and none came through. I should have used what I'd learned from Uncle Ben. He'd always told me if there was such a thing as a get rich quick scheme, Uncle Bazz would have been had a patent on it.

Fuck the system. I was going to grant myself what the system wouldn't. The system fucked Momma. It fucked hundreds of thousands of retirees and people too poor to afford medical insurance. It fucked the street people. It was time we fought back and fucked the system as a community, instead of just me. I was going to put an end to the hard-hearted Babygirls of the world. I was going to help transform the Babygirls into self-assured, confident women of distinction. First, I needed a plan of action, and then an army to attack.

What would Uncle Bazz do? Hmmm? What would Uncle Ben do? I laughed. I didn't know what he'd do, but I knew what he'd say.

"Babygirl, take your little black behind down to the library and read about someone who looks like you, who has successfully done what you are trying to do. Learn from their mistakes, and benefit from their successes."

It took another two months, but I'd studied the lives of three very special women: Winnie Mandela, Harriett Tubman, and Assata Shakur. I'd read the book by Winnie Mandela about her struggles. It was titled *Part of My Soul Went With Him*, and it was deep. That sistah was gangsta. These studio hoods and trigga-happy chumps on the streets today were toilet paper compared to Winnie. She took up the fight of her imprisoned husband. For twenty-seven years, she fought the system. She even kept a suitcase packed so she could go quick whenever the police would come to arrest her. While forced into exile and running the African National Congress, she still raised her children.

And then there was *The Harriet Tubman Story*. Oh, my God. She was off the chains. She escaped to freedom from slavery and went back to the Southern plantations several times to free others. The power structure struck no fear in her heart. Her only fear was not saving the Black race.

She put her gun to the head of any slave who tried to go back to the plantation. Believe it or not, she had to do this a few times because folks changed their minds while on the run and decided they really didn't want to be free.

She fought off dizziness and had these sudden sleeping spells. Although sick and alone on foot, she still kept going back, successfully helping thousands to flee the whip.

Harriet Tubman said some powerful stuff when she said, "I could have freed thousands more if only they knew that they were slaves." It was statements like this one that made me think until my head hurt.

I went on to read *Assata*. Now, that sistah was the strongest and deepest sister in the movement. I mean, this sister was and is so feared by the system that right now today she is one of the three reasons why Cuba can't get the longstanding United States trade embargo lifted. Fidel Castro gave her political exile in

1979 and has since refused to give in to United States government bullying.

This sister was unarmed and had her hands in the air when police officers attempted to assassinate her, shooting her twice. The system made it difficult for her to recover from her wounds by denying her adequate medical attention. She spent six and a half brutal years in prison for some shit she didn't do, before escaping. Even now, living in Cuba, she refers to herself as a twentieth century escaped slave.

No matter how many times they were raped and beat down by the system, these women never gave up fighting. That's the way I was going to be.

CHAPTER 23

SHABAZZ

I hadn't peeped his game yet. He'd been brought to the SHU, the seg unit, the hole, the tombs, what the fuck ever you wanna call it, straight from the streets. He was right next door to me and had been for a good two months now.

At first I figured the nigga was hot or he was just plain scared. Only time a nigga came straight from the streets to the tombs was when he was a hot-ass snitch or a scared li'l bitch.

With the respect he was commanding, I didn't know what to think. You would've thought ole boy was the second coming of Jesus the way the cons throughout the hole were sweating him for game. I thought he was a little soft 'cause he was givin' the shit away for free. Shit, all real Gs knew the game was meant to be sold, not told. But ole boy was droppin' unity and pro-black speeches like he was Malcolm X re-incarnated.

I called him Prophet 'cause that's what I heard everybody else callin' him. Being that he seemed to be the expert on so much shit, I decided to give him a holla. Besides, I'd already counted the 1,976 pieces of gum that littered the multi-colored metal ceiling and walls of my six-by-nine hell.

I was being held on the first of five tiers in the tombs. The most common term for the hole was the tombs or the coffin. Cons hollered up and down the tiers all day and night, "Black officer, why you wanna keep us in the coffin, sir?"

I listened in as chess moves were called out. The concrete and metal floors served as the board, and the pieces were made out of empty milk cartons.

136

JIHAD

I'd gone from being able to hold my breath for a count of seventy-five to a whopping one-fifty. I ran out of things to count, and I was afraid I'd pass out if I tried to break my breath-holding record.

Next, I tried roach racing. Yeah, I know that is some nasty shit, but if I could've got them nasty little fuckas to act right, I could get paid back on the prison compound. I could see the fellas now, lined up around the pool table in the rec room with their little matchboxes, waiting to put their roaches on the table. Hell, I took action on anything and everything else, why not roach racing? Since the little suckers wouldn't cooperate, I turned to the only thing that wasn't nailed down or running away from me on multiple legs.

I'd been at it for two days now, and I wasn't doing too good, so I reached out to him.

"Yo, Prophet, you 'wake? Pro-phet." I dodged the dried-up bubble gum and banged my fist on the drab gray metal cell wall.

"Hold on."

I knew he was doing push-ups or sit-ups by the hard-breath counting I heard from his cell. I really didn't care about interrupting him. I needed his ear 'cause this Bible thing was confusing.

"All right, I'm finished. What's up, Light-skin?"

I don't know how it started, but everybody called me Light-skin. I wasn't mad, though. At least they didn't call me white boy or some other such nonsense.

"I been in the tombs right at three months now, and I been trying to get into this Bible, like you suggested."

"Self-elevation, that's what I'm talking about, Light-skin," he said.

"I can't elevate past all these 'thees' and 'thous'. I see why we got Catholics, Baptists, A.M.E., Episcopalian, and all the other sects of Christians. Hell, they don't know what God was laying down through the Prophets with all

137

this double talk."

His hollow sounding, deep voice answered, "Just like anything, you have to first understand the game, and then you get to know the players."

"Say what?"

"Okay, first you have to ask yourself, what is God's angle?"

"Angle?"

"Yeah, angle. There's always a method and meaning to the madness. Everything is done for a reason, not a season."

"I feel you on that."

"Light-skin?"

"Yeah."

"Why do you think He sent His word down through men?"

"So we would know right from wrong?" I was quick to reply.

"Something like that, but more so to give you examples of what's to come if you act a certain way. He gave us free will to decide for ourselves whether to take heed of His lessons or do the opposite."

"I know that."

"Do you really? Most people, so-called saved and not saved, talk about their personal relationship with God, but in the next sentence, they trying to play God by judging others, as if their shit don't stink."

"That's all well and good, but I still don't see how anyone can make sense out of the words and parables in the Bible."

"The 'thees' and 'thous' are irrelevant. You have to make the Bible your personal memoir. Reach deep down inside yourself and bring those stories into your realm of existence. For instance, use Bush as Pharaoh, and the natural catastrophes that have befallen the world as God's plagues and warnings."

"My personal memoir, huh?"

"Yes, I'll give you an example. Name someone in the Bible, anyone."

"Jesus."

"Okay, let's call him J'Love."

"Nah, that's too much like J'Dove."

"How about J.C. then?"

"Cool."

"J.C. was the hardest and most gangsta brotha of all time. Single handedly, he started a revolution, one against the vicegerents of evil."

"Vice-who?" I asked.

"Vicegerents, deputies, governors of evil. Just like now, back then the government was the biggest representation of evil. They oppressed and enslaved the masses by propagating ignorance and causing the people to fear their wrath. But, J.C. bucked the system. He told the people they had nothing to fear from the government. 'You are the government,' he said. Fear God and God alone, for it is only His wrath and fury that deserves such an emotion."

"I bet J.C. wouldn't have said that in modern times," I said.

"Why do you say that?"

"Bush would have had J.C.'s character assassinated in the media, and then he would've charged him with some trumped-up, fictious weapons of mass destruction-like charge. Next thing you know, J.C. would have been in an electric chair, dying all over again for our sins," I explained.

"Bush couldn't do anything that righteousness wouldn't counter. J.C. wasn't scared of Bush's ancestors, no need to be of him. Bush couldn't do anything that God wouldn't allow. When Bush's bombs and armies can defeat a hurricane or a tornado, then talk to me about his power. Remember Moses stood up to mighty Pharaoh, and look how he fared.

"J.C. was so gangsta that when He had the people's

ear, He didn't ask for money or chickens to fatten His stable. He didn't have a fancy chariot while everybody else was on foot. He didn't build a mansion over on the north side. He kept it grimy, right in the hood."

"Yeah, and He healed the sick and brought the dead back to life," I interrupted.

"True that, but did He bring the physically dead back and heal the physically sick?" Prophet asked.

"Of course," I said.

"How do you know?" he asked.

"Everybody knows about Lazarus and the others. It's right here in the Bible."

"Yeah, you're right. It's in the Bible, but let me ask you this: What is more dangerous and in need of treatment, a mentally dead person killing others with his ignorance and rhetoric or a physically dead person who is not a threat to anything but the soil he rests under?"

"I know where you goin' with that, Prophet, but Lazarus was Jesus's best friend and he was dead and stankin' for three days."

"When you were out there, I mean out there bad, strung out on H, I bet you smelled worse than three-day-old death."

I nodded like He could see me. Hell, I could have used three-day-old death to freshen the air around me back then.

"And you were dead to the world as we know it, right?"

I nodded again.

"I'll take your silence for affirmation. The black man in America is old, drunken, drugged out with ignorance, stankin' Lazarus, but we know him as Leon or some other name. And he will be that way until God breathes truth and understanding into him. It is then and only then when he will rise from his grave of ignorance."

"Okay, okay," I said, nodding again.

JIHAD

"You see, Leon is Lazarus, and J.C., representin' God to the fullest, breathed that truth into his three-day-dead self and he rose, and still he rises a little higher every time a book is put into his hands. Do you kind of understand what I'm saying?"

"Yeah, I think so," I said before continuing. "But if King James would have painted Jesus and the Prophets black like they really were, Leroy would be in the White House instead of the crack house."

"That may be true, but he didn't."

"That's why we so fucked up now," I said.

"What you just said is one of our biggest problems as a people. Our blackness doesn't define us. What is in our hearts is what makes us who we are. So what, Jesus and most of the Prophets come from a tropical geographical land mass that was solely inhabited by people of color? You see, Light-skin, we have let another people pass on their own insecurities and ignorance to us."

"You mean beat it into us."

"That too, but we don't need another people to use their means of measure to justify our beauty and greatness. We need to put the soul back in the way Jesus walked and Moses talked. We need to write a street bible so the youth of today can rattle off J.C's lyrics instead of Jay Z's. We need to drop it like it's hot to the beat of 'I got 99 problems,' but knowing God ain't one. We need to nickname Moses, call him Mo', so the bruhs can relate and elevate they minds to a level of seeing, believing and being the leaders, leading the people from the projects of an impoverished mentality to the Promised Land of the free and educated mind."

"Hell yeah, drop that shit on 'em, Prophet," another inmate yelled from another hell.

"Keep that shit gangsta, so them young studs out there bangin' will see the light before they see the dark behind these cages," another voice shouted.

141

BABYGIRL

I was feelin' him like tight, new wet pussy. Oh, my bad, God. Forgive me for that. Oh shit, that's the first time I talked to God since I cursed Him for letting that shit happen to my moms.

CHAPTER 24

BABYGIRL

This wasn't the first time I had a confrontation with the Parrots' bulldyking owner, Stevie Brown. Back a couple years ago, the day I auditioned to work at the Parrot, some girl who didn't look a day over fifteen ran toward me with blood on her lip and a broken nose.

"Please don't let her hit me again," was all she said before Stevie dropped her purse beside my leg and came from nowhere, grabbed the child by the ponytail, and yanked her to the ground.

I had to hold Stevie while the girl ran out of the club. Stevie cursed me out for "getting into her business" as she called it. I didn't say anything. I decided to let her have that little bit because I was twenty, close to broke, and I needed the job to take care of Uncle Ben.

The girl Stevie had jumped on turned out to be her part-time lover and the biggest money maker at the Parrot exotic dance club. Back then, the fifteen-year-old-looking girl turned out to be twenty-two, two years older than me. Her stage name was Madness, and if you saw the way she turned men out with her dancing and the other services she provided, you'd know why. Madness and I had become friends. I guess you could say I sort of adopted her. Although she was older, she looked to me for reassurance and guidance when it came to her kids, her way of life, financial decisions, and just some of everything. I was the only one who didn't judge Madness for sleeping with the Hitler-like Stevie Brown, and I was always ready to get into Stevie's ass when she jumped on my girl.

A year later, this country white girl with hips and an

143

ass like a sistah came to work at the Parrot. The girls hated her instantly. She was white, thick, and had the nerve to have braids in her hair. A couple months after she started working at the Parrot, the white girl got into it with another one of the girls for not taking her braids out. The fight was close until another of the girls jumped in and started pulling the white girl's hair. After I broke up the fight, I couldn't get away from the white girl, whose stage name had been changed by the other girls from White Chocolate to Snow. They thought the name White Chocolate was offensive. Why, I don't know.

Pretty soon Snow and I became pretty cool. I didn't hang with her like I did Madness, but we had each other's back at the club. Now, when Stevie started fucking with Snow, I knew it was just a matter of time before she tried me. This woman was a sadistic, power-tripping bitch. I stayed at the Parrot as long as I did because I didn't want to leave my girls. After I started the SAID foundation, I told my girls to come on. I knew Snow was going to come with me. If I told her to jump off a building with me, I think she would have. The girl wasn't quite right in the head, but she was still my girl.

It was crazy how I had to protect the white girl from the sistahs and the sistahs from the white girl. What kind of shit was that? And to top it off, I was younger than Snow and Madness. They were the same age.

I told Madness that as long as she screwed Stevie, I wasn't getting into any domestic disputes, and I wouldn't be there to defend her when I left. Nevertheless, she stayed at the Parrot. I still could not understand how a woman so beautiful and with so much game could let herself be taken advantage of by Stevie Brown. Madness obviously didn't know how beautiful she really was. Her almond eyes were the same color as her long auburn-streaked her. She was over six feet in heels, and she put you in the mind of a bronzed Wonder Woman. If I was into women, which I wasn't, I'd do her. It wasn't her exotic look so much as it was the way she floated that turned men and women's heads. Her calf and leg muscles had this soulful rhythm as she walked.

I knew Madness would buck the Parrot in a heartbeat. All I had to do was pay her what she was used to and treat her like a woman and not a toilet.

When I used to dance at the Parrot, three o'clock in the morning meant one thing—tally-up time. After an exhausting shift, we'd all sit on the stainless steel metal benches and chairs in the dressing room and count out our tip money. Madness usually took the longest to count because she made the most money. It wasn't any secret that behind the curtain in the VIP room, she fucked, sucked, licked, and dipped for the right amount. She was the only one who could trick in the club and wouldn't catch a beat-down from Stevie. Screwing that man-looking white bitch on call earned her that right.

I don't know if it was the last ass-kicking that Madness took from Stevie in the dressing room for all the girls to see or my reassuring her of her inward and outer beauty that made her leave the Parrot. Of course I wasn't taking care of no grown woman, but I did teach her to take care of herself. This first step started with her learning to fall in love with herself through self-awareness. She caught on fast, and in no time she was engulfed in books about African and African-American revolutionary women and strong men of antiquity.

The real reason Stevie was hurt when Madness finally left, was because she could no longer screw the number one girl in the club. It wasn't like she cared about Madness or anything. Stevie was forever on a power trip. Being a woman and owning the number two strip club behind Fantasy Island, and sexing the most popular stripper in the club made her feel like a man, I guess.

I had no intentions of getting into it with Stevie, although she had Madness's face looking like a run-over Mr. Potatohead. I just wanted to scare the bitch into giving me Madness's stuff.

"Muthafucka, you ain't got to put your hands on me. I know where her office is," I said to the black T-shirt, tight-ass jean wearing faggot security guard as I walked through the crowd back to Stevie's office in the rear of the club. The guys getting table dances and watching the girls do their thing hardly paid any attention to me. A woman dressed like me, wearing jeans, a baby tee and some heels was considered way overdressed in the Parrot.

Stevie dropped the dumbbell she was curling on the gray concrete office floor and jumped up from the weight bench when I came barging through the door.

"I'm right outside, Ms. Brown. Call me if you need me," tight jeans said.

She almost took one step too many before she said,

"I have asked you nicely one too many times, now I'm telling you to leave my girls the hell alone."

"Bitch, if you don't want that finger stuffed up your ass, you'd do best to get it out of my face," I said.

"Who the fuck do you think you're talking to, tramp?"

I looked around the small office in back of the Parrot. "Your momma ain't in here, so I must be talking to you."

A cloud of smoke entered the room as the door opened. "Boss, you all right?" tight jeans asked.

"Close the damn door!" she hollered back.

Stevie Brown was an ex-cop, ex-bodybuilder, and if she kept fuckin' with me, she'd be an ex-bitch. She owned one of the hottest strip clubs in the ATL, and by the sound of it, she thought she owned the strippers too.

I knew I shouldn't have been there, but it was better me than Madness. I only came to clean out

Madness's locker. That's the least I could do after the ass-kicking she took from Stevie when she quit dancin' at the Parrot to team up with me and Snow.

I should have snuck the bitch while she was pulling the T-shirt over her head. I shouldn't have even been in the crazy bitch's back office, but what could I do? My chances were better with her than with the big ape who roughly escorted me back here in the first place.

Now clad only in a small white bra, Levi's jeans and some silver-spurred black cowboy boots, she continued, "This is what you are going to do." She paused, cracking her pink knuckles and thick, manly neck. "You are going to apologize to me and ask for my forgiveness." She flexed her steroid-induced bodybuilder arms as she undid the belt and unbuttoned her jeans. "And then you are going to lick my—"

The bitch had my fist in her mouth before she could say it.

"Ooh, that felt good. You made—" She had a death grip on my neck. "—me taste my own blood." She licked her bloody teeth. "Now I am going to let you taste mine," she said as her silver cowboy belt buckle clanged against the floor and her jeans dropped over her tree trunk thighs, revealing aqua panties with a nasty-looking red stain in the middle.

I tried to punch her in the crotch, but she grabbed my wrist, causing the blood in my arm to seek another route.

"You know you like it. Don't pretend you haven't licked pussy before."

I was almost unconscious before she'd lowered my head and legs just far enough for me to reach the razor I kept taped under my heels.

"Ain't nothing worse than a funky bitch on her cycle," I said as I came up windmilling my free arm across her body.

"Ahhhhhhhhh! Shhhhhhhhhhhhhhhit!" she screamed. I

coughed and fell back on her cherrywood desk as she let go of my neck and grabbed for her bloody left breast. "Rico!" she screamed at the door.

You would've thought I was Julia Childs the way I straddled her and went to slicing that bitch like an onion. A moment later, the door burst open. I sidestepped Rico, and the big ape grabbed the wrong arm, the one without the razor. In one smooth sweep, I sliced his wrist.

"I'll kill you," he shouted while freeing me so he could grab hold of his blood-spurting wrist.

"Not if I kill you first," I replied.

Only a couple dudes paid attention to the ruckus going on in the back of the club, or so I thought. That was normal. Nothing short of a bomb would get the crowded house to notice what was going on back here. It was Amateur night. Half of the women were auditioning for a job and a thousand dollars in prize money. There were over eighty naked women shaking their asses to Nelly's hit, "It's Getting Hot in Here," and it damn sure was. That's why I was getting the hell out of there.

I'd made it all the way to front door before a pink-and-brown hairy arm came across my face, dropping me to the ground right in front of the exit. Next thing I knew, I was kicking and screaming while being dragged outside.

The next day, I woke up to a blinding light and beeping sounds. I thought I would die from the pain. Where was the morphine? Shit.

A doctor explained that I was in Grady Hospital and I just had a fractured arm and some bruised ribs. Yeah, he had the audacity to smile and put emphasis on the word "just." Just fuckin' hell. I "just" was in a world of pain. I "just" wish I could have put my foot in the doctor's mouth after he told me I was "just" lucky it wasn't worse. If I wasn't in so much pain, I would have told him he could "just" kiss my ass.

After he increased the drip on the bag and the pain subsided in my chest, I organized my thoughts. I was thankful my face and my Tina Turner legs weren't scarred.

I knew there was a God when the pot-bellied, pasty-skinned detective came to interview me. I could see the lust in his beady dark eyes before he was even at my bedside. I would find a way to use him. And when I finished I'd throw him away like the rest of the trash I dealt with.

"Young lady, you should be thankful that Ms. Brown is not pressing charges. You cut her face up pretty bad, and you almost cut her left breast off."

Okay, he was definitely the "I'm always right" type. You know, the kind of boy in a man's body that talks big and strong to cover up his self-hate and low self-esteem.

"As of now, the state is also refusing to press charges, but," he pointed a little stubby white finger at me, "that doesn't mean that charges will not be brought up later." He smiled. "Basically, it's up to me and what I uncover while this investigation ensues." He winked at me. "If you know what I mean." He might as well have come right out and said what his smile screamed: *As soon as you get out of that bed, get on your knees and suck me off, and I'll forget about this case.*

Oh my God, I had Dickless Tracy investigating me. He must've thought I was a nigga, as Uncle Bazz would say. He had no idea that he was dealing with a black queen, and although I was black, I was still a woman. There was no jury in this country that would convict me of assault after the beating I took from I don't know how many 200-plus-pound hillbillies and Toms on the inside and outside of the Parrot.

"Do you want to tell me your side, Ms. Lawson?"

I was glad he said my name because right now, I didn't know which driver's license I used at the Parrot. I was so used to everyone calling me Babygirl.

"No, sir, I'm terribly confused right now." I shook my head. "I barely remember that night."

"Well, if you do, give me a call. My cell phone number is on the back," he said, handing me a white laminated business card that had DETECTIVE FIRST CLASS FRANCIS O'LEARY in big bold, black letters. "Oh, by the way, my cell phone is always on, so you can call me anytime of the day or night," he said, walking out of the room, leaving the faint smell of Brut cologne behind him.

With a name like Francis and with a build like a big-bellied Homer Simpson, I could see why his self-esteem was non-existent.

A couple days later, I was at home recuperating. I was sitting in front of NASA reading an article in *Forbes* magazine when Family Mutual life insurance jumped out at me. The VP of sales for the southern region made a whopping 1.3 million last year in 2002. Family Mutual was the same company that owed me two-million dollars for the policy I never was able to collect on after Momma passed. Oh, they'd have to make a large contribution to the SAID Foundation in the near future. I mean very near. I could barely wait.

I grabbed my phone right before it vibrated off of my cluttered desk.

"Sisters Against Ignorance and Deprivation. May I help you?"

"Hi, Babygirl, this is Snow."

"Hey, girl, how are you?"

"I'm beautiful. Did you get the flowers?"

"Yeah, and tell the girls at the Parrot I said thank you."

"No, they all thank you. I still can't believe what you did. The way you stood up to Stevie was beautiful."

Not that I cared, but I still asked, "Is she okay?"

"You haven't heard?"

"Heard what?" I asked.

"Well, other than her face looking like a quilt, she's fine. But now she's crazier than ever. Word is she's doing everything to make sure you don't make it to your next birthday."

"Girl, I ain't worried about her."

"Well, you should be. The woman is psycho. The girls tell me she's going around bragging about how you'll regret that you ever came through the Parrot's doors."

"Since you have to deal with Stevie, how is it going to affect Madness and I, as far as business is concerned?"

"It won't. I don't have to deal with her. She has to deal with me. We're about to get paid, and Stevie is going to be our mark. And the bitch won't even see us coming."

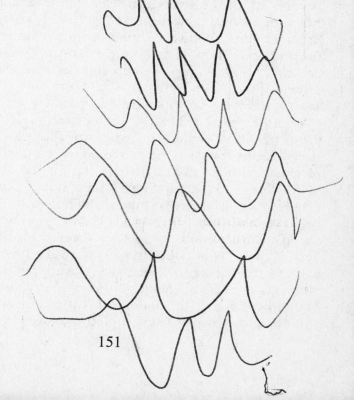

CHAPTER 25

SNOW

Five years went by as if it were five minutes. Back in the mid 90s, life was wonderful. My parents had just celebrated twenty-five years of marriage back home on our farm in Jefferson City, Missouri. I was in my last year at the University of Oklahoma. I majored in mortuary science, exactly as my father had.

After graduation, my plans were to return home and help my dad run the funeral home he was in the process of purchasing. I was a daddy's girl all the way. He loved me way more than he loved my crazy sister.

My mother had never worked anywhere but in the garden of our back yard. Her blindness never stopped her from doing anything. She was totally not a public person. She was very quiet and preferred to be at or around our home, cooking, cleaning, doodling in her garden, or listening to soap operas, *Oprah*, or a Lifetime movie.

That's why it was such a surprise to me when she called me from a 314 St. Louis area code. It was a little after six A.M. when I hung up the phone in tears. I didn't even pack. I just called a cab, threw on some clothes, grabbed my purse and left for the airport.

Let me back up for a second. I am one of two children. I had a younger sister, who was the exact opposite of me. She was drawn to negative people, things, music, and places. I loved her dearly, but she hated me. She couldn't get over how much more beautiful, intelligent, and well loved by everyone I was. She was very plain-looking, and not very smart.

Growing up in Jefferson City, Missouri, my sister and I had always been called by our first and middle names. She was Julie Ann, and I was Jennie Mae. Only the people she hung out with called her Julieliscious.

One day, I was sitting at the kitchen table studying for finals, about to graduate from Thomas Jefferson High. Mother was listening to an episode of *Days of our Lives*. My father was sitting in his favorite chair in front of the living room window, reading a Patricia Cornwell novel, when Jennie Mae—I mean Julie Ann burst through the front door wearing a way-too-short hot pink cheering outfit. She was always wearing clothes to try to attract the type of attention that I attracted naturally.

She announced that she was dropping out of school. She told our dad that next month on her sixteenth birthday she was going to pursue a career as a rap artist. My mouth hung open as I entered the living room. Dad continued reading. He never even turned around. The only thing I heard was the silence before Dad finally opened his mouth. He told her to make sure she had somewhere to stay the day she quit school, because she would no longer have a home here.

She simply said, "Okay," and ran up the stairs.

Less than two years later, Jennie Mae—I mean Julie Ann was living in St. Louis with a black guy who was beating her and forcing her to sell her body to pay for the crack-cocaine she was strung out on. She'd taken one beating too many when she broke down and called Dad, pouring her heart out.

Dad was totally non-violent. He didn't even own a hunting knife. That's why I couldn't believe that he'd taken a gun. After confronting the guy, a fight broke out and Dad ended up on the marble kitchen floor with a bullet in his head.

I felt like a part of me died that day. Dad was my best friend. I tried to love my sister, but the hatred and murderous rage that was built up inside me made it virtually impossible. I hated her for what she did to our family. I hated her for being such a pretentious, selfish, know-it-all, spoiled brat who always cried to Dad for help when she was in trouble. I hated her for being Julicious instead of what Mom and Dad named her. And of all, I hated her for what she did to Dad.

Mother my father's sudden death extremely hard, as e d. She never blamed Julie Ann for a moment. But e didn't embrace her either. It was as if Mother had into a cocoon so she wouldn't have to deal with the in and void that comes from losing a spouse. I was orried about her, but I was having a hard enough time staying sane myself.

After Dad's funeral, Jennie Mae—I mean Julie Ann checked herself into a rehab. Eleven months later, Frank Lester was acquitted of murdering my father after Julie Ann lied on the stand and said that Dad accidentally shot himself in the midst of a scuffle between him and Frank.

A week after the trial ended, I had just gotten home from the hospital when Julie Ann showed up at the front door. I was already mentally and spiritually drained from staying up and praying around the clock for Mom's speedy recovery from the mild stroke she had suffered the day after the not guilty verdict was passed down.

Julie Ann tried to explain why she did it, why she lied, going on and on about how Frank's son got to her while she was under police protection in the rehab before trial. She said that André, Frank's son, threatened to kill me and Mom if she didn't lie on the stand. It all went in one ear and out the other. After impatiently listening to her sorry excuses, I calmly told her to leave and to never come back.

She dropped a letter next to the blue wooden swing at the top of the porch before she left silently.

I didn't feel as if she deserved to know what had

happened to Mom. Mother had been in perfect health. She ate all organic foods. She exercised, and other than a rare cold, she'd never been sick. The day after Jennie—I mean Julie Ann left, I received a call from Dr. Pierce. He told me that Mom was just fine and I could come get her in a couple of days. Although she'd made a full recovery, I didn't.

That night, I had a nervous breakdown. It came right after I read the letter that Julie left on the couch the day before mother passed.

Dearest Jennie Mae,

I've always loved you from afar, although I refused to acknowledge or show my feelings. My case manager at the Betty Ford recovery center helped me realize that I love you, and I've always loved you. It was me that I hated. I hated not being you.

Every time Dad praised you, in his next sentence he would berate me. The more he told me that I should be like you, the more I rebelled. I thought if I was your opposite, I'd be noticed. I know that sounds stupid, but that was my way of thinking.

I never meant to be raped by half the football team at Jefferson High. I never told you, Mom or Dad, but this is the real reason I dropped out of school. I was scared to go back. I was afraid no one would believe me. I just wanted to disappear, so when I saw the opportunity to get out of Jefferson City, I took it.

A guy let us in the back door of the strip club, Paradise City. It was there that I met Frank. He was dressed really nice. He was very funny and intelligent. He told me that he owned a record company. He even gave me a fancy plastic business card that verified what he said. He told me that I had the look of tomorrow, and that he'd love to manage my career.

The following day, I met him at a studio and I rapped

for him. He said I was a little rough but he loved my style, and if I wanted to be a star, I had to be ready to hit the road in a couple weeks.

Next thing I know, I was in St. Louis getting raped and beaten by him and his son. They forced me to smoke crack. All it took was one pull and I was in heaven. I finally found a way to escape my pain, my loneliness, my despair. Nothing or no one else loved me. The only time I felt love was when I inhaled the smoke made from these little off-white pebbles. They let me escape to somewhere nice and warm, and it was crack-cocaine that comforted me when no one else could or would.

I never meant to sell my body so I could get high. I swear to God I am sorry for ever being born. I've done wrong by everyone that has ever come into my life. I know I've deserved everything that has happened to me, but Dad didn't deserve to lose his life defending me.

I thought I was protecting you and Mom when I lied on the stand.

I will completely understand if you never talk to me again. Soon you and Mom will be out of my life forever.

Sincerely,
Your sister,
Julie Ann Thomas

I know it sounds crazy, but I don't remember much after reading the letter. I do remember cursing the quack doctor out after he told me that my mother and sister were dead. All I know is that there was a fire at the house.

If only I had been stronger. If only I hadn't sent her away when she tried to pour her heart out to me that windy, cloudy day on the front porch of the house we grew up in. If only I had listened to what my sister had to say that day, I might not have gone over the edge of sanity.

156

JIHAD

I felt as if I was—no, my sister was fighting the deep water with one arm while the other was reaching out to me, and I just sat in my comfortable lounge chair with my big lens movie star sunglasses on by the deep end of the pool, watching her slowly drown in agony.

I may have been partly responsible for my sister's drowning, but I was not going to be responsible for letting the person that pulled her under get away. No, Frank Lester and his son were going to pay dearly. I had a goal, a mission.

My doctors kept me on anti-depressants. They said I was delusional. I wasn't about to try to change them, but I had to make them think that I was rational. I really was. In six months, I proved to them that I was back to normal.

It took a little over a year, but I'd done it. I made myself beautiful. I completely changed the way I looked. Now I was the beautiful sister. I was a new person, having shed ninety pounds. For a year, I ran three miles a day, and I had a boxing trainer. The black-and-gray bag at the gym was Frank Lester's body. The red speed bag was his face.

I used some of the life and home insurance money for the lipo and tummy tuck surgeries. The plastic surgery and electrolysis removed the freckles and hair on my face. The collagen injections and fat replacement surgery helped to make my lips full and my behind round. Instead of curly, shoulder-length red hair, I now wore dirty blonde African braids.

By year four A.D. of Julie Ann, I was renting a nice older Victorian style home in the historical Grant Park area of Atlanta, working as an exotic dancer at the Parrot. I'd been there close to a year, biding my time, watching and waiting. I was in no rush. I had the rest of Frank Lester's life.

CHAPTER 26

BABYGIRL

Instead of going into the Buckhead SAID Foundation headquarters, Snow and I sat outside in the morning sun, sipping on lattes at Starbucks downtown on Peachtree. She was explaining this master plan that she came up with a couple nights before. While she spoke, I couldn't help but think how well she fit in with the SAID Foundation. She had a lot of game, she was white, and she was hungry.

I told her that I was planning a way to handle Stevie, but in honesty, I was so caught up in the childcare and education programs that Madness and I had started for homeless mothers, I completely forgot about Stevie. Thank God, at least Snow was working on bringing money in, I thought.

After thirty minutes of listening to the details of Snow's master plan, I came to the conclusion that there was no way that in two days she could have come up with the intricate details of how we'd start a war between Stevie Brown and Li'l Dre. After she finished, I asked, "What do you get out of all this? I mean, I know our agreement, but this is different. You are taking a lot of risks."

"I take risks every time I leave my house. I just want to make sure we can continue building SAID. I'm fine with the seventy-five percent split three ways and the other twenty-five percent going back into SAID. We should make out good at Frank's place."

"Frank's place?"

She shook her head. "I meant Li'l Dre's place," she corrected herself.

"Who is Frank?"

She waved the air. "Nothing but a bad memory."

"Yeah, I have those too."

"Doesn't everyone?"

Yeah, I nodded. Snow had game. I could tell by the way she didn't bat an eye as she casually lied about this Frank character. Whatever her ulterior motive for helping me handle my business, I was getting paid in the process. Snow's business was of no concern to me as long as she pulled her weight.

Li'l Dre was this big-time Biggie Smalls-looking drug dealer who lived in the strip clubs around the city with his entourage of flunkies. He took one or two girls with him almost every time he left the Parrot. I could've sworn I saw Snow leave with him once or twice in the past. From what Snow told me, he was trying to press Stevie into selling the Parrot to him.

Two weeks after the three of us agreed to put Snow's plan into action, I got the call while watching the television show, *America's Next Top Model.*

"I'm watching four different music videos on separate TVs in the back of Li'l Dre's shiny green Chevy Suburban."

"What?"

Snow laughed. "I'm not in the vehicle with him. I'm almost two car lengths behind. I told you about the television monitors because it just amazes me how frivolous and flashy drug dealers are."

"What's his location?" I asked.

"He's pulling up to the VIP outside Fantasy Island."

"I'm on it. Stay by your phone. Madness will call you when she's ready."

"What about the footage I have of Stevie?"

"What footage?" I asked.

"Remember, the digital pictures I told you I paid a guy to take of her."

"Oh yeah, I forgot. E-mail them to me, along with how much you paid to have them taken," I said before hanging up.

If Stevie went Mike Tyson on me over Madness, ranting n r a v i n g about how I had stolen her prize stallion, like she was her pet, then she was definitely going to be at a George Bush level of war by the time she found out I was the one responsible for all the drama that was about to be dropped into her life.

Madness's name showed up as I pressed speed dial. "Girl, it's off and poppin'. You ready to make this paper?"

"Always," she answered.

"He just pulled up to Fantasy Island."

"Cool, I know the owner, Al Frazier, real well."

"Really?"

"Nothing like that, girl. We just cool. He really cares about the girls who dance at the Island."

"Why didn't you stay there?" I asked.

"Money and respect. I wasn't going to use his spot as my motel. I respected him too much for that, and you know tricking accounted for at least half the money I made."

"No, I didn't know that." I did, but I wanted her to tell me whatever she wanted me to know.

"Come on, girl, don't go getting all goody-two-shoes on me. You know how I got my name."

"No, I don't," I lied.

"When I wrapped my lips and tongue around their manhood, men would cum and go before the next song. One guy started asking for me by the name Madness because he claimed I drove him mad every time I blew him. The girls used to tease me about the name until I decided that Madness was a cool stage name. I'm not proud of that now, but it is what it is, and that's the way I put food on the table for my babies."

"That is a hell of a name. Girl, we can talk all night, but I better let you go so you can handle your business."

JIHAD

"I'm getting in the car now, and yes, before you third degree me, I checked everything off the list and burned the paper in the sink."

Although she'd done it before, I was a little nervous about sending her into Fantasy Island and convincing Li'l Dre to take her back to his place. I didn't do dope boys, and Snow, Madness and I had made it a rule not to scheme or scam another hustler, especially a drug dealer—too dangerous. And I heard some freaky shit about Li'l Dre's fat-ass. I would have been the bait, but Madness insisted. She wanted to play an important part in taking Stevie down. She hated her more than I did, and getting into Li'l Dre's place made all the difference in the world in ruining Stevie.

I knew I wouldn't be able to sleep, so I made it a Blockbuster night. I needed to laugh, so I rented and watched Richard Pryor's *Here and Now,* Eddie Murphy's *Raw,* and an old Red Foxx standup concert. I must have dozed off, because I woke to the feel of something wet on my feet.

I jumped halfway to the ceiling. "Rock," I screamed. The dog was licking my feet. I must've scared him half to death, the way he ran into my wall, causing my Maurice Evans original to fall onto the floor, breaking its glass enclosure.

"Damn, Rock, you got spit all over my foot," I said as if Madness's one-year-old Pit Bull was going to respond. I was dog-sitting until this shit was over. Rock was her third child, and she didn't want him at her house until we'd finished handling our business. Madness's twin girls were spending the summer in Indianapolis with their great-grandmother.

I looked at my watch. "Six o'clock. Oh shit." I grabbed the phone off the glass coffee table in front of me. Three missed calls. Fuck, how did my phone get on vibrate? I pressed the number two. The phone rang.

"Madness!" I answered.

"Girl, where you been?"

"I'm sorry. I fell asleep with the phone on vibrate."

"Girl, Li'l Dre took me to an apartment in the sky that was bigger than Wal-Mart. I was scared at first because the building had security like a Wells Fargo truck. Actually, that worked out even better."

"How is that?" I asked.

"Because Li'l Dre sent his boys home. Anyway, I thought I was going to have to blow him. He'd drunk a whole bottle of Cristal back at the club, and once we got here, he decided to stop drinking. Girl, I know I've done others uglier and bigger than Li'l Dre before, but I was getting nauseated just thinking about putting my mouth on his asthmatic ass."

"So, what did you end up doing?"

"I used your 'I like to role play' trip on him."

"Works every time," I said.

"Yeah, I see. Anyway, I slipped the mickey in his Grand Marnier and he was out in minutes. I handled the rest before I called Snow and had her meet me in the parking garage.

"I brought her up to Li'l Dre's penthouse. She stood over him in a daze, but once I got her attention, she put it down. You hear me, girl? Snow took out the fake packages of dope and went upstairs and put it down. She was in and out in fifteen minutes, and I was out in sixteen."

"Okay, let me get to work. I'll have a check ready for you when you wake up," I said before hanging up.

A couple hours later, I was sitting at NASA playing with the images of Stevie that Snow had E-mailed me. It took me a couple hours to doctor the photos, but I did it. After printing them out, I looked over my eight- by-ten masterpieces. Perfect, I thought. At least I had a career as a smut photo journalist with the *National Enquirer* if all else failed.

Because I didn't want detective Frank O'Leary to

know where I lived, in an innocent-sounding sexy voice I asked him to come by the hotel room I was staying at. When he asked why I was staying in a hotel, I told him my apartment was being painted. I knew his balding, pot-bellied ass would come in handy someday.

A couple hours later, I met the detective as he strolled through the lobby of the Embassy Suites hotel downtown wearing a brown, off-the-rack, wrinkled, too-worn-for-the-Goodwill pinstripe suit. It was almost comical the way he attempted to suck in his belly and stick out his chest once he saw me.

"Ms. Lawson," he said to my breasts.

I used one of my fake names. "Call me Lena," I said as I led him to the elevator. I almost laughed at the way all that authority was so easily sucked out of him.

I reduced him to the little boy he really was just by running a long red fingernail down his sleeve until I reached his hand.

"Don't you think we should talk at the station?" he asked.

"No, I need to speak with you off the record." I licked my shiny, cherry-red lips, letting my tongue linger a little longer than necessary. "I think you'll be interested in what I have to say," I said at the same time I turned my ankle, losing one of my candy apple- colored three-inch heels.

"Let me get that."

He knew damn well he couldn't bend his fat-ass down that far. I saved him from even trying such a feat, on a moving elevator at that. "No, I got it," I said and waved as I turned and bent down, straight-legged, slightly brushing my behind against his bulging blue slacks.

Once we were inside the room, I gestured for him to have a seat at the desk near the window. I sat in front of him on the king-sized bed.

His eyes went to the manila envelope on the desk,

and then they attacked my legs. I crossed them in a way that would give him a glimpse of my shaven pubic area. The particularly bright red, low-cut dress I had on wasn't made to be worn with underwear. I'd read somewhere that the color red was the biggest turn on for men.

"Detective." I got up and slowly walked toward him. Beads of sweat danced in the creases of his wrinkled fore-head while his eyes followed my waving hips.

"Sweetie, I want you to get a warrant and," I reached around him, cuddling his face between my tightly bundled thirty-six C cups, "search the home of the man in these pictures." I leaned back and handed him the envelope with photos of Li'l Dre sleeping next to what looked like three rectangular packaged kilos of some type of illegal narcotic.

He sat up in the chair and switched on the light on top of the desk. "Where did you get these?" he asked, all businesslike.

"I took them out of the office at the Parrot and hid them in the ceiling above a toilet stall in the dressing room the night I was beaten."

"This is the real reason you were attacked." He spoke like he was telling me something I had never thought of.

"Really?" was my simple, dumb girl response.

"Why didn't you tell me that in the hospital?"

Oh Lord, not the Dickless Tracy act again. "I had to get the pictures from the Parrot first." I spoke in my highest-pitched dingy girl voice.

"You may have to give a statement."

I took a step closer and wrapped a lock of his thinning hair around my finger. "I'll do anything, and I mean anything, if my name can be left out of this."

"I don't see how we can."

I took a step back, standing wide-legged, and gently ran my fingers up my thighs, slowly inching my dress up.

"Maybe you can say someone made an anonymous call and—" I let out a slow, breathy moan. The muscles in my left arm came alive with a vibrating, jackhammer-like motion as my fingers massaged the lips of my shaven love nest. "—left you this package somewhere. Oh, I'm so," I paused then whispered, "moist."

"All right, all right, it's done. I-I'll do it," he said, standing up, putting his gun on the desk, and feverishly unbuckling his belt. He pulled down his pants, revealing pale, hairy chicken legs.

"You'll do what, Daddy?"

"I'll bust the fucker. I'll bust whoever you want me to," he said while using his hand on his curved, dull-arrowed penis.

"I bet you wanna bend me over this desk and stick your rock hard manhood inside my cave of wet ecstacy."

"Uh-huh, uh-huh." Drool dropped to the carpet from his open mouth as he bobbed his head.

"Ahhhhh, Daddy, ohhhhh," I cooed as I played with myself, gently moving my fingers in a figure eight motion around my forbidden zone.

He waddled toward me, sounding like a broken bell with his keys and whatever else jingling inside his pockets.

"Come to Papa," he said with one arm on his Johnson and the other reaching out to me.

I removed the hand that was skating over my love nest as I stepped into him. He closed his eyes and took to sucking the three wet fingers I put in his mouth like a newborn baby. Why I wrapped my hand around his stiff, pinkish-purple Oscar Meyer Weiner, I don't know.

"Ah, ah, ah, ohh, ohh," he moaned. I felt him throbbing as I took over where his arm left off. His face lit up nearly the same shade as the dress I had up over my waist. His body started jerking. I stepped to the side just in time.

"Ahhhhhhhhhhhhhhhhhhhhhhhhh," he screamed like an off-key opera singer before exploding onto the beige carpet.

Before I left him in a disheveled heap on the bed, I said, "Close your eyes, Daddy." I gently ran my fingers down his face. "And imagine being able to cum in my mouth and in my tight, wet, hungry pussy." I stepped back. "Daddy, it's all yours after you take care of our Li'l Dre."

JIHAD

CHAPTER 27

MADNESS

After spending the night and half the morning going over and revising the day's plan with Babygirl and Snow, I was exhausted. I stood in line at the Jiffy Lube looking like one of the girls who greets you when you get off the plane in Hawaii, with my aqua blue Phat Farm African safari print sarong wrapped around my hips like a second skin.

"Excuse me."

I turned around. "You don't have to touch me to get my attention," I said to the guy who put his hand on my shoulder.

"Hey, hey, I'm sorry, queen. Don't go Laila Ali on me," this fine, young, high yellow, sun-bright Michael Jordan said while stepping back and putting his large, well manicured, ringless hands out toward me.

Despite my bad mood, I gave him a fake smile before apologizing. "Sorry, it's been one of those mornings."

"I understand. I didn't want anything. Just wanted to offer you my services."

Oh my. Shaquille O'Neal feet in dark brown Mauri closed-toe sandals. I hated men in open-toe sandals—too gay looking.

I continued eyeing him up and down.

Matching Tommy Bahama slacks, no bulge. Oh well. Forty-eight-inch chest on a six-foot-plus muscular frame. No jewelry on his fingers or neck, unless you count the silver Movado with the mother of pearl face he wore on his wrist. Three buttons from his neckline was where the reddish-brown hair on his chest was trying to escape the loose-fitting, short-sleeved silk summer shirt

167

adorning his window front mannequin physique.

His rugged face was accentuated by a black goatee and full, brown puffy lips. His bowling ball head looked like a bright sun in the cloudy morning light.

A mutt, probably. Hmmm, I pondered while continuing to eye him up and down. Black-Cuban, Black-Indian, Black-Brazilian or something or the other, but without a doubt, definitely Black-fine.

"Excuse me."

"Okay." I put my hand on my hip and stuck a baby-oiled, bronzed leg out. "Will you stop saying 'excuse me'? That is not my name."

"And may I ask, what is your name?"

He could have been Michael Michelle's brother with his features. She was the sexy female that starred on the show, *Kevin Hill.*

"Queen? Are you there?" he asked.

"I'm sorry. My name is Marcia Michelle," I lied.

"Pleased to meet you, queen." He tenderly but firmly shook my hand. "My name is Cole, Cole Waters. Okay, no jokes about the name. I heard them all," he said while flashing that lightning-blinding smile.

Yeah, he could definitely get it, I thought. I wondered how Kitty and Clit would like some Cole Water sprinkled all over them.

"What's so funny?" he asked.

I must have been laughing out loud. "You were saying something about your services."

"Forty-seven, number forty-seven," a clerk called out. Hell, it wasn't ten people in the Jiffy Lube and they were on forty-seven, and since I had taken a seat next to Cole, I was number who cares.

"Yes, I take it you're here for an oil change," he said.

I nodded.

He leaned in close, licked his lips, and said, "I would love to change your oil."

"Oh, really?"

"Yes, really," he said.

I was tempted to ask him if he wanted a Coke with that Colgate smile, but instead I asked, "You think you're the man for the job?" I ran a long, bright red fingernail down his muscled arm. "I don't use any of those synthetic oils."

"Of course not. I only work with the highest grade of oil. My oil will make your engine purr," he momentarily closed his eyes, "like a kitty cat in Dairy Land."

I smiled. "You know, Jiffy Lube checks and replenishes all fluids."

"I go a step further."

"And how is that?"

"I warm the fluids," he said, licking his lips and rubbing his hands together, "and then I slowly fill all of those areas that are lacking. See, I don't use any machines. I am a complete hands-on type of guy."

"You sound like you might just know what you're doing."

"Hold on, I'm not finished, queen."

I loved the way this man called me queen.

"There's more?" I asked.

"But of course. What is an oil and lube job without a tuneup? Your engine will run smoothly, and it will be self-lubricating for at least one," he paused, "hundred," pause, "thousand," he closed his eyes and put one long hand on some electrically-tingling spot right above my knee, "miles when I'm finished."

Two hours later, I walked out of Cole's building with my lips touching my ears. I hadn't planned it, but he stupidly left his pants beside the bed when he showered. What could I do? It would have been rude for me to turn down such an invitation to scribble his driver's license info and social security number on a scrap of paper.

BABYGIRL

I could have made a Frosted Flakes commercial, the way I felt after sixty-one minutes of WWF knock-down, drag-out, no holds barred, no disqualification, licking, eating and sucking, earthquake fucking. I was wet all over again just thinking about how that man knelt down like he was bowing to the queen of England on his carpeted bedroom floor. It's hard to explain just how Kunta locked his Michael Jordan hands on my naked legs and lifted me up so my second set of lips were at his eye level. Resting my legs over his Vin Diesal shoulders, he took those LL Cool J lips and that Wesley Snipes tongue, and licked and tenderly sucked Kitty and Clit until my body had a fit of multiple convulsions.

I damn near pulled the stainless steel ceiling fan down. You would have thought I was the Last Supper the way he ate me. Lucky for him, he didn't have any glass or porcelain in the room. If he had, my screams would have shattered them into a million dancing pieces. The man's momma should have named him Cure instead of Cole the way he made all my problems go away.

Oh, and you know I had to set it off. As soon as he put me down on trembling legs, I got on bended knees, and with my African soup coolers, I put a lip-lock on his super-sized Superman, and started my Universoul Circus tongue act. When I looked up at him, I would've sworn he was one of Jerry's kids from the look on his face. I ain't even gon' talk about his turned-up, bent- the-wrong-way hands and arms.

"Speak English, muthafucka," I hummed while he made deep, guttural seal sounds until he exploded. After sliding on a Trojan and licking his hand, he turned me around in one smooth motion, slapped my ass, slammed that monster up in my cave and thug- fucked me like he was a jockey riding in the Kentucky Derby.

I came again in the parking lot just reminiscing about the last hour. I took a deep breath and threw my arms up as my sweet nectar ran freely down my inner

170

thighs. It felt so good to be me and free, I thought as I got into my white Escalade.

I don't know why I put myself through it for so long—dancing, tricking, Stevie, everything. Yes, I do. I smiled at the thought of my two beautiful babies. The day they were born I swore to protect, love, and never let them want for anything.

I felt a dark cloud suddenly come over me as I thought back to my childhood. This is one horror story that Kyla and Kira would never know. Besides, my babies were nine going on nineteen, and they were just fine not knowing Mommy's past.

The twins were the real reason I left the Parrot. I only worked three nights a week and pulled down an average of two thousand a month. Most people who knew me thought of me as a high-priced ho, but if I cared what most people thought, I'd be one paycheck away from the welfare office like most people. A ho was a woman who gave it up for free. Didn't matter if it was on the first night or the last, if you didn't get paid then you were the ho in my book. I was not a ho.

And how about the women who walk around talkin' about how they love their man? Well, last time I checked, Georgia Power wouldn't accept love to pay a bill. Krogers wouldn't accept love at the check-out line, and when Kira and Kyla needed new clothes, Bank of America wouldn't cash love.

So yes, love was the feeling that I gave at the club. Love was when Big Buck, my vibrator, had a fresh set of Energizer batteries in him while he massaged Clit and Kitty. Love was the biggest ho of them all. Oh, but you better believe I always had a special wet spot in my coochie for some well-done, Grade A, tender, seven-inch-plus Shaka-Zulu-warrior black man. And for those women who say size doesn't matter, they ain't never had no Olympic gold medal-worthy, work- it-like-a-salt-shaker marathon D-I-C-K.

BABYGIRL

Just last month, this creature came in the club and made a scene.

"Ho, you fuckin' my husband," she said with her paws on her grizzly hips.

"No, the ho would be you." I pointed a two-inch pink nail in her face. "And maybe the bitch that shitted you out," I casually and calmly said.

Security caught her before she attacked. While they were escorting her out of the club, I said, "If I am fucking your husband, he pays and pays well for that five minutes of pleasure that you obviously can't or don't provide. I don't cook or clean, I just make him cum. Now, you tell me, who's the ho?"

If I wrote a book on how to please a man, I'd be on *Oprah*. Women didn't understand that pleasing a man is more mental than physical. You have to understand him, get into his big head before you even entertain the smaller one. The physical is important, but it is a far second to the mental.

That's why when I worked, it was all about him in the club. Every step I took was about and for him. Everything from my walking to my breathing was sensual. A fantasy with me was better than crack-cocaine. I provided that moment of ecstasy that dope fiends talk about. I'm not arrogant, far from it, but I am real.

Everything I did was for my little girls. That's why I left the club that night. I had been looking for the opportunity, but it wasn't until I met Babygirl that I knew I could make it without Stevie and her Parrot.

My girls were getting older, and soon they'd find out what Mommy did. I did what I did so they and I would have the best of everything and at the same time I would still be able to devote four days a week totally to them. I spent so many years and so much time hating and masturbating, I forgot how to love anything or anyone besides my babies. Although my father had come back into my life when I needed him most, I still couldn't trust or love a man.

Thanks to Babygirl showing me through other women's experiences that my struggle was just a part of the black woman's struggle to define the essence of our being, I felt good about myself, and for the first time ever, I knew what it meant to love myself.

After rediscovering myself through stories passed down from women who shared my pain and much more of their own, I felt a responsibility to give back to the women dropping it like it's hot for a five-dollar hit. I wanted, no, I needed to help the women out there living under cardboard boxes and blanketing their children with their bodies on cold, rainy nights. I had to help my sistahs learn to be strong and not let any man do to them what was done to me.

"Sorry, baby," I said to Usher as I put him on mute while I was heading home, driving down I-285.

The phone rang only once before she picked up. "I see you fixed the mysterious vibrating phone problem," I said.

"No, I just bought a new one."

"How did you know the guy was going to Jiffy Lube this morning?" I asked Babygirl.

"Good surveillance," she said.

Oh well, whatever, I thought before continuing,

"We pulled into the Jiffy Lube a few minutes apart. I rubbed my butt up against him a couple of times before he tapped me on my shoulder, and the next thing ya know, we're at his condo in Li'l Dre's building.

"Girl, you were right. That brotha was fine, and he was hung like a flagpole. Girl, I was ready to salute and pledge allegiance to the brotha's dick after he put that thang on me."

"Girl, you a fool," Babygirl said.

"Anyway, I put the manila envelope with the pictures of Stevie under Li'l Dre's doormat. I still don't see how you made the pictures look like she was planting dope in Li'l Dre's apartment."

CHAPTER 28

BABYGIRL

I was on my way to my office at the SAID headquarters when Dickless Tracy called me from Li'l Dre's apartment. He spoke fast and direct. It took a moment before I realized he wasn't on the phone anymore.

I didn't hear the horns blowing behind me. I was sitting in the middle of early morning rush hour traffic with my mouth open and my hands tightly gripping the steering wheel of my little beamer.

"Hey, lady, you all right?" some guy asked, while knocking on the driver's side window.

I rolled down my window. "I'm sorry, I'm fine. Just received some terrible news," I said before rolling up the window and putting the car in first gear and taking off.

What the fuck happened, I wondered while I drove as fast as the rush hour traffic would take me over to Snow's house. I got to her house in record time. It took me only thirty-two minutes to make the drive in the bumper to bumper morning traffic.

I nearly broke the glass, knocking on her front door. "A kilo, a whole kilo of crack-cocaine." I said as I barged right past her. I was standing inside the sparsely decorated sunken den of the restored gray- and-blue Victorian home that Snow leased. "That was flour in those packages I gave you. Knock, knock," I pounded on the sky blue wall.

"Did you forget we were planting baking flour in Li'l Dre's apartment, not the real thing?" She was standing in front of me with a dumb look on her face. "Did you forget about the pictures you took of Stevie? The ones where I made it look like she was talking to a cop in what

175

looked to be the front of Li'l Dre's building? Did you forget that we were leaving the pictures I transposed of Stevie planting the dope inside of Li'l Dre's condo under his mat after he made bond on the phony drug arrest?

"Did you forget the credit cards, driver's license, and other information I created? Did you forget that we were doing all of this so when Li'l Dre got out of jail after seeing the pictures, he'd think Stevie set him up and while they were trying to take each other out, we'd assume her identity and bankrupt the bitch?"

She put her arms out in front of her. "Relax, Babygirl." I could not believe this happy-ass, blast-from-the-past, Woodstock-acting bitch had the audacity to put her hand on my arm. "Everything's beautiful," she said.

I must have been in temporary shock, because she still had use of her hand after placing it on my arm. I jerked away from her touch a second later. "Relax? How the fuck can I relax, you everything's-beautiful-new-millennium-flower-child bitch? You've jeopardized everything we've worked for, not to mention my life. Now I have to find another way to handle that psycho dyke."

"Will you please calm down and let me explain?"

I stood with my arms folded and my foot tapping the hardwood floor.

"André Lester moved here from St. Louis close to five years ago." She took a deep breath before motioning me to have a seat at the kitchen table. "Him and his father, Frank Lester, turned my baby sister out on crack and took turns pounding on her insides. He said he loved her." She paused to wipe the tears from her eyes. "My sister, Julie Ann, was forced to perform beastial acts with animals and men for crack-cocaine. She was beaten when she refused, but Frank told her he loved her.

"She was only sixteen when she left home with the smooth-tongued, pimping drug dealer and his perverted, womanizing son."

I reached out and took Snow into my arms then moved her over to the couch, where she explained the murder of her father, Lester's acquittal, her mother's and her sister's passing, and her own bout with depression in a psychiatric hospital.

"I really admire you for your courage and fearlessness, Babygirl. You are truly beautiful. I know you don't trust me. I wouldn't either after what I did, but . . ." She stuck a lone, clear-painted finger in the air. "I can and I have helped you more than you know, and I will continue if you let me."

"Help me?" I stood up and placed a hand over my chest. "No, I don't think so." I shook my head. "At least not before we finish what you started. Looks like we have to take a trip to St. Louis. We need to do something about that cancer who calls himself Frank Lester. Damn, he must've been twice your sister's age when he took her to St. Louis."

She nodded.

I put an arm around her shoulders. "From now on, you have to come correct and shoot straight with me if you want my help. I need to know everything, and I mean everything you've done up until now."

She hugged me. "Thank you, Babygirl. I don't know what I would have done without you."

"You'd still be dancing at the Parrot, thinking about when and how you'd be able to do what we're doing now."

"I'll be right back," she said, running up the stairs. This girl had taste, I thought, as I admired the colorful abstract paintings that decorated her living room walls.

A minute later she was back in front of me. "Here." She put a check in my hand.

My eyes were big as pies. "Girl, stop playing with me. You don't have this kind of money," I said, handing the check for one hundred thousand dollars back to her.

"Yes, I do. My mother and father each had half-million dollar life insurance policies. The house I grew up in was paid for, so I banked the eighty thousand Allstate paid out for the damage. Even after paying for three funerals, the hospital bills that my insurance didn't pay, taxes, a tummy tuck, liposuction, electrolysis, plastic surgery, a dietician, a personal trainer, and a boxing trainer, I still had almost four hundred thousand left over. And in the two years I've been living here, all of it is still drawing interest in Bank of America."

I just listened to her, completely dumbfounded.

"I used money I made from dancing to buy the kilo of crack-cocaine that I hid in André's bedroom."

"You mean to tell me Li'l Dre sold you the same dope that you planted in his condo?" I asked. "Damn, you bold, girl. What prompted you to do all this?"

"While recovering inside the psych ward at Grandview Psychiatric Hospital, seeds of revenge started to grow in my mind. I figured it would be easier to get close to the carefree younger Lester. When I learned that his father had sent him to Atlanta, that made it even better. You came along and helped me grow the seeds into a full-blown plan of revenge."

"Better how?" I asked.

"Atlanta was neutral ground. It was not his turf, and definitely not mine. And his father wasn't there to watch over him."

"Makes sense." I nodded.

"Like I was saying, back in the hospital I knew I had to get close to him. The only way to achieve that was to change my look. The reason I decided to make myself beautiful was because I knew Frank and his son were attracted to beautiful white women.

JIHAD

"While getting in shape and having the cosmetic surgeries, I hired a private investigator to follow André. I learned about his drug dealing, and where he lived. I also found out that he spent most of his leisure time in strip clubs getting lap dances and trying to buy special services from the dancers. Of course, being a country white girl from Jefferson City, Missouri, I couldn't dance. So, I hired a dancer to teach me when I got to Atlanta. Since beautiful women were his weakness, what better way to get under him than to get literally under him? It didn't take long to catch his eye."

"Girl, a white girl built like a sistah, getting his eye was the easy part. But how did you get that much dope? And where did you get the idea to plant it in his condo?" I asked.

"From an episode I saw on *L.A. Law* when I first moved from Missouri to Atlanta."

"I record and watch every episode. Which one was it?"

"It was the one where the guy plants crack-cocaine in the home of his ex-wife to get custody of their ten- year-old son."

I interrupted, "And she gets a life sentence only to be overturned on appeal."

"Yes, that's the one. So I took it upon myself to do some research on the minimum mandatory sentencing guidelines and the drug laws. After discovering that one kilogram of crack-cocaine would send André away for the rest of his life, I knew what I had to do.

"He was the only person I knew of who sold crack-cocaine."

"Talk about poetic justice. Did you have to sleep with him?"

She put her head down. "Yes."

I reached over and took her hand in mine. "I'm sorry. It must've been painful to be with a man who abused your sister."

179

"You don't know the half of it. After I got home both times, I scrubbed my skin raw while I cried in the bathtub. But I was and still am willing to do anything to destroy him and his father. It took a year of buying an ounce at a time to collect enough until I had one ounce over a kilo. Since then, I've been biding my time, waiting for the right opportunity. And when you got into it with Stevie, I knew my time had come. I really am sorry, Babygirl." She touched my hand.

"Everything about you and what you are doing with your SAID foundation is beautiful. I'll support you any way I can. That's why I'm giving you this check, and that's why I did what I did for you."

"What did you do for me?"

"Oh, you'll see. Anyway, I know you have to pay Madness, and I want to help your program. If my sister had a support system like what you are providing, she may still be alive today. Who knows?" She shrugged.

"Thank you, but the only way I will accept it is if you accept my three conditions."

"What are they?" she asked and smiled.

"Like I said earlier, you have to be straight with me from this moment forward. Two, you let me and Madness help you get Frank."

"And what is the third?" she asked.

"Three, you help us take down Stevie."

"Agreed, but first I have to tell you what I did for you."

CHAPTER 29

MADNESS

"We interrupt this program for a breaking news update," an invisible voice interrupted my soaps.

"I'm Rhonda Tate from Fox 5 news and I am standing here with Detective Frank O'Leary."

I just finished running on my treadmill. I was sweating naked in my exercise room, sitting in the lotus position. I was about to put in a Pilates tape when I yelled, "Francis, not Frank," at my fifty-seven-inch plasma screen television.

"We are coming to you live from the front of the Palisades luxury high-rise condominium building across from Lenox Mall in Buckhead." The reporter turned detective. "Detective O'Leary, can you explain to our viewers what happened earlier?"

He took the microphone out of her hand and made the most disgusting sound, clearing his throat. "Yes. Acting on an anonymous tip, I took it upon myself to head up a full investigation of the suspect in question. After delving into the nefarious activities—"

"Spell 'nefarious,' dumb ass," I yelled.

"—of one of the most dangerous and violent drug dealers in the southeastern United States, I concluded that André Lester, known by his cohorts as Little Dre, had to be dealt with and dealt with expeditiously."

Pulling the microphone toward her, struggling to free it from his grasp, the reporter gave up and asked, "And can you tell us what he is suspected of?"

He pulled the microphone back to his chin. "One hundred and fifty-seven minutes ago, my team of investigators uncovered twenty-nine Saran-wrapped packets of crack-cocaine . . ."

"Shit!"

"Also on the promises, we recovered four semi-automatic hand guns registered to André Lester."

"Premises, dumb ass!" I screamed in laughter.

I dialed the office, Babygirl's apartment, and her cell phone three times. No answer. A whole kilo of crack? Shit! Shit! Shit! He was fucked. We were fucked. Babygirl was definitely fucked. He'd never get a bond. That meant he wouldn't be able to take care of Stevie, and Babygirl was in double deep shit.

I was out of my yoga position and in my den, standing up, right in front of the wall where my other television hung. I turned up the volume.

"Where is André Lester now?" the reporter asked.

"We are not quite sure at this particular time." My heart was in my toes.

"He's still at large."

They'd never find him using the picture that flashed across my screen. Li'l Dre was so damn dark and menacing looking, I would never have known it was him. Li'l Dre was one of those high yellow-ass Negros. Five hundred pounds ago, back in the days when he could see his dick, he might've been cute.

The caption that ran across the television began with the words "He's a black male."

No shit. When a brotha was suspected of any wrongdoing, he was always a black male, but when a white man was a suspect, it was always just a male suspect.

The caption described him as six feet, 260 pounds, considered armed and dangerous."

"Shit," I shouted. "That fat midget muthafucka is my height, and the Negro ain't seen two-sixty since he was two. Who'd they get their info from, Stevie Wonder?"

"So if anyone has any information on this man's whereabouts . . ."

182

"I know his whereabouts, and thereabouts, and what it's about to be about. Oh, and stank bitch, my height and weight is the least of your worries. How 'bout I let you suck thirty pounds of nut out my dick."

I jumped off of the couch and turned around. Li'l Dre stood there in beige Tims and baggy jeans with the pockets drooping at his knees. The black-and-white Michael Vick Atlanta Falcon jersey he wore could've covered my entire dining room table.

I felt like the air was being sucked out of my house as I stuggled to breathe.

Half of his hair was braided, the other half stood up like a rooster. He stood there with an unlit blunt in his mouth and a crooked smile, holding onto a green leather leash connected to the collar of a big-ass, tongue-breathing German Shepherd.

Oh, God. My babies. What would happen to them? Who would take care of my babies?

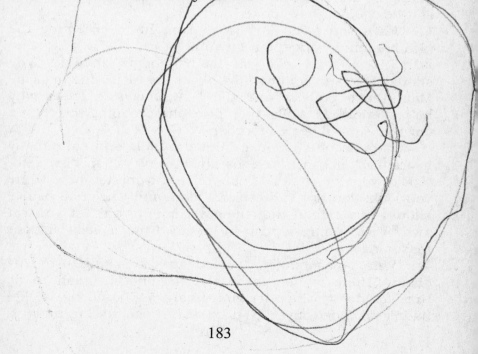

CHAPTER 30

SHABAZZ

"The trial starts in a couple weeks on Monday, the eighteenth of August. Pretty soon you'll be moved to a county jail," my attorney explained.

I was sitting in the client-attorney room with Jonathon Dalton Parker, the white Johnnie Cochran of the South, going over strategy for my upcoming murder trial.

"It's about time. I'm just ready to get this shit over with. Man, it will be a relief to eat warm food that doesn't move. I don't see how Mumia Abu Jamal does it, sitting in the tombs of his cell-hell on death row for some shit he couldn't have done."

"Have you given any more thought to accepting the plea bargain I worked out for you?"

"J.P., I done told you I ain't coppin' to shit. Why should I cop to another five years for defending myself? Man, that's bullshit and the D.A. knows it. That's why he's offering me a five-year plea and dropping the charge down to second degree murder."

He pulled his chair around the table and sat directly in front of me. In a tone barely above a whisper he said, "Look, you know how this works. No matter how white you look, you are still a black man, and you of all people should understand that the government can't let you get away with killing a man in prison. I mean, look at their reasoning."

"What reasoning?" I stood up, knocking over my chair. "There is no reason for an innocent man to do time for doing what the guards are supposed to do. If I hadn't defended myself, I'd be worm food rotting under a pile of dirt in an unmarked grave in God knows where. I may be in prison, but I'm still protected under the Constitution." I knew that what I was saying was bullshit, but I just couldn't bow down.

"Shabazz, you preaching to the choir," he said, putting his hand on my shoulder. "If they let you get off, then your case could possibly and probably would, set a precedent for others who've killed out of self defense to get their cases overturned. Imagine the fallout and the expense the government will have to eat by bringing those cases back to court?"

"That ain't my problem. Damn, J.P., you sound like one of them. You the only dude I trust outside these walls. Don't go selling me out."

"I'm not selling you out, but I've been doing this for a long time, and when it comes to federal cases, nine times out of ten I avoid going to trial, and I get the best deal I can for my client. It isn't a point of guilt or innocence when the federal government targets an individual. When they bring charges, you are guilty by default. Besides, you know the statistics."

"Yeah, they have a ninety-seven percent conviction rate," I said.

"So take the five-year plea, Shabazz. You've served almost eleven months. You'll be home in a little over three years."

I shook my head before picking up my chair and sitting down again. It sounded like he really cared, but I knew I didn't mean shit to him, for real. It was all about his perfect record. Jonathon Dalton Parker had never lost a murder trial, and didn't want this one to be his first.

"Can't do it," I said, shaking my head. "All my life I've settled. I let myself be a slave to the streets, drugs, and my own mind. Since I've been locked down in the tombs, I've been reading and reflecting on my life and just life in general. And I've decided never to be a slave to no one ever again, not the streets, the system, the needle, or anything else."

"We'll lose if we go to trial," J.P. shouted.

I leaned back in my chair, took a deep breath, exhaled, and crossed my arms before explaining, "I can't lose what I've never had."

"What kind of nonsense are you talking about now?"

"Freedom." I shook my head. "Never had it. Don't know how it feels. But I do know that I feel good," I said, patting my chest, "standing up for something I believe." I wore the smile of life on my unshaven, stubble-ridden face. "You may never understand, but it's better to die for something than live for nothing."

J.P. sighed defeat. I smiled victory.

As I walked back to the tombs, I felt like I'd just shot myself up with a needle full of feel-good. I felt like I was really living up to Shabazz, the name I gave myself after reading the *Autobiography of Malcolm X* when I was a kid back in juvey hall.

Yeah, I pounded my chest with my fist. I was walking in the footsteps, doing what the greatest black or white man that ever lived would do. If Malcolm X El- Hajj Malik El-Shabazz were in my place, he'd stand up and fight the power just like I planned to do.

I was back in my six-by-nine hell when the metal wall I was leaning on started vibrating from the banging Prophet was doing. Over the last ten plus months, I told Prophet mine and Babygirl's life stories. He asked a lot of questions about Babygirl. So much so, that I would have thought he was up to some gangsta shit if I didn't know any better. But he had proven himself to be looking out for our best interests.

"So what happened, King?"

I'd come a long way in a short amount of time, I thought. When Prophet and I first started talking, I was Light-skin, now I was King. Yeah, that shit felt good. I could get used to being called King, instead of

186

nigga, Light-skin, white boy or any of that.

"Uh, he told me if I didn't take the plea, I was more or less dead in the water."

"What are you going to do?"

"I'm going to be like you. I'm going to be a One Free muthafucka in spirit and mind, if not in body."

"Stay strong, King. I promise you that everything will work out the way the man upstairs wants. Just keep it real and stay true to yourself and what you know to be righteous."

"I feel you, and I appreciate you raisin' a brotha outta the state of nigga-ism I was in."

"All praise is due to God. I'm just a man trying to get my blessings wherever I can find them."

"I hope He blesses the twelve jurors into coming back with a verdict of not guilty."

"Don't hope, King. Speak what you want into existence. Hope is what got black folks to the wonderland that we live in today."

"Wonderland?"

"I wonder if I can get that job. I wonder if I can get that bank loan. I wonder if I can buy that house. If David sat back in a state of wonder, not sure of his self and not sure of his God, then it is very likely that Jesus, who was a direct descendant of David, would have never been born. And we wouldn't be here right now having this conversation."

Prophet was a bad muthafucka. He should've been a teacher, a writer, or a preacher. Wasn't no fakin' in his frontin'. The brotha was the real deal.

I was knocked out when the marshals startled me awake, rattling the bars a week later.

"Jackson, get dressed and come forward. Hands out front."

My trial started in four days, I thought, as I was being cuffed before they would let me out of my cage. A brown arm reached through the bars in the next cell. He grabbed hold of my hand.

"King, I just want to let you know that I love you, man."

I didn't know what the fuck to say. No man had ever said those words to me. I let go of Prophet's hand and hurried off with the two U.S. marshals before he could see my eyes watering.

"Yo, King Shabazz, be you, do you. Don't forget. Be you, do you, One Free for life.

"Everybody on the first tier," Prophet shouted.

"Stand up, look out your bars. You see that black king walking. Hear me when I tell you that you are looking at a soldier in God's Army," Prophet shouted as I strutted out of the tombs with tears free-flowing from my eyes. The chorus of rhythmic cell door banging and shouts of "Be you, do you" followed me all the way to the front of the prison.

It didn't make sense that the marshals had to take me from one prison to another when they could've just got me from the tombs on the day my trial started, but I knew I had lucked out when we drove up to the Marriott of prisons a couple hours later. Inside the Bartow County Jail, I could still smell that new jail scent of fresh air.

I was housed in a two-tier glass dorm with twenty-four two-man cells. There were six stainless steel tables in the prison dormitory common area. The stools under the tables were filled by biker and stock broker bookish-looking white boys. They were playing cards, chess, checkers, and just sitting around telling lies and waiting on the phones. It was the first time I'd ever been a minority in the five and a half years I'd been in prison. There were only four brothas besides myself in the filled to capacity unit.

I lucked up and met a brotha that went by the name Tom-Tom. Let him tell it, Prophet was his man from way back in the day. Tom-Tom was from the same side of town in Chicago that Prophet was from.

"Yeah, word up, that's my nigga on the fo' reala. We go way back to yesteryear," he said, throwing up gang signs. "I was down with the movement before he took out the ex-mayor of Chi." He opened up his orange jumpsuit, revealing a tattoo that took up his large chest. "Yeah, you see it, baby."

The word 'one' was in red, blue, and green calligraphy, and it took up the whole left side of his chest. The word 'free' covered the right side.

"One Free for life. Feel me," he said.

"Like a migraine, black man," I replied.

"So, you was in the hole wit' 'im?" Tom-Tom asked.

"Eleven months," I said, remembering how proud I felt when Prophet explained why he helped to start the national One Free movement in the early 90s that had black folks all around the country changing their last names to One Free in hopes of uniting the black family.

"Right, right, that's peace," he sang while nodding.

"I don't see why Prophet ain't running one of those super churches."

"Come on, Black, you was down with the man and you didn't know he was Muslim."

"Nah." I shook my head. This guy done played himself for real. He may have been from the same city as Prophet, but he didn't know him. I continued, "I hate to bust your bubble, but Prophet knows more about the Bible and can break it down better than the Pope."

"No question, he's like that with the Holy Quran too, feel me. You think he gon' speak French to you when you only speak English?" Tom-Tom said.

"Look here, I don't mean no disrespect, but we have to be talkin' about two different people."

"I doubt that," Tom-Tom said.

"The Prophet I know is definitely a Christian. He believes in Jesus."

BABYGIRL

Tom-Tom swayed real cool-like, crossed his arms like an old school B-boy and smiled. "Black man," he pointed at his chest, "I'm Muslim. Don't believe CNN. Believe me when I tell you we believe in Jesus.

"Hell, Jesus is the reason that all the One Frees fight for a new season, one of awareness of self through knowledge that black folks put down on paper. Ya understand me?"

I nodded, deciding to just let him talk. The brotha was entertaining, if nothing else.

"See, we building underground railroads in Bible schools and mosques all over the country, teaching the new youngbloods what the schools refuse to."

"And what is that?"

"Knowledge of self through mastering of our true history as written in the blood of the ancestors, transcribed by brothas who look just like me and you. Well, maybe not you. No offense, Black."

"None taken," I said. "So, what? You got black-authored textbooks now?"

"Oh yeah, we got books with all types of text in them. We got kids studying everything from the colorful street fiction of Donald Goines, Iceberg Slim and Thomas Long to the conscious truth works of Carter G. Woodson, George Jackson, and Dr. Ben, ya understand me."

"How can our people benefit by reading street fiction?" I asked.

"How can they not? You gotta keep it real and speak the language that the new youngbloods can feel. I know Prophet broke that Bible down to you using Street 101. That's what we doing with this street fiction. It's getting our kids to read. That's the first step. The next is explaining to them what they reading so they can make informed decisions on whether to follow the negative or positive images they reading about. Feel me?"

For the next two nights, I had insomnia, lying up in

my top bunk with my hands behind my head, staring at the paint dots on the beige cement ceiling. I was thinking about Prophet, his One Free movement, and religion. My trial was furthest from my mind until

J.P. came to see me the day before court.

We were in a small, brightly lit room adorned with red indoor-outdoor carpet. A large, heavy-looking, dark wooden door separated us from the officers standing guard outside. J.P. and I were sitting at a small metal table.

"Babygirl has gotten herself into something so deep I'm afraid I can't even help her get out of it."

"What?" I jumped up, knocking my chair over.

"She's mixed up with Frank Lester and the St. Louis Black Mafia."

I picked up my chair, plopped down on it and put my hands over my eyes.

"From what my sources tell me, I don't think she realizes who she's dealing with." Being a Slim Shady, palm-greasing, slick-talking, ponytailed wonder-boy attorney made him privy to the priest-like confessions of the underworld.

I took my hands from my eyes and sighed with a heavy heart. "Tell me everything."

After he finished, I wanted to throw up. I didn't know what to do. I had no choice but to beat my case now. My Babygirl needed me.

The next morning, I walked into the courtroom wearing a too big, black JC Penney sport jacket, a white button-down shirt, and some tight beige pants. Despite my appearance, I still held my head up high.

The jury consisted of eight women and four men who shared my skin color, but not my ethnicity. In spite of this all-white jury in a predominantly black city, I still remained optimistic.

With God with me, no man can stand against me, I

kept silently repeating until I saw the face of a woman who looked exactly like the pictures of Prophet's wife I had seen when he passed them to me in the tombs. When she nodded and smiled, I knew it was her. But why was she in Atlanta and not Chicago, and why was she at my trial?

CHAPTER 31

SNOW

I lived, ate and breathed revenge. Nothing else mattered. I was truly sympathetic to Babygirl's plight, but at the end of the day, after all else was said and done, the only thing I needed was for Frank and André Lester to suffer a fate worse than hell. And if they died in the process, I would gladly give my life to follow them to the fiery pits just to watch them burn and scream.

Babygirl put her hand over mine as we sat at the dining room table. "I want you to take your time and explain everything to me. Everything from the moment you entered Li'l Dre's building," she said.

I got up from the table, went into the small, flowery-wallpapered kitchen and opened the refrigerator. "Can I get you something to drink?" I asked while pointing a bottle of Coors in her direction.

"No, I'm fine."

I sat down and took a long, slow drink from the bottle. "Before I even got up to the apartment, my heart was pounding and I was sweating profusely," I said as I began retracing my footsteps back to the night Madness let me in André's penthouse apartment.

"Sweating?"

"It was the excitement. I'd spent so many sleepless nights daydreaming, anticipating, masturbating, and waiting for the time, the moment when I could begin to execute my detailed plan of vengeance."

"Ooookay," she said, leaning forward and resting her elbows on the glass kitchen table and her chin in her hands.

I took another drink. "Madness was as solemn as I was excited. We rode the elevator up to his penthouse

193

suite on the twenty-third floor. I was on the verge of a beautiful, massive volcanic orgasmic eruption as I studied his obese, sleeping figure sprawled over the green leather couch facing a wall of windows that overlooked the downtown Atlanta skyline. It took every ounce of strength I possessed not to take off my backpack, go into his kitchen and get the largest, shiniest, sharpest knife I could find, walk back over to the couch, cut out the crotch of his green velour sweatpants, slice off his dick off and force feed it to him while he bled and screamed in agony.

"Madness tapped me on my shoulder right as I shuddered."

"Why were you shuddering?" Babygirl asked, wearing a weird look on her face.

"From the beautifully electric orgasm I had while I stood over him and fantasized his death."

"Okay, girl, that is entirely too much information," she said, sitting back in the chair and crossing her arms.

"Since I'd been pulled out of my reverie, I decided that I'd get back to the business at hand."

Babygirl's eyebrows danced as she said, "Thank God."

"I removed the backpack from my shoulders, unzipped it and removed the three flour-packed packages and placed them on the couch next to his loudly snoring body. Oh my God, it was unreal. His mouth hung open like a walrus, and drool ran down his chin. He sounded like a cartoon character."

"Right, so what did you do next?"

"I zipped my backpack up, slung it over my shoulders, and took the stainless steel steps of his winding staircase two at a time."

"Where was Madness?"

"Who knows?" I said with a shrug. "I guess she was downstairs somewhere, waiting on me. Anyway, in his bedroom, I took pictures. But of course you know that."

"Uh-huh," she said with a slight nod.

"Anyway, you should have seen that bedroom. Two French glass double doors with custom blinds hanging from them. These doors led out to a private balcony."

"I got the picture. The room was mad tight. What else did you do?" Babygirl asked.

"Okay," I slid my chair closer to the table, "I made sure I wore gloves and left everything as it was before I rummaged through the drawers on each side of the bed."

"Did you find anything we could use?"

I shook my head. "No, he had a gun in each drawer and one under his pillow. Disappointed that I hadn't found anything else, I walked inside his tunnel-like bedroom closet. That's where I hit the jackpot."

"Money, jewelry, what?" she asked.

"No, a brown-handled three-eighty Baretta."

She fell back in her chair and threw her hands up in an exasperated gesture. "Another gun." She shook her head. "What kind of jackpot is that?"

"I'll get to that. But first you have to understand, it was where the gun was."

"I don't follow."

"You will in a minute. It's mid-July. The temperature doesn't get below seventy-five degrees at night."

"And?"

"The gun was in the inside pocket of a leather bomber coat at the back of the closet."

"And?"

"It seems obvious that he wouldn't miss the gun. He probably didn't even know it was inside the coat."

"Sooooo."

She liked dragging out her O's, it seemed.

"You took the gun?"

"Yes, I did."

"Taking Li'l Dre's gun was not in the plan."

"Maybe not yours, but don't worry. I have every angle covered. Just listen. So, I closed the closet doors and went back to the middle of the room. I put the gun in my backpack and I removed the Ziploc freezer bag."

"And this would be the bag with the cookies in it, right?"

"Cookies? What cookies?" I asked.

"Girl, that's the terminology used for an ounce-sized cookie of crack," she explained.

"Oh, okay. Well, yes. The Ziploc bags were where I kept the twenty-nine Saran-wrapped crack cookies. So anyway, I slid the bag under the television in the middle of his armoire. Babygirl, you should have seen it. The furniture maker must've used a whole California redwood tree to make that thing."

"Oh shit, no you didn't."

"Didn't what?"

"Your stuffy, everything's-beautiful ass cracked a joke."

"Please, I'm very funny, at least when I wanna be."

"Oookay. Soooo, what did you do with the dummy dope you used for the pictures?"

"I put them out with the garbage right after I got home the next morning."

I could tell that Babygirl was getting impatient because of the drum solo she was tapping on the linoleum dining room floor. "You still haven't told me why you took the gun from Li'l Dre's condo."

"I know. I was just about to get to that."

"Does taking the gun have something to do with the one more thing you told me I needed to know earlier?"

"It has everything to do with it. I did what I did because you are a beautiful person and I owed you."

"Owed me for what?"

"For giving me the opportunity to make Frank and

André Lester pay."
"I am almost scared to ask."
"No need. I'll tell you."

CHAPTER 32

MADNESS

My cell phone was on the love seat. It was too far to reach.

"Babygirl," I said, hoping the voice command on my cell phone would kick in and dial her number.

"You don't look like you happy to see Li'l Dre. Is it the hair? If so, you gon' just have to excuse the way it looks. Li'l Dre was getting his hair braided when he gets this phone call from someone telling him that his pad was being busted by the po-po." He spoke of himself as if he were talking about someone else. It was weird. I didn't know what to do or what to expect. How did he know I had something to do with the bust? For probably the first time in my life, I didn't know what to say. I just stood there naked in front of the TV in the den. My eyes were glued to him as he walked from one end of my spacious sunken den to the other with his German Shepherd at his side.

"Funny thing is, Li'l Dre don't shit where he eat. So the next thing Li'l Dre did was ask himself, hmm . . ." He put a finger to his forehead. "How is it that the po- po could find all that crack at a place that ain't never had drugs in it?"

"What are you talking—"

He put a finger to his mouth. "Shhh." He continued pacing the den with his dog walking beside him. "Now, where was we? Oh yeah, I was saying that someone set him up. Now, who would do such a cruel thing? I mean, who placed so little value on their own life and the lives of their children to do something so suicidal?" My babies. Oh God, please let my babies be okay, I silently prayed. Scared, petrified, and frightened could not begin to describe what I was feeling at that very moment.

He continued his methodical pacing. "Do you have any idea why anyone would want Li'l Dre off the streets?"

I shook my head before I started to say "Babygirl," again hoping my phone would dial her cell number. Before I could complete her name, he stepped forward and backhanded me, knocking me into a flower pot in front of the double glass doors that led to the deck.

"Did you think that being stupid got Li'l Dre where he is today? Bitch, André Lester does the fucking around this piece. It don't go the other way around."

"Please don't—" I tried to beg him not to harm my babies when he kicked me in the stomach. I coughed and panted, trying to catch my breath. I wanted to live just long enough to make sure my babies were all right. I didn't care what he did to me, as long as he didn't hurt my babies.

"Shut up, bitch. Li'l Dre ain't finished."

I cringed as he and his dumb tongue-lapping dog stood over me. Looking down, I noticed the gray carpet was turning red with my blood.

"Obviously you thought I was stupid. You thought I wouldn't put two and two together. You thought I wouldn't figure out that you did some funny shit that night I took you to my honeycomb hide-out penthouse condo. You thought that you hoes could fuck with me. You think you and that bitch, Babygirl, can fade Li'l Dre and stop his flow? Oh, I got plans for that bitch too. Yeah, baby." He rubbed his hands together. "I want that ho real bad."

I was too scared to move, so I just lay next to my brown safari print ottoman, wincing in pain. He took off his belt and undid his pants. His fat, dark, ashy legs reminded me of a chalkboard as his black-and-red tent-sized boxers dropped to the floor.

"I don't remember you sucking my dick that night. As a matter of fact, I don't believe you did. I think you owe me a suck and fuck with interest."

"Why are you doing this?" I cried before he stomped on my legs with his heavy boots. I grimaced in pain. Tears ran down my face.

"You dumb, question-askin' bitch. You gon' make me kill you. If I don't tell you to speak," he said while bending down and pointing his finger in my face, "then don't say a got damn word."

Were my babies all right? Did he do anything to them?

He grabbed my hair and pulled. "Get on your fuckin' knees, bitch, and pay your bill."

I crawled on my knees to him. I was kneeling between his legs when he let go of the leash.

"Stay, boy," he commanded, pointing at the dog who was now sitting right next to me.

"Act like you know, bitch," he said, slapping me in the face with his semi-hard penis.

"Babygirl," I called out before I closed my eyes and imagined that I was on a white sandy beach with Mr. West, my ninth grade math teacher.

"Ahhhhh, yeah bitch, make it do what it do. Make it do what it do. Suck this muthafucka. Yeah, got damn. Lick them balls, bitch. Lick-lick-lick 'em like a cherry Charm pop." He still had a handful of my hair as he pushed my head into him with so much velocity I thought I would choke. I began to get dizzy. I started to gag. His penis was too deep in my mouth.

"Ahgg," I grunted. I tried to move my head off and away from his penis, but his hands and arms held my head like a vice.

"Ahgg." Again, I tried to speak, but I couldn't talk with his dick in my mouth. Finally, I erupted.

"You nasty, stank bitch." He yanked my head off his dick and looked down at the mess I made on him. He turned to his dog. "No, boy. Stay. You bet' not eat that shit."

I was lying on my stomach with my arms posting me up. I was still throwing up even after he pushed me away.

"Bitch, look what you've done. Funky-ass bitch. I can't believe you done threw up on my shit." He kicked me in the face before grabbing a handful of hair and pulling me to my feet. I could taste blood as he led me to the kitchen by my hair.

"This ain't even close to being over, bitch. Wipe this shit off me before I stomp your ass into the ground."

I grabbed a dish towel and rinsed it out. I wondered if he saw the knife at the bottom of the sink, sticking out from under the plate I'd used for breakfast. I prayed that he wouldn't rape me.

"Bitch, you bleedin'?"

I must have started my period when he kicked me in the stomach earlier. My fear overshadowed my bleeding and the pain I had from the beating he'd been giving me.

"Don't worry, bitch. I don't do red pussy."

Thank God. I thought it would be so easy, getting that knife out from under that plate. I continued to rinse the dish towel as I gathered my courage. Fuck it. I dropped the towel, grabbed the knife and twisted away from him.

*****

"Bitch, wake up," I heard a voice say through the waterfall.

I jerked and turned. I panted, trying to catch my breath. The room smelled like weed. I was soaking wet from the cold water that had just been poured on my face. Once everything came into focus, I turned my head from left to right in the smoke-filled room.

I was bent over, lying face down on my ottoman. I couldn't move. There was some kind of tape wrapped tightly around my waist, back and hands. I saw the mess I had made on the other side of the room. There was some kind of bar attached to my legs that kept me from closing them.

"You just won't learn, will you?" he said as he smoked his blunt and paced the floor of my den.

"I told you that you couldn't fade Li'l Dre. Bitch, you fuckin' wit' a sum' bitch so bad that he kills concrete and burns water for fun. Li'l Dre makes Satan look like Mother Teresa. But yet and still, you try a muthafucka. You think I didn't see that big-ass knife sticking out from under your nasty-ass dishes?"

I had to blink to stop the blood from trickling into my eyes. He must have hit me in the head with something as I turned around to cut him.

"Before I was so rudely the fuck interrupted by you and your punk-ass attempt to gut me, I was saying, I don't do red pussy, but G-Spot does."

Who was G-Spot? And where was he? Right now, I didn't care if I lived or died. I just wanted him to do to me whatever he was going to do and get it over with.

"G-spot, come here, boy. Meet your new bitch."

"Please don't," I cried as I tried to wiggle off the ottoman.

I heard him take a long pull from the blunt before coughing and saying, "Boy, get that pussy."

I felt the dog's sharp claws as he climbed onto my back.

I screamed.

CHAPTER 33

BABYGIRL

I knew I had to keep a close eye on Snow. Something was definitely not right with the girl. The woman had an orgasm while standing over the man who molested her sister. Thinking about her enemies just made her wet. Like I said before, she was doing way too much and not telling me nearly enough.

I'd just come back downstairs from using the restroom. Snow was still sitting at the kitchen table with her hands folded.

"Okay, I'm back. Now, what is this great thing you did for me?" I asked.

"Let's see. Where should I start?"

"The beginning is always good."

"Well, I sort of placed a call to your detective."

"My detective? I don't have a detective."

"You know who I mean. O'Leary. I made an anonymous call to him."

"When?"

"A couple days ago."

"What did you say?"

"I told him that a large drug deal was going down between Stevie Brown and André Lester on Thursday evening, July twenty-ninth."

"That's today."

She smiled. "I know."

"Okay, go 'head with your story."

"He tried to get me to come in and give a statement. Of course I refused. Just in case he put a trace on the pay phone I was calling from, I spoke quickly. I told him that he'd have to hit André's place the morning of the deal to get the drugs."

"Oh shit, that was right now, this morning."

"Everything had gone exactly the way I planned," Snow said.

"You planned? I think you better tell me the rest of your plan," I said.

"Well, like I've repeatedly told you, I really appreciated you helping me, so I decided to help you. Before I made the call to your detective, I drove past Stevie's house just to make sure she was still home."

"What do you mean still home? And what did
Stevie have to do with you calling the detective?"

"So many questions."

"So few fucking answers," I replied, starting to get impatient.

"I followed her from the Parrot at five in the morning, and to answer the second half of your question, Stevie has everything to do with me calling your detective."

"Ooooooookay, tell me how."

"Well, after making the call, I got into the car I'd rented the day before and drove until I found a service station with an outside restroom. I grabbed the Wal-Mart shopping bag from the passenger seat and went inside to change. Minutes later, I emerged as a heavy- set brunette housekeeper.

"The sun was just starting to come up when I pulled into Stevie's driveway. I parked behind her car. When I didn't see any lights on or movement inside, I walked around the house. Once I spotted a large enough basement window, I kneeled down and took the glass cutter and the suction cup out of my purse. I cut a hole, removed part of the window, climbed inside, took off my wig, and put on some rubber gloves. Next, I took the Ziploc bag out of my purse."

"Don't tell me you planted dope in Stevie's house too."

"Why would I do that?" she asked.

"I don't know, but you said you pulled out a Ziploc bag, so I thought . . ."

"Oh, I understand. So anyway, I left everything in a pile on the basement floor, except the Ziploc bag. That I carried up the stairs with me."

"Sooooooo, if there wasn't any dope in the bag, what was in it?"

"I'll get to that in a minute. Let me finish telling you the story."

I nodded, thinking this woman took forever to get to the point.

"I heard voices as I came to the top of the stairs. I thought that was strange because she was alone when I followed her home. I was just about to turn around and retrace my steps when I heard a cartoon character-like voice say, 'Obey your thirst.' "

"A Sprite commercial."

"Right, so I peeked out from behind the basement door. I could hardly believe my luck. Stevie was on the couch under a white sheet. That's when I carefully opened the Ziploc bag and removed the gun."

"The gun?"

"Remember the three-eighty I told you I took from André's coat pocket?" I nodded.

"Right as I was about to enter the room, I remembered the wine glass. I had to creep back down the stairs and go into my purse and get the empty glass out and carry it back up the stairs. I thought about pulling the sheet from over her head and waking her up so she could see it coming, but instead, I just entered the den, walked up to the couch, and shot her in the head three times. *Bang-bang-bang!*" She used her finger to re-enact the scene.

"Oooookay."

"Her body didn't jerk or anything like they do in the movies. She just laid there as blood and who knows what else stained the sheet she was under.

BABYGIRL

If there was ever any question in my mind, after seeing the animation on her face and hearing the excitement in her voice as she described in graphic detail how she killed another person, now I had no doubt that the bitch had flown way over the cuckoo's nest.

I wanted Stevie out of the picture, but not this way, I thought. I didn't know what my next move was going to be, but I knew I had to get the hell out of that house and away from Snow's crazy ass.

I got up to go, but she put her hand on my arm.

"Don't you want to hear the rest?"

I sat back down. "There's more?"

She looked at me like I'd asked the dumbest question in the world.

"Yes, there is. I have to tell you about the wine glass."

"What about it?"

"I took it from André's apartment that night. I made sure his fingerprints were all over it. Anyway, I set the glass down on the coffee table in front of the couch in Stevie's den. So see, I took care of Stevie for you, early this morning. Now you don't have to worry about her anymore."

"I don't know quite what to say."

"The look on your face says it all." She smiled.

I wondered what look that was. Was it the one that screamed out for me to get up and run? Or was it the look that said, "Bitch, you need a hug very bad, but not from me." Or was it the one that shouted, "Bitch, your coo-coo for Cocoa Puffs ass needs some help really, really quick, and really, really bad?"

"So what do we do now?" she asked.

I wanted to say "We don't do a damn thing, but let me get the hell away from you as quick as I can." But instead, I said, "Hold on, let me check my phone. We've been here for a few hours now, and I know I have messages." I figured that would give me enough time to think of a way to get the fuck up out of that woman's house without her suspecting anything funny.

"Shit!" I screamed. "Oh no." I put my hand over my mouth.

"What's wrong, Babygirl?"

"That fat son of a bitch, Li'l Dre got to Madness."

"What?"

"Listen." I put my cell phone to her ear so she could hear Li'l Dre cursing. He was obviously doing some type of foul shit to my girl. I grabbed Snow's shoulders and stared in her eyes. "Look, bitch, I don't give a fuck how crazy you are. You got me and Madness into this shit with your backward-ass, wrong-way plan. Now you're going to do what the fuck I say, when the hell I say, until we find her. Do you understand me?"

She nodded.

"Bitch, answer me!" I screamed.

"I'll do whatever you want."

"I ain't playing. Don't fuck with me, Snow." I pointed a finger in her direction. "You are white crazy all right, but believe me, you don't want black crazy all over yo' ass."

This fat muthafucka done made this shit personal now, I thought as I grabbed my purse.

"Come on, Snow, you need to tell me every fucking thing you know about where this fat fucker hangs out."

She started to say something but I interrupted.

"No, not here. Fill me in while we drive. We have to find my girl before it's too late, if it's not already."

CHAPTER 34

MADNESS

"What did I tell you to do? I mean what the fuck did I specifically tell you to do?" some tall, dark man shouted at Li'l Dre.

"You said to uhm—"

"Uhm? What the fuck is uhm? What have I always told you about speaking the Queen's English? Now answer the damn question."

"You said—"

"I know what the fuck I said. I told you to bring her to me. I didn't tell you to kill the ho."

"But she ain't dead," Li'l Dre pleaded.

"Might as well be." The man pointed to the floor where I had one eye closed and one half open until the man turned toward me. "Look at the bitch."

I could feel their eyes on me. Fear made it difficult to maintain my shallow breathing. I wanted to open my eyes so bad, but I couldn't let on that I was awake. I didn't know where I was, how long I'd been there, or how I'd gotten there.

"Did you fuck her?"

"No."

Li'l Dre must have drugged me. My whole body was numb. My mouth was dry. I needed water.

"Don't fuckin' lie to me. Just 'cause you my son don't mean I won't fuck yo' ass up."

Oh shit! He was Li'l Dre's father. What the fuck was going on, and what did Li'l Dre's father have to do with all this?

"I'm not lying, Pop-Frank."

"Frank Lester, you fat muthafucka. What I tell you about that weak-ass shit? That Pop, Daddy bullshit is for

208

sissies. Are you a sissy, huh, are you?"

He shook his head. "No, Pop." He sounded like he was about to cry. "Frank! I meant Frank."

I barely held back the scream that was threatening every nerve ending in my body as someone lifted my left wrist.

"What are these?" Frank asked.

"Burn marks from the tape," Li'l Dre replied.

"I should have dropped you on your head when you were born. I told you not to lie to me, boy."

"Frank, don't," he said in a high-pitched voice. "I didn't. G-Spot fucked her."

"Do it, Frank. Do it," I wanted to say, although I don't know what I wanted Frank to do, but whatever Li'l Dre thought his father was about to do, he sounded really scared.

"Just because you my own blood doesn't mean I won't bust a cap in yo' fat-ass. If I ever even hear your name mentioned in any conversation that has anything to do with an animal fucking a woman, I will kill you. Is that clear?"

Oh God, the dog. No. God, if you truly exist, please take me now, and watch over my babies.

"Yes sir, Frank. So what do we do now?" Li'l Dre asked.

"We wait."

I knew trying to pray to God was a waste of time. He'd just proven what I'd always suspected. There was no God. If there was, He would not have let me go through it all over again. I tried not to think about him, her, and my past, but I couldn't help it.

*****

I was, I think three or four when the woman who gave birth to me first told me that my father had abandoned us. She and I had our own room in a small ranch style home in Doraville, Georgia. Nine people shared one restroom. St. Mary's Church owned the house that we lived in with the two other Dominican families.

When I asked her why we had to live with other people, she told me that it was because my father had left us and she didn't make enough money to take care of us by herself. I asked why we didn't just go back to Santo Domingo and live with Grandma-maw and Grandpa-paw. She told me that conditions were much worse there than they were here in the States.

She met her husband at a singles function at church. He was some sort of big wheel at St. Mary's. I remember thinking that she could have done a lot better. He was much older. He was a man of medium height, sort of stocky, plain looking, and he was white. I was in the first grade when she married him and we moved into his two-story older home in Stone Mountain, Georgia. His house was like a church. There was a Bible on every table in the place. A picture of Jesus hung on a wall in every room. Even when I went to pee, Jesus stared at me, hanging from the cross on the bathroom wall.

From the moment I met her husband, I didn't like him. He was always telling me and her what to do and what not to do. I couldn't watch cartoons. I couldn't go outside and play with my friends. I was always at church. It was the same routine for the first two and a half years we lived there.

I was nine when she started working in a Christian bookstore. This was the first time I was ever left at home alone with him for any long periods of time. And this was when he started touching me. When I told her, she beat me for lying. Scared and feeling alone, I kept my mouth closed for the next four years.

I was thirteen and two months gone when I found out that I was pregnant. I was frightened out of my mind. I just knew she was going to kill me. I didn't know what to do. The only family that I knew of in the States was my father, and all I had was his name.

At first I thought that my father wouldn't help me, that he didn't care because he left us so long ago. But with nowhere to go and no one else to turn to, I spent the next two evenings at the church calling all of the Murphys in the white pages. No one who answered knew of a Straybor Murphy.

One Sunday when I walked out of the church with her husband and her, this man in a white suit and a brown fedora hat came up to us. We were right in front of the church. Her hand flew up to her mouth. The sharply dressed man ignored her, her husband and every one else talking and making their way to their cars. He knelt down in front of us and held out his arms and said, "Nea, I heard you've been looking for me."

I nodded. Tears welled up in my eyes.

"Well, sweetie, I've been looking for you."

I ran into his arms and cried. I didn't care that he'd left us to struggle. I didn't care that he'd missed twelve of my birthdays. Nothing mattered. He was here now, when I needed my dad the most.

I never went back to that man's house for clothes or anything. I told my dad that I was pregnant and how her husband had molested me for years and how she didn't lift a finger to do anything about it, but she lifted a belt to beat me when I came to her for help. I knew my story sounded crazy, her husband being so religious and active in the church, but Dad never doubted me. If it weren't for me begging him not to, Dad would have killed him. He already didn't like white people.

When I asked him why he'd abandoned us, he looked at me like I was speaking Chinese.

He couldn't believe she'd never told me the truth. He explained that he had been in prison for eleven years for driving the getaway car in a liquor store hold- up where someone was shot. He had only been out of prison for a few weeks before we found each other. It just so happened that I'd phoned his aunt's home and she got him the message that I'd called. If it wasn't for caller ID, he would not have known how to find me.

The courts made her husband take a DNA test, and after it was confirmed that he fathered the twins growing inside of me, he was charged and convicted of statutory rape.

The morning after the rapist was sentenced, my father had a massive heart attack and died.

Four months after Dad died, the twins' father left prison after serving his sentence. It was then that I wished I had let Dad kill him. I think seeing a white man get a slap on the wrist for raping a black child, his black child, and him being helpless to do anything about it, is what really killed him.

It was just fortunate for me that I got to know at least one good man in my lifetime. So now, the only supportive family the twins had is my paternal grandmother whom lives in Indiana. I just had to hope that she and my babies were all right.

CHAPTER 35

BABYGIRL

"Do you have a gun?" I asked.

"Doesn't every single woman that works in the nightclub industry?" Snow replied.

"I don't know every single woman in this business, do you?"

"I didn't mean it that way."

I pulled out my Glock from under the seat of my blue Beamer. "I call this my negotiator," I said as I held the nine-millimeter out to her.

"Nice. I guess you want me to go get mine."

"Uhhhhhhh yes, I think we may need it."

Snow opened the door and was halfway out of the car when my phone rang. The word UNKNOWN flashed across my caller ID. I waved for Snow to go on and get the artillery while I hit the button on my cell phone.

"Hello?"

"I believe I have your dog," the voice on the other end said.

"Sir, you must have the wrong—"

"Save yourself, Babygirl. I'm already dead. Fr—" Madness shouted in the background.

"So, you want to play games now, huh, bitch?" I heard a muffled male voice say.

A loud popping sound was followed by a desperate scream. I swear, I wanted to climb through the phone and kill the muthafucka responsible for Madness's suffering.

"I'm sorry about that. You know how these bitches in heat get right after another dog mates with them."

What the fuck did he mean? Another dog? I know he

213

wasn't saying—I had to squeeze my eyes shut to stop the tears of hate from riding down my face.

"No, I don't know, but I do know this: Whatever you do to my girl, I will do to you ten times. And if you kill her, I will hunt you down like the beast you are, kill you slowly and painfully, and bring you back to life nine more times to keep killing you."

Laughter exploded in my ear. "What movie did you get that from? It sounded real good. If I was three years old, I might get scared. But if you want to see her before I start drawing a picture on her back with a lit cigar, you'll do as I say."

Shhhh, I made the sign with my finger to my lips as Snow returned to open the car door.

"Keep talking," I said into my cell phone.

"It's 12:43 now. Be at Geraldine's Fish and Grits inside the Kroger Plaza on Memorial and North Hairston at 1:30. Oh yeah, and I don't have to tell you what will happen to your dog if I even think you're being followed."

"Fuuuuck!"

"Who was that?" Snow asked after I clicked off the phone.

I banged my hand on the wood-grained steering wheel. "Shit," I cursed while looking at my cell phone.

"Was that André?"

I shook my head and shrugged my shoulders. "I don't know." I put the key in the ignition and turned.

"Whoever it was, we have to meet him in forty-five minutes."

"Say hello to my little friends," Snow said in a sad excuse for a Scarface imitation as she pulled two miniature cannons out of a black leather duffle bag.

"This isn't the time to make jokes, Snow. Because of us, Madness is in deep trouble."

"Sorry."

"Never mind," I said before asking, "Are those the

214

biggest guns you could find?"

"Yes, and the most powerful of their kind in the world." She paused to admire her choice of weaponry.

"These are single action, gas operated Desert Eagle Mark XXVI .44 magnums. They hold nine in the clip and one in the chamber."

"And you need all that fire power for what, now?" She held one finger up before replying, "Hold on, you haven't seen the third one."

She pulled a sawed off shotgun out of her bag. It was about the length of my forearm.

"I call this one Mr. Lester."

I wasn't about to ask her why she named her gun.

"It's a modified SKB 486, twelve-gauge double barrel."

After she put the guns back in the bag, I slid the *God's Son* disc by Nas in the CD chamber and drove off.

I could blame Snow if I wanted, but it was no one's fault but mine. I recruited Madness. She trusted me. I convinced her to quit dancing. I promised to take care of her. I got her involved in this mess with Li'l Dre. Now I had to woman up and get her out of it.

I wasn't sure of anything except for saving Madness. Her girls needed her. I couldn't bear to even think about them growing up without their mother.

There was no doubt in my mind that someone was going to die today. I didn't want it to be me, but if that's what it took to save Madness, then that's what it would be. I probably should have been scared. There was no telling how many thugs carrying guns they had. I wished I had Googled Frank Lester, André, and Snow. I Googled everyone. I couldn't believe I didn't do a background check on them. Too much of what Snow said didn't add up.

As we got off of the freeway exit, I looked out my rearview mirror. The black Suburban was maybe three cars behind us. I first noticed it when I got on the freeway twenty minutes ago. Maybe I was being paranoid. And then again, maybe I wasn't.

I couldn't help but think of how ill-prepared and unorganized I was. I always planned. I never went off half-baked, and now I was running around like a hungry fat man in a desert chasing a pork chop.

I looked in my rearview mirror before getting out of the car. There was no sign of the black Suburban.

"Come on, Snow. Let's do this," I said, putting my nine in my pants pocket and carrying my purse to conceal the nine's handle.

I wished I had asked Snow for a big T-shirt like the one she had on. She put her cannons in the front pockets of her Levi's. Her too-big, black-and-white Marvin Gaye T-shirt hid the guns and her behind well.

"Snow, hold up," I said before she walked into Geraldine's Fish and Grits.

I fumbled through my purse for my ringing phone.

"Hello."

"Naughty, naughty. You brought a friend."

"She's cool."

"Lucky for you and your dog, I know who your friend is. It should take you thirty minutes to get to the Firestone tire store on the Cheshire Bridge Road side of Lenox Mall."

"Lenox Mall? What kind of game—" The phone clicked off. I put my hands behind my head and yelled,

"Shit! Shit! Shit!"

"Was that the someone we were supposed to meet?" Snow asked.

"Supposed to meet is right. He hung up on me before I had a chance to say anything."

"What did he say?"

"Get in the car. I'll tell you while I drive."

I know I should have been nervous or scared, but I wasn't. I didn't care about anything but saving

Madness.

We made it to the Firestone just on time. We waited ten minutes before my phone rang.

"I'm tired of these damn games!" I screamed into the phone.

"What games?"

"Uncle Bazz? Is that you? Is it really you?"

"Babygirl—"

My phone beeped.

"Hold on. I'll be right back, Uncle Bazz."

"Hello."

"Good, no cops. Celestron, FirstScope telescope, huh? Serial numbers have been sanded off. Must be stolen. Naughty, naughty," the voice said on the other end.

"He's in my apartment," I mouthed to Snow.

"You know where I'm at. If you want to see your dog alive, you'll be here in five minutes."

"She's not a fucking dog. She is a black woman," I yelled.

"Tell me you have a plan, Babygirl," Snow said.

"The plan is to save the life of a friend. One who shouldn't be caught up in yours and my bullshit."

"What can I say? I'm sorry. I agree with you. What else do you want to hear?"

"Shit." I almost got rear ended as I slammed on the brakes in the middle of the flowing traffic.

"What's wrong?"

I grabbed my phone. "Uncle Bazz, you still there? Shit, shit, shit, shit," I said when no one answered.

"Who is Uncle Bazz?"

I ignored her as I scrolled through my received calls. "Private number. Damn." I said out loud.

A few minutes later, we were outside my apartment with our guns drawn. My front door was wide open as we timidly approached.

"Ladies, come in," a man said as he stepped out into the hallway in front of my damn door. "Are those guns really necessary? Come on, I'm a lover not a fighter. Drop the guns, I'm unarmed."

"Where is Madness?" I asked with the barrel of my nine kiss-close to his nose.

For a man about to die, he was extremely calm and in control. "Oh, your dog, right?" He nodded. "She's in a house not far from here.

"You heard him. Mr. Lester said drop the fucking guns," a deep female voice behind us said as she held what felt like a gun to the back of my head and probably Snow's head as well.

Snow and I slowly bent down and laid our weapons on the carpet. Frank patted us down, picked up the guns, and took them into my kitchen where he put them on top of the refrigerator.

He started walking back into the den. "I am Frank Lester. Unfortunately for you, Babygirl, I am André Lester's father. You wanted to know why I'm in your apartment. Well, I came to your home to show you—" Frank was in my face now. His pig-pug nose was touching mine. I stood my ground, my eyes locked onto his. "—that this," he made a sweeping arc with his arm, "your apartment, your everything is now mine, bitch. This is my world, and I just let you live in it."

Frank looked over at Snow. "You didn't tell her, Julieliscious."

"Tell me what?"

"That you my bitch now. And until further notice, your mouth," he pointed down, "and that pussy will be my toilets, just like Julieliscous here, was for so long until I dismissed her."

I shook my head. "No, that was her sister. She's Jennifer, Jennie Mae."

He waved a hand full of jewelry in the air. "A nose job, a face lift, different color hair, and a boob job can't hide the fear that only I can put in a bitch."

He stepped over to her, pulled up her shirt, and

forced her to turn around. "See those scars. The plastic surgeons did a good job, but if you look close, you can still see remnants of my art work. I'm the cigarette burn Van Gogh. Her back became my connect-the-dot burn mark canvas every time she tried to leave me or just did some dumb shit I didn't like."

I noticed the skin discolorations when we danced together at the Parrot, but I never thought to ask Snow about them. And now she was trembling so bad, I thought she was about to have a seizure.

He walked back over to me. "I'll fire a ho in a New York minute," he waved his index finger like a pendulum, "but nary a bitch ever, eeeeeeeever leaves Frank Lester." He turned to Snow. "Tell her, Julie."

"No one ever leaves Frank unless he wants them to," she said in a monotone voice.

CHAPTER 36

FRANK LESTER

I'm getting too old for this gangsta shit. I'm fifty-one. I been pushin' weed, coke, and H for thirty years. I done turned out more bitches than light switches. I done had more hoes than clothes, and all I got to show for all my pimpdom is a fat-ass son who is so busy sniffin' behind pussy that he can't see a set-up when it's looking him square in the face. I think I've always known that a bitch would be his downfall.

Out of all the hoes I done had, I can't name one who ever got me off my square, except maybe his momma. Even when I wasn't in control, I put across the perception that I was. The key to ho control is fear, F-E-A-R. I instilled the fear of me in the core of a bitch's very being. If it ever came down to it, my bitches would choose me over God.

A ho get out of line with me, I had no problem knocking the ape shit out of her. I'm not saying make it a habit to beat a bitch, but you have to rule your pimpdom with an iron fist to stay ahead of the game. A bitch is only loyal until you stop feeding her fear.

Don't get it twisted, now. I'm an entrepreneur, not a low-level pimp or a street-level drug dealer. I should own a haberdashery for all the hats I wore. I'm a college recruiter, street professor, business owner, and pharmacist. I took young, dumb, full of cum bitches off the streets and out of the fucked-up-ass school system and gave them an identity. Most of them were on the chubby side or plain Jane, low self-esteem, poor hustlin' bitches until I gave them a scholarship to Sidewalk University. It took sometimes years of training before they earned their degrees from SWU. Once I took a bitch in, she was in until I put her the hell out.

I had some of my seasoned bitches teach the young ones how to walk, how to carry themselves in all situations, and how to talk the Queen's English. I couldn't stand a ghetto-ass talking bitch. Slang was meant for men to shoot the shit with other men, not for the pleasure of ho jibber-jabber.

I ain't gon' lie, I took my students on a trip through hell. I did some disgusting and cruel shit to harden their hearts and to create a level of fear like none they'd ever imagined. If the fear of a God no one has ever seen could make Muslims run into a crowd of people with live bombs strapped on their backs, imagine what the fear of Frank Lester could make a bitch do. And if the President can trick a nation of muthafuckas into thinkin' he's sending their sons to war to fight for democracy and freedom overseas, and they dumb asses ain't got neither of the two at home, imagine what a nigga like me can do to the minds of the few, the proud, and the weak-minded bitches of my choosing. Going to prison was a Caribbean Island vacation compared to what I'd do to a ho who brought my name up while she was in custody.

As always, there's that one bitch who'll try a nigga. That's when you have to step up to the plate and make sure you have your strongest bitches witness what you do, so they can quietly tell the others. You ain't never heard a bitch scream until you burn a hoes pussy shut with bubbling hot tar. After you pour water on the bitch to wake her up from fainting, imagine the pain a bitch goes through after dipping a soup ladle in hot tar and painting a bitch to death. This all happens quick enough for you to pour chicken feathers over the bitch for being a coward and not accepting her fate like a true bitch in the St. Louis Black Mafia. I had more than a few bitches doin' hard time for everything from trafficking to murder. That's why I put so much time in schooling a bitch. By the time I was ready to graduate a bitch to the St. Louis Black Mafia, she had her own whip, a cell phone, and her personal clientele. The only hard leg I had working for me was my son, André. Other than being led around by his dick, he was a good businessman like me. Instead of recruiting young bitches from strip clubs, he was fuckin' 'em. Wasn't nothing wrong with long-dickin' a fine bitch, but if she wasn't bringin' in no paper for you or helping you come up, then there's a problem. I didn't raise him to be no trick.

He knew how I felt about niggas being on the team. A nigga is gon' get jealous and try you more than once. You can't whoop a nigga's ass like you could a bitch. A nigga is like a Pit Bull. You never know when they'll turn on you. But a bitch, if you train her right, she'll die for a muthafucka. A bitch is made to be ruled. That's some natural shit.

And André's hardheaded ass knew what I said was the gospel. As far as I knew, he had a crew of young boys moving product.

I did all I could do. He was a grown-ass man. If he was man enough to do shit his own way, then he should've been man enough to not need Daddy to clean his shit up. I thought sending his ass to Atlanta to set up shop five years ago would prepare him to take over this shit when I retired.

"Daddy, you all right in there?" Jordan, the fat bitch I had standing guard in the front room over that Babygirl bitch and Julieliscous, asked.

"Yeah, baby, I'm coming out now. I feel five pounds lighter," I said before flushing the pink-handled toilet.

That's another thing I loved; when my bitches called me Daddy. Used to make my dick hard. I never let André call me Daddy. That was some bitch shit, and I raised a man.

After I got the call telling me some shit was about to

go down, I brought two of my top-bottom bitches from St. Louis on the plane with me, just in case some gangsta shit like what just almost happened jumped off.

That Babygirl bitch frightened me so bad I almost shitted on myself. I saw straight up death in her eyes when she had the nine to my nose a little while ago. That was one feisty bitch that I couldn't wait to break my dick off in.

After walking back into Babygirl's front room, I began to explain to the bitches, "Bitches, I can have Jordan here put a bullet in your head, or you can let her escort you to the limo that should be outside now." I pulled out my phone and tried to call to make sure the limo was indeed waiting.

"Raggedy-ass Sprint phone. I can't get no damn service." I was about to make one of the bitches give me their phones when I decided to lay down some ground rules.

"Don't try any funny stuff. I'll be right behind you bitches. And you don't want to play with your dog's life, now, do you?"

Both them bitches just stood like statues in the middle of the front room. Jordan's ugly big ass was smiling at they backs, sitting on a bar, holding a .45 in her lap. What the fuck was wrong with these bitches? I know they heard me. Bitches were gon' make me show my pimp hand.

I walked over to the bitches and threw a Mike Tyson upper cut to Julieliscous's stomach. She slumped to the floor, holding her stomach.

"Bitch, I asked a question. I expect a muthafuckin' answer."

"You think hitting on women makes you a big man?" The Babygirl bitch had more nerve than a toothache, questioning me.

I looked at the bitch like she was speaking a foreign language. I took a step back, unzipped my purple slacks and took out my dick. "No, this makes me a big man." I looked down to the floor as I put my shit back in my pants. "Julie, you better tell this bitch about me."

She was busy on the carpet, trying to breathe. I guess I knocked the wind out the bitch.

"How the fuck did you end up in Atlanta as a dancer?"

"I don't," she strained to catch her breath, "have to answer to you anymore. I'm not scared of you, Frank Lester. All you can do is kill me, and if I can't have you or kill you, I want to die."

I wasn't even gon' entertain what I thought that bitch was insinuating. "Oh, I wondered what happened to you after you killed your mother and your sister."

"They wouldn't forgive me for Daddy's death. I couldn't live with that."

"Can you blame them? Shit I wouldn't have forgiven yo' crackhead ass either. Hell, you killed your own damn daddy."

"They didn't know that."

"First you gave a statement to the cops that I killed him, and once we got to court, you testified to him shooting himself while he and I fought for the gun."

"You made me kill him."

"I didn't make you do shit."

"But you were struggling with him and you said—"

"I know what the fuck I said, but that don't mean you had to do it. Hell, you could have shot me."

"I would have if I knew that you were going to put me out after the trial."

Did this funky ass bitch say she would have shot me? No, she wouldn't have even thought about choosing her pale-ass daddy over me.

"Why, Frank, why?"

"What the fuck else was I supposed to do with a junkie bitch who killed her own damn daddy for anotha' nigga? You's a dirty-dog-ass bitch. I ain't had no more use for you after that."

"But I loved you, and I still love you. Please, Frank," she pleaded while crawling on her knees to me.

I stepped back. "Please what?"

"You said that I was yours for life. You told me you'd stand by me. You promised to put me up in a nice apartment overlooking downtown St. Louis."

"Bitch, that was game. I had to play you like that. I couldn't tell you the truth, now, could I? You would've cracked under pressure and let them crackas convict me for some shit you did."

"But you did kill my father."

"Tell that shit to somebody who don't know no better."

"I mean you made me do it."

"I ain't made you pull no trigger."

"You told me to. You said if I loved you—"

I cut her off. "Did I make you kill your mother and sister?"

"I was never charged."

"But you killed them."

"No, Frank, you killed them."

This bitch was all the way gone. I must've fucked her head up pretty bad. This bitch talked like she really believed the shit coming out of her mouth.

"Me?" I pointed to my chest.

"Yes, you. You were in my head. You made me wake up in the middle of the night after they were sound asleep."

This bitch was just as calm.

"You led me down the stairs and into the kitchen, over to the stove. Turn all the ranges and the oven on high, you said. Blow out every pilot light, you said. Remove the two long candles and their brass holders from the kitchen table, and place them on the window of the oven's opened door, you said. Take the book of matches from the kitchen drawer, light the candles and go back to bed, you said."

This bitch should have been in one of those brains- on-drugs commercials.

"I knew you would come back for me. I felt so proud watching you fighting the flames to save me. I held my arms out to you when you lifted me from the bed, remember? You looked so handsome in your black hat and fireman's uniform. I felt like you were carrying me over the threshold like we were newlyweds when you brought me out of the house in your strong arms."

"You look gooder than a muthafucka, but you one shot-out-ass, crazy murdering bitch. Them doctors at that crazy hospital released you a lifetime too early."

"I bet you didn't know who you was teaming up with," I said to the pretty black Babygirl bitch.

"Frank, I'm not fat and ugly anymore. Look, I would have never killed you. I just wanted you to love me," she said.

I dove to the ground. "Jordan, she got a gun," I screamed right before the shot rang out.

CHAPTER 37

BABYGIRL

Snow was more than a little touched. She was all the way gone. I was in awe as I learned the details of her past. Listening to her and Frank was like watching a high definition Lifetime movie in slow motion. The sound of her pleading, childlike voice made me wanna get down on my knees and pull her into my arms. On the other hand, his condescending, arrogant tone made me want to lash out and stick my long fingernails through his dark chest, yank out his black heart, and stomp it into oblivion.

Where she concealed the palm-sized pistol or how she pulled it out without Frank noticing was a mystery to me.

She could've easily shot Frank, but instead, she put the gun in her mouth and blew her brains over me, part of the den, and the foyer. That was the moment I realized that there were fates much worse than death.

In Snow's case, loving her tormentor was her living nightmare. Just like Two Can San used to say, Satan is definitely among us. Who else but Satan could trick a person into following him off the cliff of sanity? I had no doubt that Frank Lester was the living, breathing, embodiment of evil.

After looking down at my blood-and-brain spattered pants, I looked up into the eyes of death. I didn't flinch or waver from Frank Lester's stare.

A few seconds later, he looked away, bent down and grabbed his ankle. "Got damn crazy bitch almost made me sprain my damn ankle," he said. Although I had my back to her, I figured he was looking over at the bald-headed, fat Jermaine Dupree-looking sistah who held a gun to our heads earlier.

"Jordan, cover the bitch a second. I'm gon' look out in the hall to make sure the ho ain't got any nosy neighbors.

Seconds later, he came back in. "Jordan, bring the ho."

He stopped and pointed a finger in my face. "Bitch, if you think I won't bust a cap in that fat-ass . . ." He slapped my butt.

I flinched. I had to close my eyes and count to five to stop myself from going instant muthafucka on him.

"You just try a nigga," he explained.

If he thought all women were bitches and hoes, what did he think of his own mother? All type of thoughts ran through my mind as the big-tittied, bald- headed Jermaine Dupree escorted me down the elevator and out of the building, with Frank following behind.

"Jordan, sit her behind him." Frank pointed at the driver. "You sit across from her and I'll sit here in the back."

"We ready, boss?" The driver spoke from behind the glass in the front seat after we were all in the black stretch Hummer limo.

"Pop the clutch, dog. Let's ride," Frank said.

He thought he was so hip with his jazzy language. I knew I should have been terrified, but I wasn't. Quite the contrary, I was very calm. I used to wonder how I'd react if and when I faced death. Now I knew.

For a man who boasted such an endless supply of women, he was sure trying to stare a hole in my shirt. The eye-lock he had on my breasts didn't even faze me.

"Boss, I'm sorry to hear about Treon."

"Shit happens." Frank shrugged. "Goes with the territory. She shouldn't have been sleeping on the couch when she was supposed to be watching out for Stevie."

Oh shit! Snow killed the wrong one, I thought, as I mouthed the word "fuck."

"Do you want to hear some music, boss?"

"You got that new Fi'ty?"

"Are you talking about "I Got The Magic Stick"?"

"Nah, Fi'ty Cent's new joint, with that cut "Candyshop" on it."

"Yes, you are referring to the *Massacre* album. You from St. Louis, I would have figured you for a Nelly fan, boss."

"Don't get it twisted. Nelly my muthafuckin' nigga. But that nigga Fi'ty get me so hyped up, I just wanna King Kong fuck a bitch or off a bitch. Either way, I get my nut off listenin' to that kill-a-nigga-stomp-a-bitch gangsta shit."

A fifty-year-old rap groupie. I could see him at a 50 Cent rap concert looking like Mr. Big, waving a cane, talking about "I got the magic stick."

By the way the driver called Frank "boss", it seemed like they were well acquainted, like maybe he drove for Frank on the regular. I couldn't see how that was possible with Frank living in St. Louis.

My head was hurting from the pounding bass of the music that was piped into the back of the car. Frank was bouncing and mouthing along to the lyrics. Jordan was bopping her bald-head up and down.

"I'll take you to the big dick shop. I'll fuck you with all I got," Frank sang off key as he made up his own lyrics to the song "Candyshop."

I don't know, I lost track of time, but I would say we'd been driving no more than forty, forty-five minutes before the car stopped. The driver got out and opened a long gate made of redwood and barbed wire. As he turned to come back to the car, I saw his face. I couldn't place it, but I knew him from somewhere.

We rode down the long dirt and rocky driveway. To the left was a heavily wooded area and to the right was a large, red stable surrounded by several horses grazing in an expansive open pasture. We pulled up to the front of a large, older red-brick ranch home with an attached three car garage that looked like it was recently added onto the house.

"Open the door. It's me!" Frank shouted.

Li'l Dre's gold-toothed smile greeted us at the door.

"You caught her?"

"I ain't you. Have you ever known a bitch to get away from me, boy?"

"I did," I heard a familiar female voice say.

We were in a large room with pine-wooded walls, a log cabin like ceiling and dark hardwood floors. Frankenstein must have been the owner's interior designer. Oh, and as I walked into this walled forest, the marble black eyes from a mounted deer stared at me from above the cobblestone fireplace.

Stevie turned around. She looked over to Li'l Dre.

"Maybe you need to go get G-Spot and stop up her mouth with his dick."

He nodded. "Yeah, good idea."

"Stupid ass, you know she just fuckin' with you. Besides, my dick is gon' be the first one in that pretty foul mouth," Frank said, smiling at me as he massaged his crotch.

I threw a smile right back at him. I couldn't wait. He could put that old, worm-shooting thing in my mouth if he wanted. I'd break my jaw and bust every tooth in my mouth trying to bite it off.

"Where's the other tramp?" Stevie asked.

"That crazy bitch shot herself in the mouth back at Babygirl bitch's place," Frank said, pointing to me.

"That might work out best for us," she said while rubbing the stubble on her chin. Stevie continued, "We can make Babygirl's death look like a suicide. How's this sound?" She paused and put her hands in the air.

"Jealous black female stripper goes into murderous rage, killing white lover and best friend after catching them in bed together."

"Yeah, that's some good shit," Li'l Dre said.

Stevie walked over to me. "Oh, you thought I was dead, didn't you? So sorry to disappoint you. Next time send a professional." She held up a finger and shook her head before walking around me. "Oh, but that's right. There won't be a next time. The trashy tramp you sent should have lifted the sheet. But that's after the fact, huh?" She stopped and shook her head.

"Poor, poor Treon."

"Yeah, she was one of my prize bitches, top notch like a muthafucka," Frank interrupted.

Stevie sighed. "Frank and Jordan had just dropped her off at my place while I was at work. He insisted on Treon staying at my place to watch out for me. Looks like someone should have been watching out for her."

"Got damn, put some emotion in your voice, baby, and stop being sarcastic. The bitch took a bullet for you."

"Shut up, Frank," Stevie said before turning back to me. "Anyway, when I got home from the club, Treon was asleep on the couch. I was asleep in my bedroom when the sound of gunshots woke me up. I rolled out to the blind side of the bed and I grabbed my gun off the top of the nightstand. After a few minutes, I slowly rose from behind the bed and looked out the window. That's when I saw Snow pitch something in my front yard."

"Your dumb-ass son's gun," Frank said.

"Son?" I slipped and said.

"Yes, son. For someone who thinks you're so smart, you are really stupid. How can you defeat an enemy you don't even know? See, André Lester is my son," Stevie said.

*****

"I was fifteen when I met Frank. I was on my way to

catch the bus downtown when he pulled up to me in this shiny white Cadillac Seville dressed out in gold. He ran this spiel about how I had the look and how he'd make me the next Brooke Shields. I smelled his bullshit before it even left his mouth, but I just smiled and oohed and wowed. I let him think that he convinced me to get into his car. He took me to some little studio apartment outfitted with fancy looking camera equipment and lights. He told me it was where he took preliminary photos of his models," she said.

"That was my fuck house," Frank interrupted.

"Yeah, Frank, but it was you who got fucked when we first met."

He laughed.

"I was in the bedroom when he went out to put on some music. Before he asked or forced me to, I took off my clothes in the bathroom.

"His old ass tried to play it cool. He came in the bedroom after putting on some Marvin Gaye, but I could see the bulge in his pants once he saw my naked ass standing next to his waterbed with my hands on my hips. He was undressing when I ran a finger up his arm. I still remember telling him I had to go to the little girl's room. A minute later, I walked back in the room and aimed my .25 at his dick," she said.

"That was over twenty years ago, and I still can't believe you had the balls to rob me," Frank interrupted.

"Yeah, but I gave everything back the next day."

"'Cause you found out who the fuck I was."

"Yeah, yeah, yeah, to make a long story short, Frank and I hooked up. Everything was great. I'm probably the only woman he didn't beat up on."

"'Cause you did what the fuck I told you to," he said.

"I had my period the whole time. That's why I didn't know until my fifth month that I was pregnant. After I had the baby, Frank sent me to night school. While I

232

was away, he had one of his other women take care of André."

"Correction." He put a finger in the air. "One of my bitches took care of the little nigga, not one of my women. You was my only woman. The others were my bitches, and that's all I've ever had."

"Okay, Frank. Anyway after I graduated, we decided that I'd apply to the St. Louis Police Academy and Frank would use his connections to get me in. This way I could watch the cops that were already on his payroll, and I could be his personal eyes and ears on the inside.

"Because of what he did, we couldn't be seen together. I had my place, he had his. I had more drug busts my first two years than any one blue suit or detective had in five. I made sure no one ever found out it was Frank supplying me with all the information that led to almost every bust I made those first two years. As a result of our teamwork, I made detective, and Frank and our mostly female Black Mafia family took over the dope game in St. Louis. Frank became the biggest coke dealer from East St. Louis to New Orleans.

"The streets were getting hot. Rumors of me having close ties with known drug dealers started running rampant in the St. Louis P.D. Frank and I decided that it would be best for me to charter new territory. We needed to expand our business to blacker and bigger cities, so we chose Atlanta. In 1986, I was granted a transfer.

"I was in Atlanta for three years when things got heated in the precinct. If I knew the dope boy I was shaking down was the nephew of the president of the Atlanta City Council, I would've never started taking his money. I'd been collecting money from local drug dealers for two years without a problem when this kid threatens to go to his uncle. So, I had no choice but to put two in his skull. I wish I would have known he'd already went blabbing his big mouth to his uncle. To avoid a lengthy investigation, I quietly retired and Frank and I opened up the Parrot.

"When I had everything in place and Frank felt that André was ready, we moved him to Atlanta to open up shop. For the most part, everything was pretty much set up when he got here. I had an ample supply of coke, and I had a small team of loyal young men that were waiting for guidance and product to distribute.

"So now you know the family story. Too bad you won't live to tell it."

Maybe I wouldn't, but I was going to make sure the head of this Addams family would never be able to bring any more little monsters in this world.

Frank and Li'l Dre were sitting back, lounging on the sofa when Stevie addressed them. "Boys, I'm about to go in the back room with that Madness tramp. You two have your fun with the little princess." She pointed to me. "Oh, and save some of her for me. I need to teach her a lesson or two, or three."

"As long as I can watch, I ain't got no problem with that," Frank said.

She looked into my eyes, licked her chapped lips and smiled. "I haven't forgotten the night you tried to amputate my breasts with a razor. You definitely gave me something to remember you by." She walked up to me, cuffed her hands around my ear and whispered,

"Before we burn that brown skin off that tight little body of yours, I am going to do something very special to it."

She took her hands from my ear and faced me, closed her eyes and shook her head. "And oh, I'm going to make you hurt so fucking good." She snaked her tongue out and laughed before turning her back and walking out of the room.

I'd be dead way before then, I thought. I was ready to

get on my knees and see how strong my teeth were when the front door swung open.

"Boss," he shouted.

I remembered where I knew the limo driver from. The Parrot. Rico, I think his name was. He was one of the white boys who kicked my ass that night.

"What the fuck?" Frank exploded while zipping his pants back up. He walked toward the door with Li'l Dre at his side.

"There's a car coming down the driveway."

"How many guns you got out here, baby?" Frank asked Stevie as she walked back in the room.

"Six, if you count Jordan."

Frank looked back over to Rico. "Get on that thing and tell everyone to remain at their posts until further notice."

"Everyone, this is One. Black Suburban coming down driveway. Stay at your post. I repeat, stay at your post until further notice. Over."

CHAPTER 38

SHABAZZ

I wanted to gun the big mu'fucka right through the front door, but I didn't. We pulled up to the house in the urban Suburban. I got out, armed with my stomp- a-mu'fucka black steel-toe war boots on and I carried a blonde-wood nigga-be-cool stick. That's what I called the miniature Louisville slugger bat that hung by my side.

The same woman who gave me the nod in the courtroom a couple weeks ago; the same woman who got to the assistant district attorney so I could be here now, was wearing a black God's Army T-shirt, some jeans and a pair of steel-toe boots. A briefcase was attached to one of her leather, black-gloved hands. She was right behind me as I walked the few steps to the front door, where a linebacker-sized Flintstone; a muscled, man-looking pink toe; a black-ass, purple suit-wearin' Rick James; and a baby-faced, biggie- sized, Biggie Smalls stood.

"Which one of y'all the bitch-ass nigga that call hisself Frank faggot-pussy-ass Lester? That's all I wanna know," I said as we closed the distance between us and the front door.

This big, crayon-black raisin stepped up. Call the fashion police. The raisin was a walking noise violation. His old black ass had on a screaming purple pinstripe suit with some blinding, shiny gold-tasseled purple gators on his feet. To wear some shit like that, he had to be from the deep country South. I mean Argentina, South America deep.

"Who the fuck wants to know?" The jumbo raisin replied.

"His personal black Freddie Kruger. Why, you that

236

mu'fucka'?" I asked.

The big white one took a step toward me.

"Rico." The black raisin held up his hand and shook his head.

"Don't stop 'im. Let him come get some. I'll Barry Bonds his Richard Simmons on steroids-lookin' ass," I said while standing in a batter's stance and holding my nigga-be-cool stick ready to swing.

"I'm Frank Lester. Now state your business."

"Babygirl is my business," I looked him up and down, "nigga."

"Who?" Frank asked.

"Don't play games with me. Tricks are for kids, and I ain't the rabbit, mu'fucka." I marched right up to the door and pushed my way past them. She held her head high and followed right behind me with that briefcase in her hand.

CHAPTER 39

BABYGIRL

"Uncle Bazz!"

"In living color, Babygirl."

"Hold it right there," Stevie said, pointing a gun at Uncle Bazz. Li'l Dre had his gun at his side, while Rico and Frank had their guns drawn on some lady who walked in with Uncle Bazz.

"The only reason you two aren't dead is because we don't know who you are, where you came from, why you're here, and who sent you," Stevie said.

I blinked several times as I stared at this lady. It was difficult for me to pay attention to what Stevie was saying. I couldn't believe my eyes. I put my hands over my mouth and tears escaped from my eyes.

Wow, she was beautiful. She looked almost exactly like Momma. Her dreads were the same color as her smooth, Ethiopian burnt-bronzed skin.

Uncle Bazz held his hands in the air, but she didn't. There didn't seem to be a scared bone in her body. She even walked with dignity and class. Her dark eyes were focused on me as she started walking in my direction.

"Bitch, did you not hear a muthafucka say freeze?" Frank shouted.

She stopped and turned his way. "Excuse me?"

"What, is you deaf, bitch?"

"If you see a bitch, I would suggest you beat a bitch." She took a step toward him. "Because she is obviously unruly and disobedient."

She took another step and smiled. "Surely, sir, you wouldn't be referring to me as an animal. I don't see

238

anyone in here old enough to be your mother. Maybe you were addressing the white cave woman beside you."

"I got your cave woman, tramp." Stevie came at her and threw a punch that the lady caught with the palm of her hand. She did something to Stevie's hand that brought her to her knees.

"Ahhhhh!" Stevie screamed.

"You got one second to let my mother go," Li'l Dre said with his gun drawn and aimed in the lady's direction.

After the woman released the grip, Stevie held her hand in close as she got up off the floor and walked back over to Frank.

"Ah, the offspring of Satan speaks," the lady said.

"Who the fuck are you?" Frank asked.

She held out her hand. "Relax. I just want to hand you this briefcase," she said as she came forward and set it down in front of Frank.

"What's this?"

"Open it," the lady said.

"Rico?"

"Yeah, boss."

Frank waved his gun toward the briefcase. "Well, open it up."

What was Uncle Bazz smiling for? He was the one with his hands in the air. I couldn't believe he was out. But of course, he'd found me when I needed him most. I swore if I got out of this, I would start going to somebody's church.

"What the fuck is all that?" Frank pointed to the briefcase. "Bitch?"

"Sir, with all due respect, I suggest you refrain from calling me anything other than Queen or Rhythm."

"Bitch, you ain't in no position to suggest a muthafuckin' thing but a dick up yo' ass maybe."

She took a step forward. "I already planned how you were to die today, but since you refuse to capitulate and show me the respect I demand, command, and deserve, I'll torture you until you not only apologize, but bow down and recognize the black woman as the queen that she is, little man."

"Torture who? Make me do what? Little what, and black what?" Frank walked up to the lady, looked her up and down with his gun still pointed at her chest. "I don't know who you are or where you came from, and frankly I don't give a flying fuck." He held his gun out toward Rico, who was standing by the front door with his gun aimed at Uncle Bazz. "But I do know where you goin', bitch."

Rico took Frank's gun and stepped backwards until he was by the door. Li'l Dre had his back to a window closer to me. Stevie stood a few steps behind Frank, and Uncle Bazz stood between Li'l Dre and Rico. It didn't look good. Everybody had guns but us.

"You goin' to hell, and I'm gon' be the muthafucka that sends yo' black ass there," Frank said to the woman who'd identified herself as Rhythm. He unzipped his pants.

It looked like she was smiling.

"That's after I break my dick off in you right here, right muthafuckin' now, funky-ass bitch, and we'll see who's a little man."

As Frank reached to grab Rhythm, she knee'd him in the balls. He started to double over when she ducked under him, and while she was spinning in back of him, a small knife miraculously appeared in her hand. Before he could retaliate, the knife struck Rico in the neck. Uncle Bazz dove and came up with the gun that Rico dropped to the floor.

I dropped to the carpet when I heard the shots.

"Noooo." I heard Li'l Dre's voice.

"You will respect me, little man. You will address me as Rhythm or Queen. Nod if you understand."

I looked up just in time to see Frank nod his head. In

spite of everything going on, I couldn't help but smile.

"You shot my mother. I'm o' kill yo' bitch ass," Li'l Dre said as he went toward Uncle Bazz.

"Take one more step, fat boy, and I'll snap your father's neck like a toothpick."

Who was this black Superwoman? She had Frank in some type of chokehold. Other than nodding his head and fighting to breathe, Frank didn't move. She had him paralyzed.

"André?" I heard Stevie's voice. He turned his head.

"Do as the tramp says."

Li'l Dre turned back toward Rhythm. "But Ma, I got a full clip and she ain't got shit."

"She has your father."

"I can shoot the bitch before she can kill him."

"I said no."

Without turning his head, his eyes and his gun still locked onto Rhythm, he asked, "What about you? Are you all right?"

"Hell no, I'm not fucking all right," Stevie said, holding a blood-soaked hand to her left shoulder while she spoke.

"The asshole-fucker on the ground next to Rico," she pointed at Uncle Bazz, "shot me. My collarbone hurts like hell, but I'll live."

"King, how you doing over there?" Rhythm asked.

"Better than him," Uncle Bazz responded, turning his head in Rico's direction.

Rico was in a sitting position against the wall beside the door. His unblinking eyes were staring at the ceiling and blood poured from where the knife's stainless steel handle was lodged.

I turned my neck. "Uncle Bazz, you're bleeding."

"Just a surface wound. I-I'm good, Babygirl.

I shook my head. "You don't sound good." I took a step forward before the air exploded in a chain of quick bursts.

I dove onto the floor again. Oh God, someone had an

automatic something.

"Let him go."

I was kissing the carpet so I couldn't see her face, but I knew who it was.

Rhythm released the hold she had on Frank. He fell to the ground, coughing. It took him a minute, but he was finally able to crawl over to Stevie and Li'l Dre.

"Kill the bitch. Kill both bitches, Jordan," Frank said while Li'l Dre helped him to his feet.

"Both of you, go stand next to him," Jordan commanded.

Rhythm was unreal. We were about to die or worse and she wasn't the least bit nervous. She was just as calm. She waved for me to come to her as she casually walked over to Uncle Bazz.

"Come on, Queen. She has too many bullets in that thing and they come out too fast for us not to respect her wishes," Rhythm said to me.

"Uncle Bazz?"

He didn't respond.

"Uncle Bazz!" I cried out.

He just lay there on his stomach with his head turned toward the door. I couldn't see his face.

I shook my head and cried out, "Nooo!" She took me in her arms. "Shhh."

"Ahhhhh, ain't that sweet?"

"Fuck you!" I said to Li'l Dre while I cried in Rhythm's arms.

"Bitch, I said shoot them funky bitches."

Jordan seemed to be pre-occupied with something she was looking at out a window in the den. "Frank, you better come over here," Jordan said.

"I run this muthafucka. You don't tell me to come to shit, bitch. I said empty the damn clip in them hoes."

"But Frank?"

"But my muthafuckin' ass." He walked over to Jordan

and was about to snatch the gun out of her hands.

"Oh . . . my . . . muthafuckin' . . . God," Frank said when he looked out the window.

"Close," Rhythm said.

She grabbed my hand and led me over to the window and pointed.

"That's God's Army," Rhythm said.

I let go of her hand and placed my arms over my ears and screamed, "Nooooo!" as Stevie stood up and took aim at Rhythm.

Again the room exploded with gunfire. I didn't move. I was not going to move. No, not again. I shook my head. I wouldn't run. She couldn't make me. We'd die together. I wasn't going to lose her again like I had in that little yellow house when I was a little girl. In a cloud of smoke, she fell to the ground. "Momma," I heard myself say.

The noise from the front door crashing to the floor brought me back to the present. I shook my head. I looked down. Rhythm was on the carpet beside me.

Black men wearing T-shirts just like the ones Uncle Bazz and Rhythm wore came from the front and the rear of the house.

"Mommmmm!" Li'l Dre shouted in a shrill voice. Before I could reach Uncle Bazz, the men had carried him out of the house.

"Why?" Frank asked.

"Do you really have to ask?" Jordan replied.

"Bitch, I made you."

The men in black shirts and jeans just watched the scene unfold after assessing everyone's injuries.

Jordan shook her head. "No, Frank, God made me."

"God." He looked down at her. "Bitch, where the fuck is He?" He looked around. "I don't see Him. I took yo' ugly, fat-ass in when you didn't have shit. God didn't do a got damn thing. If anything, bitch," he pointed to himself, "I'm God."

"You're wrong." She shook her head. "I had my freedom, but most of all you took what I thought no one could take. I knew I was fat, I knew I was unattractive, but every day I held my head up because I had my dignity. But you took that."

She began to explain why she had turned on Frank.

"When you first brought Babygirl inside, Rico held the ladder while I climbed up to an open bedroom window."

"You mean to tell me your fat-ass was in here the whole muthafuckin' time?" Frank said.

"Yes, and I listened to that woman whip you with her confidence. I was amazed at how calm and self-assured she was when the odds were so overwhelmingly in your favor. She never panicked. She never raised her voice or cursed. She never lost control. And when she kicked your ass, I knew then that I would die before I would let you or anyone else in this house harm that sistah. I wouldn't have killed Stevie if she had not drawn down on Rhythm," Jordan said.

"Before they knew what hit them, we took the six guards out that were posted up and around the farm. They'll be 'sleep for at least another four hours, probably closer to six. Do you want us to put these two down, Queen?" One of the men wearing the God's Army T-shirt asked Rhythm.

"No, I have special plans for these two. But I would like you to secure them to the couch over there." Rhythm held her hand out toward the long couch in the den.

"I need four kings, fellas," he said to the others.

"You heard Queen. Let's do this," he announced in the direction of the ten men who stood behind Frank and Li'l Dre.

Rhythm put a fist over her heart before saying, "I want to thank all of my beautiful black kings for everything."

"Always a pleasure to serve and protect a queen," one of the men said.

"That's our job, Queen," another replied.

The men ignored Frank and Li'l Dre, who cursed and pleaded with the men to let them go.

"King?" Rhythm said as she tapped one of the men on the shoulder.

"Yes, Queen."

"I need you to gather the cleaning crew and wait outside for us. And King James," she said to another of the men in the house, "could you gather as many kings as you think you'll need, and take the tranquilized men and lock them in the horse stable?"

"Consider it done, Queen. Will that be all?"

"No, after you're finished, please radio the kings that took King Shabazz and brief them. Afterwards, please dismiss the rest of the kings. Tell them I'll see them back in Chicago on Sunday in God's house. That will be all."

"Madness," I shouted as I watched her being helped down the stairs.

I ran to her. "Are you okay? Do you need medical attention?"

"No," she said, shaking her head. "At least not until I deal with that fat, sick bastard sitting on the couch over there."

CHAPTER 40

NEA MURPHY

Madness was the self-hate I manifested every time I shook my ass on stage. It was the self-hate I exhibited every time I gave a lap dance. Madness was the self-hate I embraced every time I fucked in the V.I.P. It was the self-hate I reached out to every time I wrapped my lips around a dick or licked a clit.

For years I suffered from selective blindness. I used my children to facilitate my madness. I told myself that the only thing I could do was lease my body out to provide for my girls. I've run across several good men. My father, for instance, but I hated him and didn't even know it. I had forgotten how to trust and how to love after my mother shunned me and my stepfather abused me.

I said the words, but I didn't really think that I loved my girls until I started reading about women who lost more than I had and still persevered.

I didn't begin to look at men as anything other than toys to be played with until I read *Last Man Standing*, the story about Geronimo Pratt, a man who fought and stood strong for what he believed. Even when his friends and one-time mentors turned on him, he kept standing. When a corrupt and racist system charged and convicted him for murders he couldn't have committed, he kept standing. And for over twenty-six years, he remained on his feet until his case was finally overturned.

After reading about him, I discovered Malcolm X, Marcus Garvey, Ossie Davis, Muhammed Ali, Louis Farrakhan, Dr. Ben Carson, André Frazier, and so many other strong men who stood up when others were laying down. The common bond that all these men shared was their love for God.

I was lying on top of a bed, bleeding from having my insides ripped open by a dog, when I figured out the method to the madness.

The madness was me not knowing who I really was. Madness didn't define me. I, Nea Straybor Murphy, defined me. Now I could and would command, demand, and stand as a black-woman- sistah-queen. I was and will always be my daddy's and my father God's babygirl.

CHAPTER 41

BABYGIRL

Rhythm embraced Jordan as if she'd been down with Rhythm's army from day one. She sent Jordan outside with the others and instructed her to wait for us there.

As the men were leaving the house, one of them turned and told Rhythm that Snow had been taken care of and that my apartment had been cleaned.

Rhythm walked over to the coat rack in the foyer where her briefcase had been moved sometime during the ruckus. "Queens, my name is Aja Rhythm One Free. You two can call me Rhythm," she said as she put her briefcase down and hugged us.

"I'm Nea Straybor Murphy," Madness replied with pride.

"They call me Babygirl," I said.

"Oh, I know who you are. You are the reason I'm here. I'll explain everything after we handle these two," Rhythm replied as she went into her briefcase. She carefully put on a pair of rubber gloves before removing and placing a scalpel in her pocket. She carried two large syringes filled with a clear liquid over to where Frank and Li'l Dre sat.

"There is a pair of gloves for both of you inside the case. After putting them on, could you two please bring me the other scalpel and the two bottles inside the briefcase?"

"What the fuck are you going to do with those?" Frank asked.

"Would either of you queens like to assist me?"

"I don't know what you are about to do, but I want to kill this fat fuck," Madness cried as she lashed out,

248

cutting Li'l Dre in the face and the head with the scalpel.

"AHHHHHHHHHHHHHHHHHHH!" Li'l Dre screamed bloody murder.

Rhythm put her syringes down and grabbed hold of Madness. "Queen, not this way."

"He beat me, made me suck him off, and he tied me up," she cried. "And, and . . ."

"It's okay, let it all out, Queen," Rhythm consoled her.

"He forced his dog to-to enter me."

"Trust me, he's about to pay. They both are. Let me show you a preview of what I have planned for these two. But first, if you are up to it, I need you to follow my lead and help me out."

"Bitch, is you crazy? What the fuck are you doing?" Frank twisted and turned as Rhythm undid the purple alligator skin belt and pulled it off of him.

Madness did the same to Li'l Dre as I watched.

"This scalpel is very sharp. Keep squirming and I'm liable to sever an artery," she told Frank as she cut his pants off of him. After Madness had Li'l Dre's sweats off, Rhythm had trouble removing Frank's socks and shoes because of the way the men had his ankles tied together.

Rhythm picked up both syringes and took the tops off. "Nea, you have to be very careful with these."

Madness nodded.

Frank's eyes rolled into the back of his head, and he let out a high-pitched, blood-curdling scream after Rhythm squirted a couple drops of the clear liquid out of each syringe onto his big toe. I put my hand over my mouth after seeing the two liquids burn right through the flesh and bone on Frank's big toe.

Rhythm ignored Frank's screams. "Queens, the acid in these syringes will burn through metal. If water doesn't interact with it, the acid is harmless," she explained.

Li'l Dre's eyes were wide with horror and his Fruit of

the Looms were instantly soaked with his own urine.

As Rhythm cut Frank's purple silk boxers off, she said, "I told you that I would make you bow down and respect the black queen, didn't I?"

Frank didn't respond.

"Did you not hear me? I asked you a question." He still didn't answer.

"I burnt half of your toe off, not your ears, but I can."

She put a syringe to his right ear.

"No-no-no-no-no Ms.-Ms.-Ms. Black Queen. I-I-I-I, wh-wh-what do you want from me?"

"For you to suffer. You've hurt so many queens in the past, now I'll hurt you in ways you never dreamed of," she said before releasing a couple of drops from both syringes onto his penis.

I had to close my ears as he screamed and violently jerked. A few seconds later, Li'l Dre's anguishing cries drowned out his father's. The couch started moving back and forth until Li'l Dre and Frank had flipped it on its back.

I welcomed the fresh air that Rhythm let in by opening the front door. She summoned one of the men while Nea and I watched Li'l Dre and Frank squirming and crying.

"King, I need you and the clean-up crew to come in and take care of this mess we made." She pointed to where we were. Nea's mouth flew open once she saw the guy Rhythm was addressing. I couldn't get a good look at the guy, but he did seem familiar.

"What about them?" His question was directed at the sweating and whining bodies of Frank and Li'l Dre.

"What about them?" she retorted.

"They're still alive," he said.

"After you bury them, they won't be. And please, bury them alive," Rhythm said as she walked toward a window in the den.

JIHAD

"Cole, is that you?" Madness asked.

Jiffy Lube, Cole Waters, the guy I put Madness on. The one who lived in the same building as Li'l Dre. What did he have to do with all of this?

CHAPTER 42

BABYGIRL

Once we left the house, me, Nea, and Rhythm went to the Ritz-Carlton downtown Atlanta, where Rhythm had a room. After a long, hot shower, I went to sleep. The next morning, I quietly got up so as not to awaken Nea, who was sleeping beside me.

By the time I showered and put on a hotel robe, Rhythm came into the room with a bag from Neiman's. I didn't even know she had left. I looked at the hotel clock; it read 1:21 P.M.

She handed me the bag and said it held a couple of outfits for us to travel in.

"Where are we going?" I asked.

"Chicago."

"Why?" I asked.

"That's where I and the rest of your family live."

"Family?"

She pulled two laminated pictures from her wallet and gave it to me.

"This one is you when you were around her age." She pointed to the picture with me as a little girl. "And this one is my mother holding me and my twin."

"Is that my mother?" I pointed to a little baby girl who looked just like me.

"No, that's me." She pointed to the other little baby girl in the picture. "She was your mother. Her name was Anaya Azure."

"That is such a beautiful name," I said.

"It means 'look to God.' "

"But how?"

"My father, your grandfather was a West African hitman who was heavily into drugs and Santeria

252

JIHAD

Voodoo. I don't exactly know why, but your grandmother sent your mother away to protect her. She told me something about my father planning to take one of us away to be sacrificed on an altar as part of some ceremonial ritual. Somehow, your mother didn't get to the family she was supposed to, and we lost her.

"As I got older, I started having these dreams of me being in places that I've never been or seen. They were so clear. I'd wake up in a cold sweat, rambling on in vivid detail about these places. At first, your grandmother didn't pay much mind to them. But after I kept having them, her husband, my stepfather started to suspect my dreams were connected to my twin.

"After reading several books on twins, my stepfather moved a cot into my room and started sleeping next to my bed. He wanted to be the first person I spoke to after I woke up from one of these dreams. A year later, all we knew was that I was dreaming of places in Northern California.

"As I got older, the dreams faded. Then one day, over ten years later, I got extremely sick. And for nine months, I had the symptoms of someone going through a rough pregnancy. My doctor couldn't explain it. He said it was all in my mind. But I know it was much more than that. I knew it had something to do with my sister.

"I was going through a lot at the time. I was leading a Chicago gang war against the government that drew national media attention. I was trying to organize a rally to help free the man I loved from prison, and I was trying to stay out of prison myself.

"It took me another six years before I was able to come out to California to see if I could find my sister. The last dream I had about me being lost in a city that I'd never been to, I remembered seeing the Hollywood sign.

"As soon as the plane landed in Los Angeles, I began to sweat. Once I got off, I was drenched. I must

253

have drunk three Evian bottled waters from the time I left the gate until I got the Hertz rental car. I had no idea where I was going, but I just drove until I was in front of this big, beautiful beachfront home in Santa Monica. My heart started to beat rapidly after I parked the car on the street. I could hardly believe what I was seeing. I can't begin to tell you what I was feeling as I looked at myself fifty yards away, dropping keys at the front door. As I ran through the gates, she seemed to rush inside.

"She'd left the door wide open. I called out, but no one answered. Loud classical music was coming from the inside the house.

"I went in and followed a hall until I saw her standing outside some windows and a pair of large, glass French doors. She was holding a large kitchen knife with both of her hands, just staring.

"I looked in and saw a man and another woman doing terrible things to this little girl. He didn't even stop once he saw me. As a matter of fact, I think he grew more excited. That's when I completely lost it. I grabbed the kitchen knife, ran into the library and started going crazy."

I closed my eyes. "Yeah, I remember seeing my mother in the room with me and outside of the room looking in, too. So that wasn't my imagination. That was you," I said in amazement.

"Yes, it was me. By the time I'd realized what I'd done, it was too late. I told your mother to stay put until I got back. I drove around for about fifteen minutes before I found a pay phone and made a call. I had to wait another fifteen to twenty minutes before the person I phoned called me from a secured line.

"After getting directions on what to do, I drove back to the house and you and her were gone. The only lead I had was the name Lavette Burgess and Babygirl. It was through my soul mate that I finally found you. He was incarcerated with King Shabazz.

"If that isn't God's hand, I don't know what is. I live in Chicago and you lived in Atlanta. Almost three million black men in the prison system, and the right two kings are next door to each other in solitary confinement.

"Your uncle went on and on about this queen named Babygirl. When he mentioned that her mother had been killed and her name was Lavette Hawkins, my soul mate sent me a letter explaining everything. By the time I sent King Cole Waters to Atlanta to find out if you were my niece, you were already in deep with the Lester family and their so-called St. Louis Black Mafia.

"While Cole was gathering information, I was doing what I could to make sure the assistant D.A. assigned to King Shabazz's case got sick, and the one we needed took over. King Shabazz's trial was declared a mistrial and he was set free just in time.

"I had fifty soldiers in Atlanta and another fifty in St. Louis weakening the stronghold Frank had on the members of the St. Louis Black Mafia."

"I still can't believe you went through all this trouble just for me," I said, teary-eyed.

"I didn't do it just for you. I did it for us. You are a part of me." She held my face in her hands. "Queen, you are the future. If you die, I die." She closed her eyes. "I loved you from the moment I found out there was the remotest possibility that you existed."

"Since I know who I am, I no longer want to be just Babygirl. From now on, I want a name that means something. I want to wear the name of the most influential women I've ever known or read about. I want to be called Anaya Rhythm Azure."

"When I tell you about my past, you may want to change that up a little," Rhythm said.

"What do you mean?"

"I did things and was involved in situations that would make what you went through seem like Sunday school."

"Tell me about it."

"I will. One day, I will tell you the story of Riding Rhythm."

JIHAD

One year LATER

Funny how tragedy brings people together, I thought as I waited for Nea. We were in Santo Domingo, Nea's birthplace.

Although she despised her mother for what she did not do, she still loved her. Before her mother passed, Nea forgave her and promised to go to her mother's birthplace and rekindle her family ties. It was on her death bed in St. Vincent's Hospital that her mother apologized and told her that her stepfather had divorced her not long after Nea left home to live with her biological father.

What a coincidence it was that Nea's stepfather died the day after Nea's mother passed. The autopsy report determined that he'd committed suicide by swallowing acid.

Before Uncle Bazz and I moved back down South, would you believe that he found his soul mate and moved her from Chicago to Atlanta? Oh yeah, he'd suffered a punctured lung back at Frank and Stevie's horse ranch, but he was fine. Nurse Nicole made sure of that. He said that she was the only woman he'd ever met besides me who had as much game as he had.

Even more unbelievable was that he'd been working a square gig for eight months straight. He hadn't missed or been late once. I know, because he worked for me. Well, sort of. Uncle Bazz was the Southern Regional Director of recruiting for the One Free Family, and he was the project manager for the Anaya Azure Memorial Hospital.

I turned around and smiled at him and Nicole as they sat in the sand and waved.

Me, well, I was rich in more ways than one. I hit the lottery for two million dollars six months ago. You could say it was rigged from the beginning. My plan almost backfired when Snow came into the picture.

Before I started executing my plot to pit Stevie and Li'l Dre against each other, I found an old friend, Two Can San, and since she was the only older white woman I knew, I took her off of the streets, cleaned her up, and moved her into a nice little apartment near downtown. I gave her a social security number and birth certificate that matched one of Stevie's relatives that she'd never known. Then from those two forms of I.D., we went and got her a Georgia I.D.

Maria "Two Can San" Wolfe was now Marsha "Set for Life" Brown, thanks to the two-million dollar life insurance policy we took out on her niece, Stephanie Brown, AKA Stevie Brown. I chose the name Brown for Two Can to add validity to the niece story we told Family Mutual upon acquiring the policy.

I knew the information that I'd copied from her purse the day I was interviewed at the Parrot a few years ago would come in handy one day. It may have sounded risky, but as much money as she was pulling down at the Parrot, I took a gamble that she would not have paid attention to the $157.67 Family Mutual was deducting from her police pension each month.

Stephanie Brown's body was the only one the police found when they acted on a tip from an anonymous informant. The horse farm that she was found on was owned by a dummy corporation was traced back to Frank Lester.

The police were still looking for Stevie's bodyguard, Richard "Rico" O'Leary, son of Detective Francis O'Leary, as well as Li'l Dre and Frank Lester, for questioning into the death of Stevie Brown.

Six months later, Stevie Brown's murder was still unsolved, and Two Can San received a fat check in the mail, made out to Marsha Brown. After the check cleared and we transferred the funds into my newly acquired

JIHAD

Swiss numbered account, we re-routed the funds and had them wired into four different dummy accounts.

It took me three more months to withdraw the funds that helped start the free hospital and clinic. I arranged for Medicare to pay for Two Can San's assisted living facility the SAID Foundation got her into.

Nea's twins were so precious in their little peach dresses as they rolled out the red, silky-looking runway their mother and their soon-to-be stepfather now walked on.

The sun was barely watching as it was about to leave us and make room for the moon while my family and hers watched the proceedings. It was still hard to believe that I not only had an uncle, but he was the Bishop Solomon "Soul King" One Free, and he moonlighted as the Governor of Illinois when he wasn't doing things like marrying people or preaching sermons.

Fifteen months ago, you couldn't have paid me to believe that Cole Waters was watching me when I was watching him. And how about him and Madness falling for each other after one afternoon of wild sex? And now they were exchanging vows.

Before there was a *Coldest Winter Ever,*
there was a **Hot Summer Rhythm**
in the Windy City
that was ignited by one no-limit, no-bullshit, 'bout- it-
'bout-it sistah that goes by the name of **Rhythm.**

The game is not to be *told* but *sold*
RIDING RHYTHM, the revolution that one sistah
started will be in stores everywhere,
May, 2006